He kissed her, a convincing kiss if she'd needed more convincing. He wasn't rough or demanding; instead, he became gentle, as if unsure, nibbling at her lips. She shivered as he licked the seam, delved within, then shuddered as he tasted every inch of her mouth.

She gave herself over to the joy of touching him, running her fingers along his chest and belly, thumbs across his nipples, knuckles along the ridge of his ribs; then she clasped his shoulders, hanging on as the world tilted and tipped when he pushed her back onto the bed and rose above her.

"No," she rasped, and he stilled, then started to withdraw.

She clutched at him. "Wait—"

"You said no. I understand what no means."

Impressed, Lily studied Rico's face. At this point, most men would have ignored her words, but Rico stopped the instant she said no.

"I meant let me touch you." He frowned. She pushed on his shoulders, and he reclined on the bed. "I want to—" She broke off, and her cheeks flooded with heat. She didn't think she could articulate what she had only just begun to want.

"Hey," he whispered and tugged on her hair, which had come loose from his roving hands. "Touch me. Any way you want."

Dear Romance Reader,

Last year, we launched the Ballad line with four new series, and each month we'll present both new and continuing stories set everywhere from medieval England to the American West—the kind of passionate, romantic stories you love best, written by the most gifted authors. At the back of each book, we'll tell you when you can find subsequent books in the series that have captured your heart.

This month, the fabulous Suzanne McMinn returns with the second installment of her *Sword and the Ring* series. **My Lady Runaway** is determined to escape marriage to a cruel nobleman, but she never expects a face from her past to become her knight in shining armor. Next Lori Handeland continues *The Rock Creek Six* with **Rico,** a man who has a way with women—until he meets the one woman who refuses to believe that love is possible.

In the third entry of rising star Cindy Harris's charming *Dublin Dreams* series, a widow meets her match in a brooding attorney and wonders if she can convince him that a true romance is certainly not **Child's Play.** Finally, reader favorite Alice Duncan concludes the smashing *Dream Maker* series with **Her Leading Man,** as an actress who dreams of medical school learns that even the smartest men can be stupid when it comes to love. Enjoy!

Kate Duffy
Editorial Director

THE ROCK CREEK SIX

RICO

LORI HANDELAND

ZEBRA BOOKS
KENSINGTON PUBLISHING CORP.
http://www.zebrabooks.com

ZEBRA BOOKS are published by

Kensington Publishing Corp.
850 Third Avenue
New York, NY 10022

All Kensington titles, imprints and distributed lines are available at special quantity discounts for bulk purchases for sales promotion, premiums, fund-raising, educational or institutional use.

Special book excerpts or customized printings can also be created to fit specific needs. For details, write or phone the office of the Kensington Special Sales Manager: Kensington Publishing Corp., 850 Third Avenue, New York, NY 10022. Attn. Special Sales Department. Phone: 1-800-221-2647.

Zebra and the Z logo Reg. U.S. Pat. & TM Off.

First Printing: November 2001
10 9 8 7 6 5 4 3 2 1

Printed in the United States of America

For Amy Garvey
Who gives me the opportunity
to write what I love.

CHAPTER 1

"Your job, Betty, is to sing. Singing pays for this room, your food, those brightly colored silks you wear. So get your exquisite, expensive rear end downstairs before I kick you out on the street where you belong."

Betty Lillian lifted the hot, damp cloth from her aching forehead and opened one eye to glare at her employer, Randolph Ward. The volume of his voice did nothing for the pounding in her head. "I'm ill, R.W. Everyone becomes ill now and again."

He stepped closer to her bed, one he often shared by virtue of his position and hers. One of these days, Betty was going to be in charge of her own bed, her own future, her own life. R.W. had promised her the world, then given her nothing but New Orleans.

"No blood," R.W. concluded after studying her like a bug on a pin. He put a beringed finger against her cheek. "No fever. Get your butt onstage. It's carnival; the crowd is thick. Once the men get an eyeful of you—that face, such hair, the body— then an earful of your voice, no one will be able to stop themselves from throwing their money into my coffers when you deal poker."

"I might manage to sing, but I doubt I'd make it through an entire night dealing cards, as well."

"You'll do what I say, Betty. Have you forgotten who took you in and made you what you are? Have you forgotten that without me you'd still be singing on that street corner in Baton Rouge, near starved and worse?"

Some days Betty wondered what could be worse than this, but most nights she still dreamed of her time alone in the dark—belly screaming, heart aching, wolves, albeit human, circling.

"I don't know how I could forget, since you remind me every day."

"Excellent." His smile was as warm as his heart. A handsome man, with a trim golden beard that matched his close-cropped hair, R.W. had sky blue eyes, which should have been kind but weren't. He had little in the way of personality unless you counted avarice and selfishness among the traits of a worthy disposition. "I'll see you downstairs in ten minutes."

He left without another glance, slamming the door behind him. R.W. knew Betty would comply. What choice did she have? What choice had she ever had?

Betty dragged herself from the bed. She *did* have a headache, but not as bad as she made out. Once in a while her life, this place, R.W., became more than she could bear.

Seven nights out of seven Betty sang for her supper—and everything else. She might have been born a poor woman's child whose daddy had left them behind without a second glance, but she'd also been born beautiful. That alone would have been a curse in her world. Beautiful, uneducated, poor women, had one option—selling that beauty on the streets or in a house built for such purposes.

But Betty had an additional asset. She could sing, amazingly well. She might not have been able to read until R.W. taught her or speak like a lady until she'd been with him for three years, but there had been music in her heart and soul, and that, combined with her body and her face, had saved her.

Betty set about making her ink black hair appear tousled, as if she'd just stepped from the bed of a lover. It didn't take long. Her hair, her curse, had always been riotously curly and unmanageable. Some nights she wanted to pull the waist-length mass into a proper bun to keep the strands out of her eyes. But R.W. would never allow that.

Her hair hypnotized, he said, and when she pulled it away from her face, she looked too thin, with cheekbones too pronounced, too high. Without her hair as a distraction, her eyes loomed large and black in her pale face, frightening all the customers—or so R.W. insisted.

Though Betty might look foreign, she was anything but. Born in the bayou, like her mother before her, she shared her mama's dark eyes and hair, but Betty's pale skin reflected the ancestry of a father she'd never known.

R.W. had hired people to teach her to move like a courtesan and to speak as a member of the Creole elite. In New Orleans, descendants of the early French and Spanish settlers formed a circle whose wealth was based on planting, banking, and brokering sugar and cotton. Their mystique hovered above the city like a cool mist over a heated summer day.

R.W., a Yankee carpetbagger if ever there was one, had hoped to cash in on the grace and refinement of the upper class. Unfortunately, certain things could not be taught. Betty did her best. She spoke French here and there, and she had always moved as if the music in her heart played to the beat of her feet, but she was a singer who'd come out of the swamp, and there was no changing that no matter how much money R.W. spent.

She finished dressing in the usual tight, low-cut, jewel-toned gown—this one garnet—then applied powder and lip rouge. Twenty-nine years old, she had a few years left but no illusions that R.W. would keep her around once her age began to show. Beauty without the voice would have gotten her nowhere, just as the voice without the beauty would get her to the same place.

Betty had been secreting coins for years. She knew better than to pilfer large amounts of money from the poker table. Such behavior led to apprehension. However, patience led to freedom.

But her patience was nearly at an end, and she still did not have the funds to get away from New Orleans and start over. She had to do something to save herself from the inevitable, and she had to do it quickly. But what?

Below stairs her music began. Even though Betty disliked singing for all that she had, the singing itself kept her sane. She took a deep breath, thought of music and only that, and prepared herself for another night as Betty Lillian, the ebony-eyed nightingale of New Orleans.

* * *

Hours later, Betty's headache pounded in time with the piano, but no one would ever know by looking at her face. In her lifetime, she'd sung a ditty as men cursed and drank and died on the saloon floor in front of her. She'd given voice to a ballad while half-naked women danced along the bar. Nothing made Betty bat a sooty, long eyelash.

So even though she'd prefer to lie down and die awhile, she laughed at every stupid joke, smiled seductively at every foolish man, and raked in every bit of cash she could as they all looked down her dress and drooled.

Men. How in hell had they ended up ruling the world?

The only male she'd ever had any fondness for was Jean Baptiste. Betty dealt another hand, and while her oglers checked their cards, she glanced at the boy playing the piano.

Two years ago, when she'd been "promoted" from R.W.'s place in Baton Rouge to this one in New Orleans, she'd heard the haunting strains of an unknown melody before she'd even walked through the door. Jean Baptiste had sat alone in the deserted saloon, caressing the keys of the piano as if it were his only friend. When she'd begun to sing, he'd stopped playing as fear filled his eyes. She'd coaxed him to play some more, and when R.W. had heard the two of them, Jean Baptiste went from floor sweeper to piano player.

The boy had lived at the saloon for years. No one knew where he'd come from or how he'd learned to play so well. They probably never would, because whenever Jean Baptiste attempted to speak, his stutter was so profound as to be painful.

For some reason, the boy's affliction annoyed R.W. no end, and he'd forbidden Jean Baptiste to talk to him or the customers. So the child got his meaning across to those who cared enough to "listen" with the use of his eyes and hands and body alone.

"Miz Lillian, if you don't mind, I'd like two cards."

Betty dragged her attention back to the table. There was little challenge for her in poker anymore. She could read every nuance of a player's face. Sometimes she wondered if R.W. kept her around more for the money she won at the game than the money his place made on entertainment.

"Certainly." She gave the grubby man from Texas his cards. She could tell by the tiny twitch of his nose that the ones she'd given him weren't the ones he'd wanted.

With only half her attention, Betty continued with the game. Jean Baptiste finished for the night and drifted over to sit at the next table until she was done. They always shared a drink before retiring. She figured Jean Baptiste was perhaps fourteen or fifteen years old and should not drink whiskey. But she wasn't his mother, would never be anyone's mother, so she kept her opinions to herself.

Time passed. Everyone folded but the grubby Texas man and Betty. He frowned at his cards as if he could change them by looking. She could have sworn he had nothing, but if so, then why was he cleaning out his pockets to keep up with her?

"Are you in, or are you out?" she asked.

"In. But . . ." He patted his pockets and shrugged. "This is all I got left."

A crumpled yellow piece of paper floated gently

toward the center of the table. "Rules of the house," she recited before the paper even settled atop the coinage. "Money only. No watches, no rings, no . . . whatever that is."

He leaned over the table, lowering his voice. "Deed to a mighty fine saloon in Texas. Even better than this one. You'd like it, Miz Lillian."

Meaning to shove the paper back at the man, she froze, her hand halfway across the table, and considered his words. A quick glance at Jean Baptiste and the boy hustled off to keep R.W. out of her way. She'd kept R.W. occupied a time or two so Jean Baptiste could do whatever it was he did when *he* gave *her* "the look."

The place was nearly deserted, though the streets still echoed music and laughter. Tomorrow was Fat Tuesday, the busiest night of the year in New Orleans. Some of that merriment always splashed forward onto Monday, since Lent would cast sobriety, or at least a semblance of it, over the city from Ash Wednesday to the rebirth at Easter.

At the table, just she and Grubby Texas remained—and that deed for a mighty fine saloon. Even if it was located in Nowhere, Texas, it was anywhere but here.

"Free and clear?" she asked.

"Yes, ma'am. I got that saloon from my daddy." His gaze shifted from her face to her cleavage. "It's mine."

Betty resisted the urge to put her finger beneath his chin and raise his gaze, but what would be the point? He'd only ogle again as soon as she released him. They always did.

There was something odd about this man and his saloon. "If it's so great, why aren't you there?"

"Me?" The word came out a squeak, and he paled.

Hmm, probably something odd about Nowhere, Texas, too. "You," she repeated. "Why are you here if your saloon is there?"

"Oh." He nodded eagerly but kept his gaze on her breasts. "Left the place with a friend."

"And will I have to put up with you whining about what I've done to the place?"

"Me?"

She started to think of him as Squeaky rather than Grubby, though both names fit so well.

"No, ma'am. I'm bound for old Mexico tonight. Not goin' back to Texas, no way, not ever."

Betty nodded. Sounded like Squeaky was in trouble with the law. Not a bad idea to go through New Orleans at carnival, then off to old Mexico. It would take an excellent tracker to find him that way. Which gave Betty an idea of her own.

"All right," she acceded. "I'll take that as a call." She laid her cards on the table.

The man's lips collapsed from a leer to a trembling pout. "B-but I've got three jacks."

"Not enough to keep your saloon." She scooped up the deed along with the money. "Make that my saloon." The deed disappeared into a pocket of her dress as she turned; the money went into her reticule.

She left the three queens on the table.

Jean Baptiste joined Betty at the bar as she finished a note to R.W. "I need to lie down, sugar. Is that okay?"

He nodded, though his dark blue eyes welled with disappointment. Oh, how she didn't want to leave him, this boy who had become so much more to her than a piano player. Just the thought made her own eyes burn, and Betty had to duck her head and let her hair fall across her face before he saw her tears and wondered.

Betty rarely cried. What would be the point? In fact, she rarely showed emotion of any kind. Such softness only made for trouble later. She had been denying her feelings for so long, she was surprised she even had any anymore. But Jean Baptiste had slipped beneath her reserve and into her heart. Once she was settled and had more money, she would send for him. The resolution soothed the sadness that had overtaken her at the thought she might never see the boy again.

"Can you give this to R.W.?" Betty held up her reticule, which bulged with the money she'd won that night. "And this, too?" She handed Jean Baptiste the folded piece of paper.

He turned to do her bidding, and acting on impulse, Betty touched his arm, then kissed his cheek. "You're the sweetest, most talented boy alive, Jean Baptiste. Don't you forget it."

Before he could question her uncommon expression of affection, Betty fled to her room and locked the door behind her.

She hoped the amount in her reticule would send R.W. into a fit of euphoria that would counteract his annoyance at her note.

My headache is worse. I must plead pain and forgo your company in my room tonight. I will make it up to you tomorrow.

Betty pulled a carpetbag from beneath her bed and packed what she could not leave behind. She smiled as she did so, because by tomorrow she would be gone.

* * *

If anyone saw her leave, they would not recognize Betty Lillian. She tamed her hair into a severe bun, then covered her face with a Mardi Gras mask. Her dress was one she'd never worn before, because R.W. had taken one look at the garment and declared that it did not reveal enough of the merchandise. Maybe that's why Betty felt better than she ever had, wearing the dress R.W. hated as she escaped right beneath his nose.

He'd come after her; of that she was certain. But he'd have a hard time tracing a woman wearing a mask and a black dress through streets ripe with carnival. He would have no idea where she was going, and even if he thought to check the stage office, he would find no trace of Betty Lillian.

She'd always disliked her first name—not flashy enough. Lillian was nice, though, but too stiff for the stage. Lily, on the other hand, sounded just about right. Now all she required was a dazzling new surname.

Hurrying onward, Betty pondered over a name. She needed to take the first available stagecoach out of New Orleans. She could not risk being caught waiting for a ride. But that became the least of her worries, because by the time Betty reached the stage office, she knew someone had followed her.

That someone could not be R.W. He would not hide; he would scream and shout and drag her back. And then . . .

Well, she wasn't going to think about "then" or she'd be too nervous to get on with "now."

Betty marched into the stage office and came mask-to-face with—

"Jean Baptiste!"

The shock of seeing him there ahead of her and the fear that he'd brought R.W. along made Betty sway. He grabbed her hand and shook his head frantically, as if he knew what she was thinking.

"R.W. isn't here?"

"N-n-n—"

He struggled gamely until Betty squeezed his hand. "Sugar, I can understand you without the words."

With a nod, Jean Baptiste grew silent.

"Does he know I'm gone?"

No.

Betty let out a sigh of relief, and the world stayed in focus. When Jean Baptiste released her hand, she discovered a smudge of blood across her palm.

"Did you hurt yourself?" She took his fingers in her own and examined a small slice in his skin.

He pulled away, wrapped a handkerchief about the wound, then slid a thin knife from his boot.

"You brought my knife?" He pulled a leather strap from his pocket. "And the sheath. Thank you."

She had not thought to bring the weapon she sometimes wore strapped to her wrist beneath her dress, a mistake Jean Baptiste had thankfully rectified at the cost of injury to himself. She'd rather the boy had not cut his precious hand on her blade, but she would no doubt find plenty of use for the knife in Nowhere, Texas, U.S.A.

"I have to get on the stage," she whispered. "I was going to send for you later."

He shook his head. "Yes, I was. Do you think I'd leave you unless I had to? I don't have enough money for us both right now."

Jean Baptiste raised an eyebrow and withdrew a

large roll of cash from his pocket. A slash of blood across the belly of his shirt and a few splotches on his pants disturbed Betty. The poor boy had hurt himself trying to help her.

She covered the money with her hand and glanced about. But at dawn on Fat Tuesday the stage office was deserted, all revelers sleeping in preparation for the gala street celebration that evening. Even if R.W. noticed her gone this morning, he would be unable to mount any kind of search on the busiest day of the year.

"I am not even going to ask where you got this."

Jean Baptiste lowered both his brows and scowled. He wasn't going to tell her, either, which was just as well. R.W., being R.W., gave Jean Baptiste room and board but little else. He had to have stolen this money, and Betty didn't want to know if he'd stolen it from R.W.

"All right, I'll need a piano player, and God knows, you can keep a secret. I guess we're in this together." He grinned. "But we're going to have to change our names so R.W. doesn't find us." Jean Baptiste's smile fell. "He'll look, but maybe not too long if we make it hard enough."

Slowly, he nodded. "I thought I'd be Lily. Do I look like a Lily to you?" In answer, Jean Baptiste cupped her cheek with his good hand. "I'll take that as a yes. But I need a last name. A common name, but pretty. I'll still have to sing wherever we go. It's all I know."

Jean Baptiste pointed at the wall behind her. Betty turned.

Edmund Fortier asks all visitors to the city of New Orleans to stop at his restaurant for their evening meal.

"Fortier? Lily Fortier." Jean Baptiste winked. "And you shall be my brother, Johnny." He frowned. "Jean Baptiste is a beautiful name, and I adore it, but in Texas I think you'll stand out. If you're Johnny, you'll be like any other cowboy."

He hooked his thumb in his belt and hitched up his pants with a shrug.

Betty laughed. "That's it. You'll fit right in. From now on, I'm Lily, and you're Johnny, always, right?" He nodded. "We'll say that the war took your voice. Then there'll be no need for you to speak to strangers until you're ready."

Gratitude washed over his face. As difficult as it was for him to talk to her, it was even harder for him to talk to those he did not know. Ridicule often followed any attempts at speech, which only made the problem worse.

"All right, then, let's see if we can get tickets all the way from New Orleans to . . . Where are we going?" She reached into her bag and pulled out the deed. "Hmm, never heard of it."

She crossed to the ticket booth. "My brother and I need to get to Rock Creek, Texas."

CHAPTER 2

"Times certainly are changing." Daniel Cash sat with his back to the wall so that his empty black eyes could watch the door of the Rock Creek saloon.

Rico Salvatore lounged opposite, his own back to the door. If Cash was watching, and he always was, no one would sneak into this place.

The abandoned saloon belonged to Cash now, and everyone in Rock Creek knew it. Since Rico, Cash, and their four friends had saved the town from the outlaw El Diablo, they'd been accepted as residents, if not upstanding citizens. Times might be changing, but not the spots on an Indian pony.

"What changes?" A drink appeared next to his hand, and Rico nodded his thanks to Yvonne, the war widow Cash had hired to run the bar. Besides Laurel and Kate, who were still sleeping off last night above stairs, Yvonne was the only woman allowed in the place. "Nate's still drunk; Jed always wanders; I still have *mucho* knives." Rico slipped one out of his boot and began to clean the mud off the sole, letting the dirt drop to the floor. No one here would notice. "And you still shoot everything that annoys you."

"Not everything. You're still alive."

Rico ignored him. With Cash, sometimes that was best. "So what is so different, *amigo?*"

"Reese is a married daddy-schoolteacher," Cash sneered. "And Sullivan is a leg-shackled, tin-star-wearing papa of four. What good are they?"

"Would you like to tell them that?"

Cash took his time lighting a cigar, then blew smoke rings at the ceiling. "Not today."

"That is what I thought."

Cash might be the roughest, toughest, meanest gunman in these parts, but he appreciated Reese. The only person Rico had ever seen Cash back down from was their former captain. And Sullivan was just spooky the way he sneaked up on people — kind of like Rico himself. Cash might be quick with a gun, but not quick enough if Sinclair Sullivan decided to slit his throat in the middle of the night.

"Life is dull, kid. I'm not made to sit around and drink, smoke, gamble, and . . ." He paused, casting a glance at Yvonne, who scowled at him from behind the bar she constantly polished.

Perhaps because Cash made her leave the rest of the saloon alone, Yvonne took out her cleaning needs on the bar. She was a bartender and nothing else. When Cash had tried to hit on her tail once, Yvonne had threatened to fix his face with a broken bottle and castrate him with a rusty nail. Cash respected that.

"Well, I'm just bored," Cash finished, leaving out his other occupation—namely, switching off bed partners between Laurel and Kate, the only two saloon girls left after Eden, Sullivan's wife, had come to town.

Suddenly, Cash sat up, and his hand went to his pistol. Rico dropped his boot and spun toward the door, knife pulled back to his ear.

"Dammit, Rico, that child is peaking beneath the doors again. Does she want to die young?"

Rico stood and put his knife back into his boot with a sigh. "Sometimes I wonder."

He went through the swinging doors and into the early spring sunshine. The wind had a sharp bite, and Rico rubbed his arms, wishing he wore a coat over his coarse black shirt. Over ten years gone from San Antonio and he still missed the heated springs of his childhood home.

Carrie Brown lurked at the side of the saloon. Every day after school she came looking for him. Rico didn't mind. She reminded him so much of the sister he had lost, he already felt as if they were joined by flesh and blood instead of mere friendship. Though he, of all people, should know that friendship forged by blood was stronger than any family tie.

"You can't keep lurking around the door, Carrie. Cash is a jumpy sort of fellow."

Her sweet face, framed by loose brown braids, appeared around the side of the building. "You won't let him hurt me. No one will ever hurt me when you're here."

Rico flinched. That's what his sister had thought, too. Such belief in him had gotten her a very early grave.

"What if I am not here? Or Cash is faster than me?"

"He isn't." She came around the corner and

threw her arms about his waist. She'd grown. Used to be she had to hug his leg. "No one is."

There was no talking to her. Rico had learned that in the past three years. She was nine now; he was twenty-five. Old enough to be her father. Poor kid didn't have a father or a mother, only a grumpy old grandpapa who let her run wild.

"Look!" she shouted, pointing toward the center of town. "Stage is in, and someone's getting off."

The stage came through once a week, and usually people got on. Once in a while, folks came and visited relatives who lived in Rock Creek or on the surrounding ranches, but very few people came to Rock Creek to stay, even though the six had cleaned the place up mighty fine.

A tall, skinny kid jumped out and glanced around. His gaze lit on Rico and Carrie, and he studied them for a moment. Although too far away to see the expression in his eyes, Rico, who'd had a lot of experience with folks of a jumpy sort, thought that the kid looked a bit tense.

But Rico forgot all about the boy when the woman stepped out. Even from here he could see she had a figure that would make grown men beg. Rico never had to. He adored women, and women adored him. All women—even the little ones.

Putting his arm about Carrie's shoulders, Rico pulled her close for a quick hug before releasing her. The child soaked up attention like a dry streambed. Sometimes Rico considered talking to her grandpapa in a way William Brown would understand, using his fists for emphasis, but Reese wouldn't let him. Besides, if Rico did, Sullivan would have to put him in jail, and Rico liked Sullivan too much to make him do that. So he kept his fists, and his precious knives, away from William Brown.

Rico didn't realize he'd stepped off the porch and begun to walk toward the stage until Carrie tugged on his hand. "Where ya goin'? I thought we were gonna play poker."

"We will, *muchacha*. I just want to see—"

"That woman!" Carrie dropped his hand. "Why do you always want to see the women?"

Rico shrugged. "I like women."

"I thought you liked me."

Rico stopped and went down on one knee so she could see his face. Immediately, she put her arms around his neck, and his throat went thick. "I—" He cleared his throat and tried again. "I do like you. But there's like and there's . . . like. Someday you'll like a boy your own age, and then you'll understand."

"You're talkin' about sex." Rico winced. He certainly hadn't meant to. Carrie pulled back to look into his eyes as she imparted her incredibly wise opinion on the subject. "Disgusting. Yuck."

His face heated. He had known women from Georgia to Texas, Louisiana to Kansas, and not a one of them had thought his touch *yuck*, but he certainly wasn't telling his angel-faced *muchacha* that.

"Oh, son of a bitch, they're coming this way."

When Carrie cursed, Rico forgot all about his sex life and the approach of the new woman in town. "Watch your mouth," he admonished. "You know your grandpapa thinks you get those words from me."

Her face creased. "But I get them from him."

"I know that, and you know that . . ."

"Mr. Reese knows, too."

"I think everyone knows."

"Then what's the friggin' problem?"

Rico groaned and put his hand to his head. "Carrie, you must stop cursing. Ladies do not curse."

"I don't want to be a lady. I want to be like you. I want to ride with the six and save the world." She pulled an imaginary pistol from her imaginary belt, aimed, and shouted, "Pow, pow, you're deader than the bad cougar cat."

"Hello, to you, too, *chérie*."

Rico glanced up to find the woman staring at Carrie and the boy staring at him. Each wore similar expressions of wary interest. He straightened to his full height. He'd been over six feet tall since he turned fifteen.

Up close the woman was stunning, though the wrinkled, dusty black dress did not enhance the shapely figure beneath it and the severe style of her hair did not complement the angles of her face. But Rico knew incredible when he saw it, and she was it. Even without that musical voice that tumbled French endearments.

Since he wanted to get that body in his bed and hear her call him *chéri*, Rico went to work.

"*Señorita*." He swept his hat from his head and bowed. "Welcome to Rock Creek."

Carrie snorted. Rico ignored her.

Straightening, he flashed a grin. The *señorita* merely raised an eyebrow, unimpressed. Rico faltered. His smile usually made women swoon—or at least smile back.

"I'm looking for the saloon."

It was Rico's turn to lift an eyebrow. "Uh . . . ah . . . well, I . . . ah . . . don't think you want to go there. It is not . . ."

"What?"

"Fit for a lady."

"What if she ain't no lady?" Carrie interjected.

"Carrie," he warned.

"I guess there ain't goin' to be any poker now that *she's* here." She huffed, put her nose in the air, and flounced off.

The woman watched her go with a slight smile on her face, as if she thought Carrie incredibly cute. Rico liked her better with every passing moment. "I am Rico Salvatore, at your service."

The woman looked him up, then down. "I can imagine."

"Excellent, *señorita*. Let me make your every imagination come true."

She rolled her eyes. "Get out of my way, *enfant*."

She attempted to walk around him, but Rico stepped into her path. The boy shoved himself between Rico and the woman, his lip curving into a silent snarl.

Rico laughed. "Very good. You are her watchdog. I understand. I will look, but I will not touch." He winked. "Until she asks."

The boy's dark blue eyes narrowed, and he took a step closer to Rico. "Johnny, never mind him." She tugged the boy back to her side. "He may hold his breath and die before I ask. Now, *monsieur*, can you point me to the saloon or no?"

"If you insist. The saloon, such as it is, stands right in front of you." He held out his arm for hers. "This way."

She made an annoyed sound. Planning to tuck her hand into the crook of his arm, Rico circled her wrist with his fingers. What he felt beneath the sleeve of her dress made him go still. His gaze flicked to her face. She tilted her head as if to say, *Try me.*

Rico dipped his chin, lifted his hands in surrender, and backed off. She strode toward the saloon with Johnny in tow.

Beneath the dusty black silk, his mystery lady had worn a knife sheathed to her wrist.

"Ah, *querida,*" he murmured. "God has made us for each other."

Lily—she'd been thinking of herself as Lily since stepping onto the stage in New Orleans—felt Rico Salvatore staring at her as she walked away. She refused to look over her shoulder and give him the satisfaction.

She'd met a hundred men like him—though none quite so handsome and virile, but plenty who thought they were a gift to any woman who walked. She'd had enough gifts like that, thank you, and now that she'd reached Rock Creek, any further gifts of such a nature would be because *she* said so.

Lily shoved through the swinging doors of the saloon and stopped dead. One of the doors smacked her in the back, forcing her to stumble in a few steps more. Her boots slid in dust. The place was a disgrace.

A frighteningly still man sat at a table directly across from the door. In contrast to the filth of the place, he was immaculately dressed in a dark suit with a pristine white shirt and lace cuffs spilling from his sleeves. He held a pistol on her, though he looked too lazy to use it. Still, the sight of the barrel pointed at her chest made Lily catch her breath just enough so that her stays poked her in the ribs. That always annoyed her no end.

"Who are you?" she snapped.

Lily could have sworn the man's perfectly

trimmed mustache twitched. But since no humor tilted those compressed lips or reached his dead eyes, she must have been mistaken.

"I might ask the same of you. Women aren't welcome here unless they're women of a certain kind, or Yvonne, of course." The tilt of his head indicated the woman in front of the cracked mirror behind the bar.

Lily glanced at Yvonne, who busily polished the scarred wood. She appeared to be Lily's age, though tired and sad and worn down. Since the war, Lily had seen far too many like her. She nodded, and the woman returned her greeting.

"So, are you a woman of a certain kind?"

Johnny stepped forward, and Lily put her hand on his arm. She'd been asked that question, in many variations, since she was old enough to need a corset. She knew how to handle men like this just as well as she knew how to handle men like Rico.

"I am *not, monsieur.* I am Lily Fortier, and this is my brother, Johnny."

"Enchanted," the man drawled, not sounding so at all. "Get the hell out."

She laughed, surprising herself. She surprised him, too, because the gun drooped just a bit and his mouth did the same.

"Ah, I see." He pocketed his pistol. "You and your brother have just escaped from the nearest lunatic asylum. I'll have Yvonne make arrangements for your keeper to round you up and drag you back."

"Why would you think I'm insane just because I refuse to get out?"

"Do you know who I am, madam?"

"Should I?"

"Well, I suppose my name hasn't quite made the sewing circles and prayer meetings. I'm Daniel Cash."

"The gunfighter?"

His smile held no mirth at all. "The same."

"What a surprise to find a man of your . . . skills in little old Rock Creek."

He frowned at her tone. "Don't you want to run away now?"

"Why ever would I do that? I don't think you realize who *I* am, Mr. Cash."

"Calamity Jane?"

She smiled, and he obviously didn't like what he saw in that smile, because he stood abruptly, his chair screeching across the wood floor, loud in the dusky quiet.

Lily reached into her reticule and pulled out the deed. "I'm the new owner of this fine establishment."

On the other side of the swinging doors, Rico cursed beneath his breath, and a trill of fear ran down Lily's spine. She stared into the dark, haunted gaze of Daniel Cash and wondered how far he'd go to keep women like her out of this place.

She never found out, because Rico, moving quicker than any man she'd ever seen, came inside, yanked the paper from her hand, and stepped into the line of fire.

"*Pardon moi?*" Lily said indignantly.

He waved his hand at her as if she were a pesky fly. "It *is* the deed for this place, Cash."

"Just because some prudish female walks in here with a piece of paper don't make my place hers."

"Actually, it does," she said.

Cash was the picture of frustration. His mouth worked, but no sound came out. Lily had seen Johnny afflicted the same way many times, and she almost felt sorry for the man. *Almost.*

Cash ran his fingers through his perfectly combed hair, making it stand on end, then kicked the table with his shiny black boot. "I'm getting the sheriff."

"Please do. That should settle this once and for all."

Cash glared at her, and she understood why he was an infamous gunman. That stare alone could make a faint heart stop. Luckily for Lily, a faint heart had never been a luxury she could afford.

Cash stomped out. Yvonne polished faster. Upstairs, doors closed, and footsteps milled about, but no one came down.

Lily held out her hand for her deed. "Is your sheriff a reasonable man?"

"I've been riding with him for about ten years, and I've never considered Sullivan unreasonable."

"The sheriff is your friend?"

"Guess you could call him that."

"And what about Cash?"

"Same."

"*Merde!*" she muttered. "*Fils de chienne!*"

Rico's blank stare revealed he did not understand the French curse words. Lily took a deep breath to calm herself. "So, by deduction Cash and the sheriff are friends."

"As friendly as Cash gets."

"Johnny, where's my derringer?"

"Whoa!" Rico held up his hands. "You cannot

pull a gun on the sheriff, and you especially cannot pull a gun on Cash."

"I'm not letting any hickish lawman take my place and give it to his pal."

"That will not happen."

She snorted. "You bet it won't."

Lily held out her hand, and Johnny gave her the tiny gun she'd bought just across the border. Sometimes a knife simply wasn't enough. She tucked the pistol into the palm of the hand that did not carry a secreted knife.

"No guns, *por favor.*" Rico looked into her eyes beseechingly. "They will only make things worse."

Lily hesitated. Rico seemed sincere, but most men—especially pretty ones—could get their way with the turn of an eyelash. Still, he ought to know his friends and this town. She *was* in the right, no matter the fame of any gunman.

With a shrug, she returned the gun to Johnny. He was better with it, anyway.

Cash returned, accompanied by a tall, dark-haired man who looked to be half something or other—in this state, most likely Comanche. She didn't care who his daddy was as long as the son was honest.

"Seem to be a problem here, kid?"

Lily glanced at Johnny, who shrugged. "My brother doesn't speak," she said. "Besides, I'm the one with the deed." She waved it like a flag.

"Ma'am." The sheriff nodded. "I was talkin' to Rico. We've been together since he was a kid."

Lily's gaze wandered all the way up Rico's six-foot-odd-inch frame. He didn't resemble any kid she'd ever seen.

"Hard habit to break," the sheriff finished. "Your boy can't talk?"

She sent a warning look in Johnny's direction before answering the sheriff. "My brother, and he doesn't speak since the war."

"Shame. Had the same problem with one of my own boys, but he came out of it after being safe here for a while. Maybe that'll happen for your brother, too."

"Maybe. But Johnny has talents beyond speech, Sheriff, which you'll discover when I get this place ready to open."

"It *is* open," Cash snapped.

"It's also filthy, smelly, dark, and disgusting."

"That's the way we like it."

"Then you can leave."

"I live here!"

"Fine. Live here. But it'll cost you."

"I hate to interrupt your fun," the sheriff said. "But could I see that deed, please?"

"Certainly."

Lily handed over the parchment, then cast a glance at Johnny. He nodded. The small gun in his pocket was trained on Sheriff Sullivan. The man thought he was going to torch her deed? He would have to think again—in hell.

The sheriff returned the deed, his expression solemn. "Looks fine to me." He cut a gaze to Johnny. "Don't ever hold a gun on a lawman, son, even if your sister tells you to. Next time, I'll be obliged to take it."

A healthy dose of respect came over Lily for this hickish sheriff. Johnny nodded his understanding and took his hand out of his pocket, empty palm visible.

"Sorry, Cash." The sheriff dipped his head at his friend and headed for the door.

"That's it?" Cash shouted, following him. "What

kind of lawman are you? What kind of friend? What kind of brother-in-arms?''

Sullivan slowly faced the shorter man. "If you have to ask me that, then you haven't been paying attention for the past ten years. She's in the right. Ain't nothin' to be done about it, hear?"

"That sounds like a threat, breed."

Rico tensed, and Lily cast him a quick glance. His jaw was set, and he stared intently at the two men. Oh, *zut!* Did they plan to splash blood all over the wood floor. That would be a lot harder to scrub out than the dirt.

Surreptitiously, she pulled Johnny out of the line of fire, but instead of going behind her, as she wanted, he stepped in front of her, and no amount of tugging would dislodge him.

"I don't threaten, Cash. We came to this town to make things right, and I don't aim to let you mess that up, whatever problem you have with women. You don't want to fight me; you're just mad at the world and always have been. One of these days you'll have to get over it or take it to the grave."

Sullivan turned his back on Cash. *Interesting.* Either the sheriff trusted the man implicitly, or he was much dumber than he looked. But he left alive, and Rico let out a long sigh of relief.

Silence descended. Lily felt gracious in victory. "You can keep your room," she said. "Either pitch in and help clean in lieu of rent, or we'll work out a reasonable rate." Rico choked. "What did I say?"

"Cash doesn't do work that might make him sweat."

"I see." She glanced at Cash's perfect clothes and well-maintained hands. She should have noticed the latter right off. "Fine, I can use money, too. What about you, Mr. Salvatore?"

"I have no problem with sweat, *señorita*." He winked. "You can count on me."

Somehow Lily doubted that.

CHAPTER 3

"Why don't you give her a chance, Cash?" Rico watched the gunman shove clothes into a bag. "She might make the place better."

Not half an hour had passed since Lily Fortier had gotten off the stage and already Cash was leaving.

"It's perfect the way it is."

"What could a clean floor hurt? And you must admit, when the cards stick to the table, it is very hard to play poker."

Cash hesitated, one of his fancy ruffled shirts in hand. "True."

"I was watching her downstairs. She seems to know her way around a saloon."

She knew how to move, too. Lily Fortier had a grace to her walk that was nearly a dance. When she talked, using her slim, long-fingered hands, he went breathless with desire. He'd had to stop watching her and flee upstairs before he disgraced himself and begged for just one kiss.

Cash was looking at him as if he knew exactly what Rico was thinking, and it disgusted him. Cash should talk. He shared women with Nate. Well, not at the same time; even Cash had standards. Rico couldn't do that no matter how many dark, bloody nights they'd shared.

Before Cash got snide and lippy, Rico hurried on. "She might bring in better liquor, even more women. She's from Louisiana; can't you tell? Maybe French women?"

Cash's eyes brightened, at least as much as dead eyes could. "You think?"

"Why don't you wait and see? Besides, Nate is in no condition to travel."

Both of them looked at Nate Lang, passed out on the bed. Why he'd come to Cash's room while they were downstairs was a mystery that would not be solved until he woke up, if then. Since he hadn't even twitched while they talked, he'd probably be out for several hours yet.

Cash shook his head and sat down next to Nate, who reacted not at all. Rico was just glad to see his friend stop packing. Whenever Cash left Rock Creek, he added a new story of death and destruction to his steadily growing reputation. Rico knew that one of these days Cash would not return, and if Nate kept following him about, watching his back, he wouldn't, either. That would cut the six down to four. Rico had seen enough people he loved die. He had no desire to see any more.

"He's getting worse," Cash said.

"I know. Since Jo Clancy left Rock Creek, no one can reach him."

"That little girl had nothin' on Nate. He might be a drunk, but he's not a fool."

Rico didn't argue, but he knew the truth. Something had been going on with Nate and Jo; he just wasn't sure exactly what. Because as soon as she left town, Nate's drinking had gotten worse, which, with Nate, was saying quite a lot.

"I think he could use some action," Cash said. "At least with El Diablo running loose he had to be near sober to hit the broad side of a barn."

"Nate could hit the knothole on a barnboard at twenty paces after drinking every one of us under the table."

"I know." Cash sighed. "And I think we're going to have to do something about it pretty soon."

Rico contemplated their sleeping comrade. Dark stubble, liberally sprinkled with gray, covered Nate's jaw and his head. He needed a shave. Rico wondered if his hands would be steady enough to do the job this time or if Laurel would be enlisted to help again. For some reason, the girls found Nate's shaved head enticing.

Every one of the men had talked to Nate, tried to find out why he drank, if not how to make him stop. But they all had their secrets from the time before they rode together, and while some of them had shared their pasts with at least one of the others, Nate spoke of the days when he'd been a preacher to no one at all.

"I can't believe Eden lets him help out at the hotel and with the children," Cash said. "But then again, we *are* talking about Eden."

Even though most good women set Cash's teeth on edge, Eden Rourke Sullivan touched a part of him no one else could. While he tolerated Mary, Reese's wife, he truly liked Eden, and Rico couldn't figure out why. Sure, she was sweeter than melted sugar, but that ought to bring out the worst in a man like Daniel Cash.

"The children like Nate. He tells them stories, plays games, rolls around on the floor and wrestles."

"That's because the floor is an old and dear friend to him," Cash said dryly.

"Nate would never let anything happen to one of the *bebés*, and he would never let anything happen to one of us, either."

"Why do you think I let him tag along with me all the time?"

Cash tossed his partially packed bag into the corner, and Rico let out a sigh of relief. Cash would stay a few days longer. Every day he remained in town was another day he stayed alive. None of the gunfighters eager to make their reputations off his would dare venture into Rock Creek, where all six men lived.

"Did you ever wonder what he would be like if he did not drink?" Rico asked.

"Nope. What's the point? That would be like wondering what you would be like if you didn't love women more than breathing. Or wondering what Reese would be like if he were a coward and not a leader."

"Or what Sullivan would be like if he could not follow a bad man over rocky ground. Or perhaps what you would be like if—"

"Watch it, kid."

"If you were not such a smart aleck."

Cash's mustache twitched. "Same goes, kid, same goes."

* * *

Nate Lang heard every word. He could pretend to sleep just as he could pretend to be drunk or sober as the occasion warranted.

Sounded like the true owner of the saloon they'd taken as theirs had shown up—and it was a pretty Louisiana woman. That should get Cash's goat and liven this place up a bit.

Rico seemed to like her, which wasn't surprising, since she wore a skirt. But the kid hadn't had a woman in this town, ever, because of the little girl who adored him. When Rico needed release, he went to Ranbourne for a few days. The kid might be a womanizing pretty boy, but he loved that little girl as if she were his own, or at least his baby sister. Nate admired that.

He'd come into Cash's room because Kate was hogging the bed again. She was a sweet enough gal, and she never expected more than Nate had to give, but while he often needed a warm body next to his in order to fall asleep, when he awoke, he needed just as badly to be left alone.

Because when he awoke he was usually far too sober, yet exhausted enough to need more sleep. When he wasn't passed out drunk, the nightmares came. Then he'd wake up screaming and thrashing.

His friends had seen that on occasion, and he'd seen them at their worst, too. No doubt Kate had seen worse things than his crying like a baby, but that didn't mean he wanted her to watch.

The only other person who had seen him break down was Jo. Nate tensed at that memory, and his entire body shuddered.

"Looks like he's wakin' up," Cash said.

Nate forced a soft snore.

"Or not," Rico murmured.

"If he starts shaking, I'm going to need your help."

"I'll be right here."

"Maybe Reese, too."

Nate fought not to wince. He hated when Reese saw him with the shakes. Their former captain never said an unkind word, but in his eyes Nate always saw guilt and sadness, as if Reese had failed him somehow. And that just wasn't so. Nate had failed himself.

Why should Nate be any different than God?

He refused to dwell on the emptiness he tried to fill with liquor—that emptiness where God had been but was no longer. Because there was no God.

How much would he have to drink today to forget that everything he'd ever believed in was a lie?

"Take our things upstairs and see if you can find us some empty rooms." Lily handed Johnny her bag.

He hesitated, and she smiled reassuringly. "I'll be fine. I think we already met the worst of the lot."

A twist of his mouth and a quirk of his eyebrow showed Johnny's opinion of that.

Calling him Johnny for several weeks in the close quarters of a stage from New Orleans to Dallas to Rock Creek had made Jean Baptiste Johnny to her. Once in a while, if she was tired or distracted, she formed the French-sounding *J* of Jean Baptiste, but as of yet, she had never let his real name tumble free. Luckily, she didn't have to worry about Johnny's spilling out her real name.

She liked being Lily Fortier. New name, new place, new life, new woman. Lily took a deep breath and did a slow twirl in the middle of *her* floor. She was going to wrestle this place into something wonderful.

"Ma'am?"

The quiet voice at her elbow made Lily freeze in mid-twirl. She'd forgotten the bartender, Yvonne. The woman must think her crazy to be dancing amid the dust and spiders.

Lily gave her a sheepish smile. "I've never had a place of my own before."

"Me, neither." Yvonne's pale blue eyes went dreamy. "I bet it feels like nothing else."

"Nothing," Lily agreed. "Is there something you wanted?"

"I just wondered if you'd give me to the end of the week before you make me leave. Maybe I can find another job by then."

Though Yvonne held her head high, her lip trembled, and her voice quavered on the last word.

"Who said anything about your leaving?"

Surprise and hope lit Yvonne's eyes, though wariness still hovered at the edges. "You'd keep me on?"

"Cash doesn't strike me as a charity-driven soul, so you must be able to do your job. Even though this place is filthy, the bar is spotless, the mirror, too, and those bottles are organized and sparkling to within an inch of their lives."

The pleased smile that pulled at Yvonne's lips

negated her shrug. "I do my best. Cash didn't want me touching anything but the bar."

"Oh, I imagine he wanted you touching something other than the bar. The fact that you didn't only impresses me more."

"I'm not that kind of woman. Yet, anyway. But I'm alone in this world, and I don't have much left to sell but me."

"My world's the same, but at least I have a voice to sell. We do what we have to do. How much was Cash paying you?" Yvonne named a figure that had Lily gaping. "A generous man."

"He was trying to work his way into my bed. I figured if he was too dumb to hear no, I'd just take his money as long as he was offering."

"I'd do the same. Unfortunately, I'm short on funds until I get this place going." Yvonne's face fell, and her sigh tore at Lily's heart. "But I have a proposition."

"What kind?"

Lily studied the woman. Yvonne had obviously had a hard life and trusted few people. Even now, the look she gave Lily was filled with wariness.

"I'm a singer. I know entertainment. I know people. I know cards. What I don't know is Rock Creek or how to stock and manage a bar."

"Those things I know."

"Exactly. So, do you want to be my partner?"

Yvonne's eyes widened, and her mouth gaped. "Partner?"

"We'll work out the details later. Primarily, I'll sing, and you'll run the bar. You don't tell me how to hit high 'C,' and I won't tell you how much whiskey to buy. Deal?"

Yvonne stared at Lily's hand as if there might be something hidden there. Well, there *was* a knife up her sleeve, but Yvonne didn't know that. Rico did only because he couldn't keep his beautiful, dark, and no doubt clever hands to himself.

Lily frowned at the direction of her thoughts, and Yvonne, who must have thought by the expression that Lily meant to change her mind, slapped her palm firmly against Lily's.

"Deal," she said, and pumped Lily's hand once.

"What kind of deal?" an annoyingly high pitched voice screeched from above.

Yvonne rolled her eyes and broke the handshake. "Meet your new boss, Laurel."

Lily glanced up just as Laurel shrieked, "Cash! Where are you!"

The girl stomped out of view, and Lily returned her attention to Yvonne, who was already headed back to the bar. "Wait a minute. Who was that?"

"One of the two soiled doves left in Rock Creek. The other is Kate."

"You don't seem to like them much."

"I have no opinion one way or another."

"Sure you do. One of your jobs is to tell me about everyone, especially people who work for us."

"All right," Yvonne acceded, though she didn't look happy about it. "I don't care what women do to get by. Like you said, you do what you have to do. But those two are just plain dumb and annoying as all get-out. 'Cash, let me touch your pretty gun. Nate, let me help you shave.' " Yvonne's falsetto voice and rapidly batting eyelashes made Lily smile. "I don't think they have one working brain between them."

"Which is how they ended up here, doing what they do."

"Right."

"Well, maybe with a little help they could become less annoying."

"I don't think so."

"We can try. Maybe if we teach them a different job they won't have to do what they do."

"Cash isn't going to like that."

"Which means I'm going to like it a whole lot."

Yvonne shook her head as if Lily had said she wanted to dig her own grave. Maybe she had.

"You're going to tell Daniel Cash there's no more women for sale in this place?"

"No, ma'am." Yvonne looked confused. "The girls will have to make that choice on their own. Once they do, they'll tell him."

"You are a dreamer, aren't you?"

"Aren't you?"

A shadow passed over Yvonne's face, then settled in to haunt her eyes. "Not anymore."

She turned away, but Lily put a hand on her arm. She hesitated, wanting to ask about Yvonne's dreams, or lack of them, but even though she felt a connection to this woman, they'd only known each other an hour, and she had no right.

"Before Laurel comes back, tell me about Cash and Rico, that sheriff, and who's Nate?"

"I don't think I'll have time."

"Be quick, then, but I need to know who I'm dealing with."

So Yvonne told Lily all that she knew, quickly. Her story not only explained why Grubby Texas had left town, never planning to come back, but why he'd been so eager to lose the saloon. The coward no doubt thought Rock Creek had been left a pile of burning buildings and dead bodies.

"I wasn't here when El Diablo came, but I guess

those boys were somethin' to see. Now most everyone considers them hometown fellas."

"If everyone likes Cash so much, how come this saloon is empty."

"I don't think anyone *likes* Cash. Except those other men, and sometimes I wonder on them. Folks are afraid of him, mostly, so they steer clear of this place. Oh, Saturdays we get busy when the ranch hands come to town. But the way Cash grumbles on Saturdays, I think he prefers to have the saloon all to himself."

"That's no way to run a business."

"He doesn't need the money."

"Well, we do."

"You tell me how to go about that and I'm right behind you."

Lily smiled. With every passing minute, she liked Yvonne more and more. "First we clean; then we decorate and prepare to open with a flash."

Before Yvonne could give her opinion of the plan, bare feet pattered down the stairs. From the roll of Yvonne's eyes and the way she hightailed it behind the bar, Lily knew who had arrived before she even turned around.

"Cash says you own this place." Laurel, of the high-pitched voice, tossed a length of brunet hair over her shoulder.

At her side, a redhead with a buxom figure blinked sleepily at Lily. Must be Kate. Lily wondered whose bed the girl had been in, then decided she really didn't want to know.

"I do own it," Lily agreed.

"You don't plan to horn in on our business, do ya?" Laurel asked. "There are only so many men with money in this town."

"I wanted to talk to you about that."

"Oh, no!" Kate wailed. Her voice, even higher pitched than Laurel's, made Lily's ears rebel. "You're gonna take away all the customers."

"Not the way you think—"

Kate started to cry even louder than she talked. Laurel put her arm around the other girl and glared at Lily.

Lily glanced at Yvonne, who shrugged as if to say, "Told you so," then polished faster.

"Listen!" Lily shouted over the din.

Amazingly, Kate stopped crying as if a faucet had been turned off. Lily narrowed her eyes. Had the girl been acting all along? If so, she was very good, which gave Lily an idea.

"We're going to clean this place up. Make it more appealing. Bring in more customers." Laurel and Kate grinned. "And we're going to have entertainment." Laurel and Kate frowned. "Singing? Dancing? Music? If things work out, down the road maybe even a play or two."

"Play what?" Kate asked. Then a light dawned. "Oh, cards."

"Well, those, too. But I meant play, as in theater. On the stage."

"What stage?"

"We'll build one."

Laurel's eyes narrowed. "Who's we?"

"All of us, working together, can make this place better. That means more customers and more money."

"More money is good. What'll we have to do?" Lily told them. Slowly.

"But if we're serving drinks and you're paying us part of the profit and things go good, then eventually we won't need to . . . you know."

They seemed to be catching on.

"I know."

Laurel looked at Kate, then Kate looked at Laurel. They both looked at Lily. "Cash isn't going to like that."

Yvonne snorted.

Lily just smiled.

CHAPTER 4

Lily left Laurel and Kate under the direction of Yvonne, who seemed to have a knack for cleaning and a military mien. She had Laurel sweeping and Kate dusting within minutes. The lure of money did wonders for the work ethic.

Still, Lily didn't think the girls would have worked on a promise unless Yvonne said so. They trusted the woman, which said a lot for Yvonne.

As she reached the stairs, Johnny appeared. He'd changed from his dusty traveling clothes and wiped his face. She could still see streaks of dust along his chin and wrists, which only made her want to lick her finger and rub the smudges away. He'd no doubt let her; the boy was starved for affection. But Lily was afraid to get too close. Johnny wasn't her child, not even her brother, and he would most likely drift off when a better offer came along. Men did that. It was their nature.

"Were there empty rooms for us?" He nodded.

"Mine?" Johnny raised his hand and put up one, two, three fingers, then jerked his head to the right. "Third door on the right?"

Yes.

"And yours?"

One, two, three fingers to the left.

"Right across the hall. Perfect." She gave in to the urge to pat his arm. "I'm glad you came with me, Johnny."

He soaked up her praise as dry dirt soaked up the rain.

"Who's this handsome young thing?"

Johnny flinched at the volume of the voice. He had very sensitive ears, no doubt a result of his musical ability.

Lily glared at Laurel. "My little brother. Look but don't touch or you're out on your ear."

"I'm no baby thief. Is he gonna help with the dirt?"

Johnny clattered down the steps and started moving the tables aside so Yvonne could wash the floor.

"Well, ain't he handy?"

Lily didn't like the way Laurel eyed Johnny's arms. For a piano player, the kid had some impressive muscles. No doubt R.W. had started him carrying crates of whiskey at the age of ten.

Another glare and Laurel moved off. Lily couldn't fix the entire world, but she'd begun sweeping out her little corner. It would have to be enough for now.

She climbed the stairs, planning to get out of her corset, as well as a few petticoats, before she pitched in and helped.

From the looks of the hallway, the upstairs would need a thorough cleaning, too. Lily sighed, hoping the rooms were habitable at least, though she didn't hold out much hope.

The first door at the top of the stairs was smaller and shorter than the others—a linen closet. Had Johnny meant her room was actually the third door or the third room door? She opened her mouth to call out the question just as the trill of a piano filled the air.

With a shrug, Lily opened the third door. The eyes of the naked man standing at the washbasin met hers in the mirror. Pale blue, they did not reflect surprise or embarrassment, only a dark sadness contained deep within. Without so much as a blink, he returned his attention to shaving his head.

Lily had never seen a man shave his head. She wondered why he did it, though with those incredibly beautiful eyes and the symmetry of his face, he must be stunning once the soap was off his head.

The rest of him was equally impressive. Thick shoulders, hard legs and . . . Lily jerked her gaze from where it did not belong.

"You must be Miz Fortier."

Lily blinked, glanced behind her for Miss Fortier, then remembered Miss Fortier was her. "Uh, yes." She thought back to the men she'd met and the names she'd heard in relation to her saloon and lit on one. "You're Nate."

His smile was gentle, an expression at odds with his height and breadth. "You've heard of me already. I'm flattered."

He had the least southern accent of any of the men she'd met in Rock Creek thus far, though the twang to his voice made her think border state— maybe Kentucky, Missouri, even the southern tip of Illinois. During the war those states had seen some of the worst violence of them all.

Nate continued shaving. His serenity baffled Lily. She had known countless men. She'd been intimate with a few. Yet none of them were as easy with their nakedness as this one. She didn't know what to say or where to look.

"Did you want something?" He paused and made a movement as if to turn around.

"No!" Lily backed into the hall. "Wrong room. I'm terribly sorry. We'll chat later."

She slammed the door and rushed to the next, stumbling inside and slamming that door, too.

Muttering in French, a habit she'd adopted when any annoyance voiced in English sparked violence from R.W., Lily unbuttoned her dress, then slipped it from her shoulders. Crossing to the washbasin, she breathed a sigh of relief to find cool water. As she raised the cloth to her dusty, hot neck, her gaze touched upon the mirror.

With a shriek, she spun about, palming her knife and holding the weapon at the ready.

Rico's black eyes lowered to the knife, then rose to her face, perusing her uncovered bodice along the way.

Lily hissed at him. "You sneaky little— What are you doing in here?"

"This is my room."

Her eyes narrowed. "Then why are you hiding like a thief?"

"Habit. I heard someone go into Nate's room. Figured it couldn't be you."

"Wrong room."

"You seem to have that problem *mucho*. Or perhaps this is not a mistake." He pushed away from the door and took two steps in her direction. She waved the knife at him, but he merely smirked, unconcerned.

"What are you blathering about?"

"You come to my room and begin to undress." He shrugged, his lean shoulder sliding seductively beneath the black cotton shirt. "It is my dream come true."

"Your ego is bigger than Texas."

Strong white teeth flashed against his bronzed skin. "That is not all that is bigger than Texas."

Lily snorted. "You *are* a dreamer. I did not come in here on purpose. Johnny indicated that this was my room."

"I wondered why your bag was on my bed. But I had hopes it was a message. You did not want to make the others jealous because you desire me. I understand."

Was he serious? The way he was smiling, she couldn't tell. One thing she was sure of: He was the most infuriating man she'd ever met, even worse than Daniel Cash. With Cash she knew where she stood. With Rico . . .

"Oh—shut up." *Excellent response, Lily,* her mind taunted, which only annoyed her more. What was it about this man that made her feel ungainly instead of graceful, foolish instead of clever, hot instead of cool?

She glanced about. The room was devoid of any personal items but her own. "This is a mistake. Obviously Johnny thought this was an empty room. I'll just move elsewhere."

"It is not necessary, *querida.* I will share."

"I will not."

"Pity. It would save so much time."

"I am *not* going to sleep with you!"

"Would you care to make a bet on that?"

"*Enfer non!*" she snarled.

"I will take that as no. But if you are so certain my heart's desire will not come true, then you would make easy money on such a wager."

"Get out."

He raised an insolent eyebrow. "This is my room."

Lily considered sticking him. She'd used her knife before. Working in a saloon gave men the idea a woman was for sale. While many were, she was not. Not that she hadn't taken lovers with no love involved. She'd done what she had to do, and if she had to split a little skin, she wasn't squeamish. But she had a nagging feeling that Rico was a whole lot quicker than she was. While he was no doubt dangerous, she didn't think he'd force her. His ego was too big for that.

"If you don't mind, I'd like to freshen up before I move to another room. Would you step outside like a gentlemen?"

"Ah, *querida*, my papa always told me I am far from a gentleman." Though his voice teased, the words brought a crease to his brow, making Lily wonder just who his father was and why the man had wanted his gunfighting son to be a gentleman. But Rico's past was no business of hers. Just as hers was no business of his.

"Fine," she snapped, tired of the game. She could be as nonchalant as Nate about her nakedness. In years gone by she'd danced in front of a roomful of men in much less than she wore right now.

She put down the knife and retrieved the dropped washcloth. But the sheath on her wrist prevented her from washing her arms. When she tried to unbuckle it, her fingers became all thumbs.

Suddenly, Rico's dark hand covered her paler one. She caught her breath. How had he come so close and she'd never heard a single footfall? The man was spooky.

"Let me." His breath whispered across her bare neck, making Lily shiver.

The heat of his body meandered along every inch of hers, though he touched her nowhere but at her wrist. A quick glance in the mirror revealed their reflections, so similar—their hair nearly the same shade, his black shirt, her black dress, eyes equally dark and heavily lashed. But whereas his skin was the shade of summer-warmed sand, hers was as pale as the petals of the flower she'd taken as her name.

Rico unbuckled the sheath with nimble fingers that made Lily wonder how inventive those hands could be. She'd had lovers, true, but never one of her own choosing and never one as skilled as she'd heard a true lover could be.

The leather loosened, but instead of backing away, he pressed the tips of two fingers to the pulse at her wrist at the same moment his mouth closed over the pulse at the side of her neck.

Her sharp gasp as arousing as the scrape of his teeth, the kick of her blood sent her heart thundering like a caged bird against her chest. The sheath fell to the floor as her hands went limp, and her head fell back against his shoulder.

He had a smart mouth, a clever mouth, a very busy mouth, that teased and taunted a path to hers. His hands on her hips, he spun her about and worked his way along her neck and chin to her empty, seeking lips.

She thought she'd go mad. His mouth tortured hers, a gentle brush, the flick of his tongue, a touch-

and-go pressure of the lips. She had never been kissed like this, and she didn't want him to stop.

So when he lifted his head, she tangled her fingers in his soft hair and yanked him back for some more.

No matter how deeply she kissed him, he did not lose control. He did not grab her or maul her or throw her on the bed and take. He did not even brush his knuckles across the bared expanse of her breasts. His thumbs stroked the sharp bones of her hips over and over again. His restraint confused her, enticed her, tempted her.

When he removed his hands, her hips moved forward of their own accord. She bumped against him and discovered his restraint did not extend everywhere. Her mouth curved against his, and she wondered why. Usually the proof of a man's desire bored her. Right now she felt anything but.

Fingers tangling with hers, he drew them from his hair, then lifted his mouth. "I want you, Lily. While I will happily share my room, I do not share my women. How much to have you all to myself?"

She came out of her soft reverie with a start, though she knew the shock would not show on her face. She'd been kicked when she was down a hundred times before, and the only way to survive was never to let them see the bruise.

So she smiled as if she meant it as she untangled her fingers from his. Then she lifted her knee straight into that part of him that did not look anywhere near as big as Texas but was certainly as easy to find.

"Bâtard!"

A few moments later, Rico regained his posture, and something dangerous flickered in his eyes. Fear flowed through Lily, as deep as when she'd looked down the barrel of Cash's pistol. She could see now why the two of them were friends.

She raised her chin and stared him down. If he meant to kill her, then so be it. But she was no man's whore.

"Somehow I do not think that means darling." After a courtly bow, Rico left the room limping.

Rico paused in the hall to compose himself. Something hard hit the door behind him—perhaps a shoe—and he heard again Lily's favorite word for him.

He'd have to find out if Mary spoke French, though having the dear, sweet wife of the man he admired most on this earth tell him the word meant . . . He figured he knew what it meant, and he was certain he didn't want to hear such a thing from Mary Reese's lips.

Rico's body still hummed, though one part throbbed. Perhaps he had deserved that, though he did not think so. As he started down the hall, his step held a bit of a hitch. He figured it would wear off in a week or two.

A shuffle near the stairs drew his attention. Nate and Cash lounged against the wall, smirking. *Damn.*

"You limping, kid?"

"Twisted my ankle."

"I don't think it was your ankle got twisted." Nate gasped in mock surprise. "I do believe the boy done got his attitude forcibly adjusted. Must be a first."

"You want me to take care of her?" Cash drawled.

Rico gave them a scathing look and tried to move past to the stairs. Each put a hand on his chest and shoved him back.

"Ten dollars he has her in bed before another week is out," Cash murmured.

"A week? He's good, but I think she might be better. I say three weeks."

"Why don't you make it a month so I'll have a fair chance?" Rico snapped.

"You're on."

For the first time that Rico could remember, he wanted to punch his friends. "You are both a disgrace."

Nate looked at Cash. Cash looked at Nate. Then they looked at Rico and laughed in his face.

Nate put his hand over his heart. "Kid, you wound us."

Cash was laughing so hard, he had to brace himself against the wall. "We're a disgrace? When did that happen?"

Rico made a disgusted sound and left them both laughing their asses off as he clattered down the stairs and away from them.

Lily locked the door behind Rico. She didn't trust him or herself. He might have insulted her, but he'd also thrilled her. She'd done the right thing. So why did she feel as if she'd done everything wrong?

In the mirror she looked different, softer somehow. Was it the glass, the light, the truth?

She touched her fingertip to her lower lip— warm, wet. Her tongue shot out. She could taste him still.

Once, just once, she would like a lover of her own choosing. Over the years she had heard all sorts of intriguing information, and one of the tidbits she'd gathered was that some men were worth keeping awhile. She'd observed people as she went about her job, and certain men had a charisma that came from within. When a man like that came to town, the women fluttered about, begging for one single touch of his hand.

Lily wasn't the begging type, but she had to wonder: What was so special about those men that made women who got excited about little as twittery as virgins?

Whatever it was, Rico had it. Because even though he was long gone, her hands still shook. And even though she'd sent him on his way with little doubt as to what she meant, if he came back, she might just let him kiss her again and to hell with his insults.

The man could kiss. He knew where to touch and exactly how much or how little. He would be a memorable experience if she took him to bed. She had no doubt he knew it, too. Rico was completely self-absorbed, a charmer but a cad. Poison, no matter how good he tasted or how delectable he looked.

Once upon a time she'd hoped for a man who could see the woman she wanted to be and not the woman she'd been forced into becoming.

Silly hopes. She wasn't any kind of fool. If men like that existed, they certainly wouldn't spend time with a woman like her.

Not that she was bad, no matter what the good women said. She didn't kick dogs or drown kittens or steal—much. She always tried to be nice to everyone and help whomever she could. Of course, most decent folks only saw her cleavage, her lip rouge, her past. They didn't care that all she could do was sing, all she knew was music, all she had to depend on was herself.

Lily liked it that way. Her mother had depended on a man—make that men—over and over and over again. She'd believed in love. She'd believed that every last one of those men would come back for her and make things right forever. She'd died believing it. Lily had lived by knowing the truth.

Love was a myth perpetrated by men to get what they wanted from women. Men wanted one thing; women had it. Life was as simple as that. If you understood the rules, you didn't get hurt. Lily might fall down, but she always got up, and she would never allow herself to care about a man so deeply that he could destroy her from the inside out. She didn't have that luxury.

The taste of Rico was gone. The face in the mirror appeared familiar again. Lily dressed in her last clean skirt and shirtwaist, tightened the hair that had been undone by Rico's busy fingers, picked up her bag, and opened the door.

The shadow of a man loomed in the hall, and she dropped the bag with a thud. He was back. Her heart stuttered and lurched. What would he do to her now?

The shadow materialized into Johnny. Lily began to breathe again. "You scared me."

He picked up the bag she'd dropped and gave her a look that questioned.

"This is Rico's room."

His curious expression became a scowl. "Hey, I didn't put my bag in here; you did." When he hung his head, she felt bad. Unlike her, Johnny was very easily hurt.

"S-s-s-sorry," he blurted.

"I was teasing." Lily put her hand on his arm. "You musn't talk, Johnny. We're alone now, but there are so many people in this place, you never know who might be listening. Until you feel at home here, there's no reason to speak, sugar. You're with me, and I understand you completely."

Johnny nodded, but sadness still haunted his eyes.

"Never mind about the room," she continued. "It was a reasonable mistake. The man keeps nothing personal in there. You'd think he barely stayed here at all."

Which made her wonder. Did he have another house? A wife? Lily recalled the little girl who had not seemed to like her overly much. A child? She'd known men who kept a room at the saloon for their mistresses and a house for their wives and children. Rico didn't seem the type, but then, what did she know of him? He'd disappeared quickly enough once she'd shown him how she felt about his offer.

Johnny crossed the hall and opened the door next to his. With a shrug, he stepped back so she could look. Though the place wasn't as clean as Rico's had been, that only proved it was emptier. She shouldn't find Cash, or someone she hadn't even met yet, in her bed accidentally.

"This'll do," she said.

Johnny tossed her bag on the bed. Lily chose to ignore the puff of dust that rose on contact—for the time being.

Descending the stairs, Lily stopped at the sight of Rico, sleeves rolled up, gray dust sprinkling his black hair like snow, moving empty crates from the main room to the porch outside. Cash and Nate sat in the corner, smirking and drinking and absently tossing cards back and forth in some game only they seemed to understand.

Johnny paused before her on the stairs. He looked from Lily to Rico and scowled, then shook his head vigorously.

"Never mind," she admonished. "I'm not that foolish."

He didn't look convinced, but then, neither was she. The boy started pulling broken boards from the wall, and that was when Lily saw the bullet holes.

She strolled to Cash and Nate's table. "Have you been shooting in here?"

"Me?" Cash looked insulted.

"If the gun fits . . ."

"The only gunfire that went on inside this place was when Brown came shooting at Rico. Remember that?"

Nate snorted and loosened his collar. He looked half-drunk already and even bigger wearing his clothes, if that was possible. Lily had been right. Nate was a handsome man. His skin unmarked, his eyes exquisite, the lack of hair only made him all the more striking.

She hoped he wasn't a mean drunk. She'd hate to have to smack him over the head with a wood plank and drag him upstairs.

"Why would someone shoot at Rico?" she asked.

"Granddaughter." Cash tossed another card on the pile.

"Hmm." Lily glanced at the man in question, but he was busy with dusty cases of whiskey. She found herself captivated by the play of muscles in his forearms, and when he leaned over to put the case on the bar, his black pants pulled tight along his legs. Suddenly, her shirtwaist seemed too hot for the night.

"Most of those bullet holes were here before we showed up," Cash said.

"Liar," Nate murmured.

Cash shot him a glare. "What are you muttering about, Rev?"

"Rev?" Lily's interest returned to Nate and Cash.

"As in reverend. Nate's the closest thing we got to a preacher, if you don't count that hypocrite Clancy over at the church. And most don't."

"You're a man of God?" She took in the bottle of liquor at his left hand and the gunbelt strapped around his waist.

"Was." He took a long pull on the bottle. "I cannot tell a lie. Some of those bullet holes came from our battle with the Devil."

Lily raised a brow. Just how crazy was Nate? "Don't tell me you shot at the Devil in my saloon."

"He shot first. It wasn't my idea."

Lily didn't know what to say. She didn't want to throw a paying customer out on the street, but if Nate kept seeing imaginary devils and shooting up the place, she couldn't let him stay here.

"Never mind him," Cash drawled, gathering the scattered cards and shuffling them with long-fingered, well-maintained hands. "He's talking about El Diablo, a very real bad guy. Or at least he was until he died. We wouldn't let Nate shoot up the place no matter how much fun that might be."

"The Devil is the prince of lies." Nate sighed, then sipped and put his head down on the table. "But God has told some whoppers of his own."

Lily glanced at Cash and caught a flicker of sadness in his eyes before he saw her looking and any semblance of emotion disappeared. "Go away." He flicked a hand at her. "Leave him to me."

"Maybe his problem is you."

His dark gaze narrowed. "I'm all he's got left besides Rico and Jed. Nothing will ever hurt him again if I have anything to say about it. So go watch Rico's ass some more, Miss Fortier, and leave Nate to someone who knows what he's up against."

Lily chose to ignore the jibe about Rico. She'd learned that with men like Cash it was best to ignore a lot. "He's your problem, then. Just make sure he doesn't shoot up my saloon, smash up my glass, or throw up on my clean floor."

"I never throw up," Nate muttered.

"Then we'll get along just fine."

The clatter of a board pulled her attention back to Johnny. He hissed in pain, then grabbed one hand with the other.

Lily hurried across the room. A sliver stuck out of his palm. She plucked it out before he could pull away, then peered at the tiny hole. No blood welled. It looked to be no more than a scratch. She let out a sigh of relief. "No more hard labor for you, young man."

He tugged on his hand, but she wouldn't let him go. Instead, she picked up the other hand and held them gently as she looked into his eyes. "I mean it, Johnny. We can't risk your hands."

"What is so special about him?" Rico's voice at her shoulder made Lily flinch. "Why are my hands dirty enough to lift and drag and bleed? What makes his better?"

"I'll show you." She led Johnny to the piano. "Go ahead, sugar. Show 'em all."

He touched those keys as if they were satin, played them as though they were golden toys. Johnny's fingers on the keys of any piano, even one that had not been played in a long, long while, were magic such as this little town had never known.

He closed his eyes, became the music, and in turn the music filled the room, became the air, swirled around, through and into every heart.

After a few moments, Lily began to sing. When Johnny played, she could not keep quiet for long. He smiled at her as together they finished "Do They Miss Me at Home," a sad, weepy song that had been around since before the war.

When the last strains died away and Johnny segued into "The Yellow Rose of Texas," Lily glanced at each person to see if she were the only one feeling the enchantment. The women stood frozen in wonder, mouths agape, eyes dazed. Cash contemplated Johnny, a considering frown pulling at his mouth; even Nate had raised his head. Rico stared, but not at Johnny.

Those dark, unfathomable eyes were on Lily, and he wasn't thinking of music. A shiver went over her when she remembered his touch, his kiss. Her gaze dropped to the V of his shirt. He'd released several buttons, and a thin line of damp trailed from his bronzed neck to his smooth chest, disappearing beneath the black material. She found herself wondering if his entire chest were bare and smooth, not a wisp of hair, only supple muscles expanding and contracting beneath perfect skin.

How would he taste now? Hot and wet? How would he taste in the morning? Warm and new? Or at sunset on the river, cool wind across damp flesh.

She licked her lips, then raised her gaze to his. Rico took a step in her direction, cursed, grabbed a bottle of whiskey from behind the bar, and slammed out of the saloon.

Johnny kept playing, lost in the music. Lily kept

staring after Rico, lost in the possibilities long after he'd gone.

He'd taste like trouble, she thought, and trouble she'd tasted enough.

CHAPTER 5

Rico was halfway to the hotel when Eden's shadow drifted past the window. He stopped in the middle of the street and took a long pull on his bottle.

He could no longer go banging in there and raise a ruckus with Sullivan. The man had a wife and four kids, one of them not much more than a baby. Oh, Rico could probably tip a few with his former instructor in the sneaking arts, but after a while, Eden would come in, stare at him with her sweet face, her knowing eyes, and want to fix whatever was wrong with him.

Rico stepped toward the cabin behind the schoolhouse, stopped, and took another drink.

He'd fare no better there. His former captain would pour him a shot, then bounce his own daughter on his knee while thinking of the next day's lessons for the children of Rock Creek. Little Georgie would giggle and babble his name—she loved Rico as much as the next female—and for a while he could forget the gnawing restlessness in his gut. Then Mary would come in, kiss Rico on the cheek, and want to fix whatever was wrong with him.

"And what is wrong with me, they cannot fix," he murmured, then drifted down the empty boardwalk on Main Street.

There was nothing Eden or Mary could do to help him—not now or ever. Probably nothing Lily Fortier could do, either, except soothe the ache and assuage the loneliness for a single night. Rico wasn't dumb. What was wrong with him went deeper than even great sex could fix and hurt a whole lot worse than loneliness.

Rico paused outside the broken-down home, which was little better than a shack, where William Brown and his granddaughter lived. For a minute he considered knocking. But the place was quiet and dark. She was asleep, as she should be. As Rico probably wouldn't be all night.

A few more pulls of the whiskey and the boiling discontent in his belly cooled, replaced by warmth and a maudlin state of mind.

Only Carrie made him feel worthwhile anymore, because she was too young and in love with him to see that she was mistaken in her devotion. And bastard that he was, he didn't enlighten her, for Carrie's love gave him a reason to get up every day.

Oh, he put on a cheery, cocky, flirtatious front. Everyone expected it. But inside he'd never felt sadder or less like flirting. He was twenty-five years old, and sometimes he wanted to just lie down and die.

The only time he'd done something important with his life had been in the war—after he and the five men who were his only true friends had begun to ride together. They had done a lot of good, saved a lot of lives. But those days were gone.

Their leader turned teacher, their scout turned sheriff, God only knew where Jed was, and Cash and Nate were trying their best to kill themselves or get someone to do it for them.

And himself? He was just drifting again, trying to find a reason why he was alive and so many others were not. Hoping to find something worth living for but pretty certain he would not.

He would have to get a paying job soon. He had little money left, and he could not hire out his gun like Cash or Nate. Just the thought made him laugh. He could sneak up on anyone but Sullivan, and he could do amazing things with a knife, but he'd never been able to hit much beyond nothing with a gun.

''There aren't too many jobs for knife-wielding sneaky people these days,'' he muttered.

Since the only person who might be willing to drink with him was Baxter Sutton, the shopkeeper, and Rico had had enough of him the first week he came to Rock Creek, he took his bottle and sneaked into his room the back way.

He could still smell her on the air. He could hear her voice drifting from below. *Madre de Dios*, what a voice! What was she doing in Rock Creek if she could sing like that?

The tinkle of the piano now and again only made Rico remember how Lily had looked as she sang, how her face had softened when she watched that kid play. As if Johnny were the most precious and remarkable thing on this earth. No one but Carrie had ever looked at Rico like that.

"Not no one, *bastardo*. Anna looked at you like that up to the day that she died."

He pushed the thought away, drowned it, as he always did, with whiskey burn from throat to belly, then yanked his mind back to Lily and the piano player.

Although the kid was probably half her age and her brother to boot, Rico had been jealous. Or at least he thought that's what the burning, churning anger in his chest had been.

So many women, so little time. He cared about each one with equal passion for a single night, sometimes a few more. And they all adored him, until Lily.

Well, there was that one occasion when he'd kissed Mary and she'd laughed in his face; then Reese had almost killed him. But that didn't count. He'd only been trying to annoy Reese, and it had worked quite well. They *were* married, after all.

So why did Lily look at him as if he were horseshit on the bottom of her shoe? Was it just Rico, or every man but Johnny who disgusted her? Why did a woman who looked like Lily, who'd lived in the wicked city of New Orleans, who'd obviously spent most of her life in a saloon, kiss like a puckered-up virgin?

Most importantly, why did he care so much? Why did he want to be the one to change the way she kissed? Was it the challenge of the first woman who'd ever been unaffected by him? Was he that shallow? Most likely. So how was he going to make himself stop wondering about Lily, stop giving a damn if she hated or loved him, stop wanting to teach her how to use her tongue?

Rico held the bottle up to the light. This should

help for tonight. Tomorrow he wasn't so sure about.

He sat on his bed and listened to the music from below stairs, never knowing if the lilt of the piano lulled him to sleep or the whiskey in the bottle knocked him out.

Either way, he awoke to the thunder of native drums. His mouth tasted like . . . Ugh, he didn't want to think what his mouth tasted like. He smelled of stale whiskey, which didn't help the state of his stomach or the pounding of the drums.

Groaning, Rico lifted his face from the pillow and opened his eyes. The room spun. The light was too bright. The thunder continued. Were the Comanche attacking Rock Creek?

He didn't think there were enough Comanches left in these parts to mount much of an attack, but one never knew. His head fell back to the bed with a thud. Let Sullivan take care of it.

"Rico, open this door or I'm gonna shoot off the lock."

There was Sullivan now. Why wasn't he out stopping the Comanche?

Wham, wham, wham. "Rico! I'm gonna count to three."

Suddenly he understood that there were no Comanche except for the half-breed pounding on the door. "Hold on," he muttered, dragging himself from the bed.

The pounding stopped—at least on the door. Inside his brain was another matter. With his hand on his head to keep it from falling to the floor and bouncing about, Rico stumbled to the door and unlocked it.

Sullivan shoved inside as if Rico would try to keep

him out. His gaze flicked over the room before his mouth thinned, and he slammed the door.

Rico winced. "*Madre de Dios*, be silent. Have some pity for a dying man."

"I already have one dead man and no time for pity. Where's Carrie?"

Rico dropped his hand, lifted his head too fast, and gritted his teeth against the pain. "What in hell are you talking about?"

"I take it she's not hiding here."

Rico's mind was not working as fast as it should, and his ears seemed to be lagging behind the rest. He stared at Sullivan, who looked more frazzled than Rico had ever seen him. Even when his friend had been sneaking around behind Jed's back with Jed's little sister, courting death every day, he hadn't looked quite this haggard.

Suddenly, Rico heard what Sullivan had said, and he grabbed him by the shirt. "Where's Carrie?"

Sullivan went still as only Sullivan could. "Let me go, kid. Make it quick."

Rico shook him, even though the movement hurt Rico more than it did Sullivan. "Answer me."

"Get your whiskey breath out of my face and I will."

Rico released him and collapsed on the bed. His legs weren't going to hold him up much longer, anyway.

"Carrie's missing. I was kind of hoping she'd be here with you."

"I haven't seen her since yesterday."

Sullivan cursed, and he wasn't much for swearing. "I wonder if she even knows."

"Knows what?"

"Haven't you been listening? Brown's dead."

Well, this just got better and better.

"Dead how?" Rico hoped all his knives were where they belonged and there wasn't one sticking out of Brown. He hadn't done anything, but with his past history, Rico doubted anyone would believe him. His friends wouldn't let him hang, but they'd still think he'd done it.

"Looks like his heart."

Rico looked at Sullivan though the tangled shade of his hair. "Bullet through the heart?"

The sheriff's forehead creased. "Don't sound so hopeful. Heart gave out. He was an old man with a terrible temper. It was only a matter of time until he popped. Why would you think someone killed him?"

"Everyone wanted to. He was an awful man and no good for Carrie. He was crushing her soul from the inside out."

"He was her only living relative. What we're going to do with her *if* we find her, I have no idea."

"I'll find her." Rico stood, and the room spun. Sullivan grabbed his elbow. "You couldn't find a horse's ass if you looked in the mirror."

"Nice." Rico yanked his elbow away and tumbled onto the bed.

Sullivan let out a snort of disgust. "I'll find the little girl. You sleep it off."

"I'm fine. I know where she is."

"So tell me and I'll get her. You'll be worthless until noon."

Rico covered his face with his arm. *Worthless.* Even his friends saw it.

"What's gotten into you? I never knew you to drink more than a few, but today you look as drunk as Nate."

"Am not," Rico mumbled.

"And you've never been lazy. Yet here you sit

with Cash, playing cards for dares, day in and day out. Find a job, Rico. Find something.''

Sullivan slammed out of the room. The clatter of his boots receded down the hall, then descended the stairs.

Find something. Easy for Sullivan to say. He'd found everything in Eden.

Rico might not know how to find a life, but he would find Carrie. He wasn't going to let another little girl die because of him.

Gritting his teeth, Rico forced himself to his feet. He rinsed his mouth, then dumped the rest of the water in the pitcher over his head.

He stepped from his room just as Lily was leaving hers. From the twitch of her nose and the flicker in her eye, he looked nearly as good as he felt and smelled even better. He was just making one spectacular impression after another with her. Right now he didn't give a damn.

"You're a quiet drunk; I'll give you that.''

"*Gracias.*'' He headed for the stairs.

"I didn't even know you'd come back.''

"It is my gift.''

"You owe me for that whiskey.''

He faced her. "Put it on my account.''

"You don't have one.''

"I have no money, either.''

"And how do you expect to live?''

"Day to day, same as always.''

A furrow appeared in her brow, as if he confounded her somehow. She opened her mouth, but he got there first.

"*Excusa.* I must find Carrie.''

"Your little girl?''

"Not mine. Though she would argue that I belong to her.''

The crease in her brow stayed right where it was, but Rico had no time to explain even if he could.

Nate and Cash waited in the saloon. When he nodded and walked on by, they got up and followed. It was then that he realized they were both dressed and armed at the shiny hour of eight A.M.

"Where are you two going?"

Cash lit a cigar. "Wherever you are."

"Why?"

"You think we're going to let you go anywhere in your condition?"

"I am fine."

"I'm the queen of Sheba. Let's ride."

"It is not necessary. I can find her."

"Listen, kid, six eyes are better than two."

"And ten are better than six." Reese stood at the door with Sullivan. They all stared at him with faces that revealed they weren't going anywhere—except wherever he went.

Rico's eyes burned. He hated the morning after.

"Too bad Jed isn't here," Nate observed as the five of them tramped outside. "It'd be just like old times."

"I think the old times are gone for good," Cash said.

"And maybe that isn't so bad." Reese headed for the stables.

Everyone followed, which was as close to old times as they were probably going to get.

Lily huddled at the top of the stairs and eavesdropped shamelessly on the five men. She could read voices, every nuance, every rise and fall of inflection. They had a bond only tragedy could forge and nothing would ever break. She envied them that.

Laurel stumbled from Nate's room. She didn't even glance toward Lily. Instead, she knocked on Cash's door and went in when Kate answered.

Lily sighed. Why even give the two their own rooms if they continued to sleep with Nate and Cash, or Cash and Nate, as the case might be? Funny, but neither of them seemed to take a turn with Rico, which made her wonder. The man oozed sex from his skin; he flirted as easily as he breathed, yet he did not partake of two willing women. He had said he didn't like to share, which she found an odd quirk for a man like him.

She needed to quit wondering about Rico. He was nothing to her beyond a way to clean this place up and get it ready to open. But first she had to see how much credit she could charm out of the shopkeepers in order to buy supplies so she could use her cash to buy the perfect dress for opening night. She had to look the part of a prosperous entertainer if she ever hoped to become one. In her business she'd learned that appearances counted for a whole lot more than they should.

A thud downstairs, followed by the murmur of women's and children's voices, something not usually heard in a place like this, made Lily descend. Yvonne, already dressed and polishing her precious bar, stared at a tall, thin, brown-haired lady holding the hand of a cherubic blond toddler. Directly behind her stood another blond, a joyous-eyed woman with a baby on one hip and three older children gathered around her.

Lily braced herself for the assault. Looked like the committee on morality had come to call. She'd met them before in every place where she'd lived—

ladies who had never had to do anything on their own but felt compelled to tell others the appropriate way to live.

They would berate her for her lifestyle, her occupation, her very being, and when she asked them how she should make enough money to live, they would quickly find a reason to leave. They knew what she should not do but were of little help in telling her how to do anything else.

"Good morning, ladies," Lily greeted with a smile. Yvonne rolled her eyes. She'd obviously met women like these before, too, and had little use for them now.

The tiny blond-haired lady came forward. The kids followed her as if they were one being. "Hello. Welcome to Rock Creek. We're so excited you've come."

Lily blinked. "Huh?"

"I'm Eden Sullivan. This is Mary Reese. We thought we'd come over and get acquainted, since all the boys went off together."

She turned to Yvonne. "You must be Yvonne. Daniel's mentioned you. I've seen you about but never had the chance to say hello." Eden indicated the children. "Between these four and the hotel, I barely get a chance to talk to Sin."

Yvonne just stared at her as if she'd sprouted two heads.

"I think we might have come a bit early, Eden," Mary said. "The children get us up with the sun. But since you work late, our arrival at this hour must border on rude."

Lily narrowed her eyes, wondering if there was a veiled insult in there somewhere. But Mary's blue gaze was as clear and friendly as . . . as . . . Lily couldn't think when she'd seen friendlier eyes, unless they were Eden's.

"W-would you like some coffee?" she asked, figuring that would send the two running quickly enough.

"How lovely!" Eden cried. "I brought some biscuits, figuring there wouldn't be much in your kitchen yet." She settled the older children nearby with some of the food, then took a chair at the same table Mary had already appropriated.

The little girls in their laps reached across, trying to grab each other's hands. Eden's girl babbled nonsense, and Mary's giggled and shouted, "Fi, fi, fi."

"All right." Eden set her daughter on the floor; Mary did the same. Then Eden handed each a biscuit, which they promptly began to gnaw, all the while grinning at each other and holding hands. They reminded Lily of happy little puppies with bones.

"Georgie and Fiona have been the best of friends since the first time they saw each other," Mary murmured. "It's uncanny."

Lily glanced at Yvonne, who looked as confused as she felt. Yvonne shrugged. "I'll get the coffee and some cups." She fled.

Wary, Lily joined the two women. She kept waiting for the sneers to begin. But they just kept smiling. It was a bit frightening.

"Sin said you own this place."

"Sin?" Lily repeated, feeling like a fool.

Eden laughed. "My husband, Sinclair Sullivan."

"The sheriff."

"Yes," Mary answered. "My husband teaches school. Have you met him yet? He came by to get Rico and the others this morning."

Lily remembered the deep, commanding voice that had belonged to no one she'd known. "I didn't see him."

"Well, you're bound to run into each other eventually. So tell us how you've been getting along with Cash."

Lily couldn't help but make a face. The two women exchanged glances.

"That's what we thought," Eden said. "But don't let him push you around. He'll try until you push back."

"I already shoved him hard enough to meet his gun."

Eden gasped. "He pulled his gun on you?"

Lily shrugged. "I'd have done the same. I think we have an understanding."

"Hmm," Mary said. Eden just looked concerned.

Yvonne returned with a tray of cups and a pot of coffee. She put it down and turned to leave.

"Don't go," Mary cried. "Stay and talk with us,"

"No, thank you, ma'am. I've got work to do."

Lily met Yvonne's eyes and mouthed, "Traitor." Yvonne smirked and left the room.

"So tell us what you mean to do with the place."

Here it comes, Lily thought, *the snide comments, the sneers, and the threats disguised as suggestions.*

"I'm a singer. I plan to perform every weekend."

"Really? How wonderful." Mary clapped her hands, and her daughter did, too. The other child followed suit, even though she was busy chewing on Georgie's shoe. Everyone beamed gentle smiles and friendly eyes. "Eden, I think Rock Creek is going to become something to see."

"I always thought it was."

"Me, too." A dreamy look came over Mary's face, as if she remembered something special and secret.

Eden had the same look. "What can we do to help?" Mary asked.

Lily gaped. "*Pardon moi?*"

"We want to help. You can't expect those men to do things right. Nate won't last long sober, and Cash never lifts anything heavier than his pistols. Though Rico might be of some use other than decoration."

"I doubt it," Eden said dryly.

"He's of great use in certain instances." Mary's secret smile left no doubt what she was referring to.

"None of which apply here."

Lily couldn't resist. "What instances?"

Mary glanced at Eden. Eden glanced at the children, then lowered her voice. "You've seen him. You've talked to him. The man's a walking, talking temptation."

"*He* thinks he is."

"From what I've gathered from the boys, Rico's main occupation, when he wasn't with them, was beautiful women—one after another."

Lily's eyes narrowed. She'd known Rico was that type of man. So why did the truth annoy her?

Mary caught her expression and glanced uneasily at Eden. "Maybe we should get back to talking about the saloon."

"I suppose," Eden allowed. "But I've often wondered about Rico. How good is great?"

"Eden!" Mary gasped. "You're married."

"But not dead. He *is* beautiful, with more experience than any man I've ever heard about. It doesn't hurt to wonder."

Mary didn't look convinced. She smoothed her hair, then her skirt. "What did you have planned for the saloon, Lily?"

Lily wasn't sure what to say. The subject of Rico now closed, the two women seemed serious about helping her with the place and not in any mood to leave.

She couldn't believe ladies like these would want to pitch in and dirty their hands on an entertainment venture. Why weren't they sneering at her, preaching hellfire, trying to save her from herself? Could it be they didn't understand exactly what she meant to do here?

"There's still going to be a saloon and gambling as well as music, dancing, and singing."

"Of course," Mary said. "How else would you make a living?"

Lily knew how most women like Mary believed she made her living. But without even asking, Mary assumed that Lily was exactly who she said she was—a businesswoman, a singer—nothing more or less.

The slam of a door and the patter of bare feet down the stairs made Lily wince. Kate and Laurel stopped dead when they saw Mary, Eden, and the children.

Lily stood and placed herself between the visitors and her employees. Kate and Laurel might be fools, but they were her fools, and she wasn't going to let anyone hurt their feelings or talk down to them in her place.

Before Lily could introduce everyone, Eden spoke. "Hello, girls. How have you been?"

"Good," Laurel answered. "You?"

The four made small talk—wary, polite, but friendly enough. Lily just stood there, unable to believe her ears or eyes. The ladies of the town and the ladies of the evening spoke to each other, knew each other's names, did not consider one the other's enemy. What kind of place had she come to? Why couldn't every place be like this?

Laurel and Kate drifted off to find breakfast. Lily returned to her seat.

"Did you think we were going to throw stones at them?" Mary asked softly.

"Or perhaps get out the tar and the feathers or a rail to run them out of town upon?" Eden put in.

"I wasn't sure." Lily met both their gazes squarely. "But I certainly wasn't going to let you."

Mary glanced at Eden. "Oh, I like her."

Eden kept her gaze on Lily. "Me, too."

CHAPTER 6

In Lily's line of work women competed—for jobs, men, money. They did not pitch in and help virtual strangers clean the grubbiest place in town. In Rock Creek, the women did. Or at least that's what Mary and Eden said.

Even the children helped. The older ones— Teddy, Rafe, and Millie—dragged loose boards outside; they also watched the younger girls until the two fell asleep on a blanket in a heap of chubby legs and sweet-smelling curls.

Cute as they were, Lily kept her distance from the little ones. Children were out of her circle, out of her reach, and there was no reason to taunt herself with what would never, ever, be.

Yvonne shook her head and mumbled whenever her path crossed Lily's, but she couldn't argue that Mary and Eden were hard workers and a lot of fun to be around. Once in a while Lily caught her smiling at something one of them said or something one of the children did.

Lily put Johnny to work upstairs. She wasn't sure how the other children would react to his silence, and she didn't want him teased. He'd had little contact with anyone his own age or younger. Until they were settled and he felt comfortable, she'd keep him away from strangers, and she would always protect him from everyone and everything with all that she had. She'd never felt so deeply about anyone, and while such strong emotions for another human being disturbed her, there was nothing she could do to stop them now.

The place nearly spotless from top to bottom, Lily put her hands on her hips and smiled with satisfaction. "Now I need curtains, food, and a new dress for the opening. Can you ladies direct me to the general store and the seamstress."

"The store is past the church." Eden rubbed sweat from her brow and left a long line of dirt across her forehead. "There isn't any seamstress, but you can get good-quality calico at Sutton's."

"Calico? I need satin, if not silk. And if there isn't any seamstress, how do you get clothes?"

Mary raised her brow. "By sewing them."

"Sew?" Lily had never so much as lifted a needle. She sat down, discouraged. She wouldn't be defeated by the little things. So she had no curtains. She'd get by. But because of her pride, she had brought very few clothes with her from R.W.'s place and nothing suitable to wear at the gala opening she envisioned. She could not sing and dazzle the crowd in a torn and tattered shirtwaist. She might be good, but not that good.

"I can sew." The quiet admission came from

Kate as she took a seat on the opposite side of the table. "My mama taught me."

Lily sat up straight. "How well?"

"Mama worked for a modiste in Charleston before the war. She was all the rage."

"Isn't that wonderful?" Eden said. "Problem solved, Lily."

Kate's face brightened. "If you get the material, I'll make you a dress. I love to sew. I've missed it."

"You know, I could use a new dress, and so could Millie. What about you, Mary?"

Mary watched Eden with a speculative gleam in her eye. "I wouldn't turn one down."

"Between working here and sewing you could make a pretty good living, Kate. In fact, I bet you'd need help." Eden turned to Laurel, who had just finished sweeping the last of the dust out the front door. "Can you sew?"

"Enough."

"Eden," Mary warned. "Cash isn't going to like this."

Laurel and Kate looked uncertain. Lily could see Yvonne's reflection in the mirror behind the bar, and she was shaking her head. Mary bit her lip. Eden just shrugged, then sat down at the table with Kate and began to plan new dresses for every female in the room.

"Thought you knew where she was, kid." Sullivan got off his horse and allowed the animal to drink from the river while he filled his hat with water and dumped the contents over his head.

The calendar might say spring, but the sun screamed summer, the chill bite of the wind yesterday a mere memory today. The five of them had ridden all over the area—from the river to Wishing Rock, even part of the way to Ranbourne. There was no sign of Carrie anywhere.

"And I thought you were an Injun scout," Rico tossed back.

His headache had not improved in the sun, and his tossing, turning stomach had only gotten worse as each hour passed without finding Carrie, as each place he knew her to frequent came up empty.

"If the two of you can't find her, she ain't gonna be found," Cash pointed out. "Chalk her up as missing and let's get a drink."

"Here, here." Nate toasted the idea with a canteen that fooled no one. Nate never bothered with water—plain or as a mix.

"She can't have gotten far." Reese washed his face in the river, then glanced at Rico. "She might even be in town. Somewhere we haven't thought to look."

Reese was trying to make Rico feel better. He knew how much Carrie meant to him. Not why, of course. Rico had told no one about his past so that no one would have a reason to look at him with the disgust he'd always seen in the eyes of his father.

He'd been a worthless son, a useless *caballero*, the worst brother in the world. He had to live with that, but he didn't have to live with everyone knowing it.

Rico had ignored Carrie yesterday so he could flirt with Lily. Who knew, he might have been kissing Lily's neck as Brown lay dying. He might have been whispering improper suggestions to her as Carrie cried.

"Kid, stick your head in the river until you're cooled off enough to quit sighing like you've lost your best friend," Cash snapped. "I've heard enough of that for one day."

He wheeled his horse and trotted off toward town, Nate at his heels.

Rico followed Cash's advice. Though it had been suggested with a sneer, the idea was a good one, because he felt much better after sticking his head into the spring-cold river.

Sitting down on one of the larger rocks that lined the water, he let the sun warm his wet hair. A moment later, Reese joined him on the right side and Sullivan on the left.

"You taught her well," Reese said. "Maybe too well if *you* can't find her."

"Why would she hide from me?" Rico hung his head between his knees. "Why would she not run *to* me."

"She might have run to you, but you were passed out or maybe busy with the new saloon owner?" Sullivan ventured.

"No to the second." Rico raised his head, then lifted one shoulder in a wry shrug. "She does not want me for any money. She does not want me for free, either."

"She hasn't been around you long enough. You grow on a woman, or so I hear," Reese said.

"She is not impressed with my face or body or reputation, as most of the others. Even my kiss only made her—" He paused, in no mood to recall how she'd told him no. He still ached in places he should not.

"So there is one woman with taste in the world."

"*Gracias, mi capitán.* Please feel free to kick me some more as I lie dying."

"Perhaps we should get in on that bet with Nate and Cash."

Rico groaned. Did everyone know about his misfortune? Trust Nate and Cash not to be able to keep their mouths shut about anything they thought was funny.

"Now, those two think you can seduce any woman, given enough time," Reese continued. "But maybe, just maybe, you can't."

Rico couldn't take that lying down, even though lying down was what he wished for. "I can, too."

Sullivan snorted. "Don't say that around Eden or Mary. They'll damage you permanently."

"Grow up, Rico," Reese said. "I've been expecting it for years. The war didn't help. Riding with us didn't, either. Maybe a woman will."

"I doubt even that would help," Sullivan murmured.

Rico scowled at him before turning to Reese. "I am grown. I have been a man since I left *mi casa* at the age of fourteen. I have taken care of myself."

"Have you? Or have we always been there for you?"

Rico thought back on the years before he had met these men. "Not always."

"All right," Reese acknowledged with a dip of his head. "But taking care of yourself, being tall, strong, wielding a knife better than anyone, doesn't make you a grown-up, Rico."

"What does?"

"That's something you'll have to figure out for yourself."

Rico rubbed his aching eyes. "That is what I was afraid of."

Reese stood, and so did Sullivan. Their shadows spread across the rocks. Though Rico was taller than both of them, he always felt smaller, and he probably always would.

Reese held out a hand to him. "Come on, kid. Let's go home."

Rico sighed. He had no home, and hadn't for a very long time. It hadn't bothered him, either, because once he'd met these men, home had always been them, not a house or a town.

Perhaps home had *never* been a place. Just as being on your own didn't make you a grown-up.

Rico took his friend's hand and let Reese pull him to his feet. Sullivan slapped him on the back hard enough to make his head throb some more. "In the morning we'll look everywhere all over again. We'll find her, Rico. I promise."

Rico nodded. Sullivan's promise was as good as a fact.

Still, he went back to Rock Creek feeling worse than he had when he'd left that morning, and that was saying a lot.

His mood did not improve when he approached the saloon and heard Cash shouting. Cash rarely shouted; he just shot, and then there was no more reason for shouting.

Ahead of him, Reese and Sullivan glanced at each other and started running. Rico followed, more slowly, because moving that fast made his head hurt. What he saw inside the saloon made his stomach hurt, too.

The women were having a lovely time, or should be if the yards of fabric spread over every table were any indication. Where dirt and dust had reined only yesterday, the Rock Creek saloon now sparkled and shone. Whereas there had been only cards and booze and men, there were now women, children, and—

"Are those cookies?" The horror in Cash's voice was matched only by the expression on his face.

Nate merely looked confused, as if perhaps they'd wandered into the wrong building or the wrong town. He sipped from his canteen and sat down to watch the show.

The children, used to Cash by now, ignored him. As soon as Georgie and Fiona saw Rico, they squealed and hugged his knees, just as Carrie always used to. Rico cleared his throat, always thick and tight the morning after he drank too much, then knelt to receive a wet, cookie-crumbled kiss on each cheek. He returned the favor, minus the cookie crumbs, and the girls joined hands and toddled back to the other children, Georgie helping Fiona all the way.

"What in holy hell is going on here?" Cash towered over Lily.

Lily looked mad, and when she began to stand, Eden put her hand out and stopped her. Rico relaxed a bit. If anyone could handle Cash, it was Eden. He moved a bit closer to the action, anyway.

"What does it look like, Daniel?" Eden asked.

"Purgatory."

"A myth," Nate stated. "I believe purgatory is life itself."

Everyone ignored him.

"We've had a hellish day, girls, and now we need a drink and a bit of companionship." He headed for the stairs. No one moved. Cash stopped and turned about. "Kate?"

She swallowed, glancing at Eden, then Lily. Her back straightened, and she lifted her chin. "No, Cash. I'm not goin' with you anymore. Lily says I can have part of the profits from Three Queens."

"What's that?"

"The new name for this place." Lily rose to her feet.

"Three Queens? Sounds like the name a woman would give the place."

"I won it with three queens."

"Figures," he sneered. "You'd have needed a flush to win it from me."

"Lucky for me, then, it wasn't yours to lose."

His dark eyes narrowed ominously, and Rico took a step forward, but Sullivan waved him back.

Cash kept staring at Lily, but she didn't back down. "The profits from this place won't feed you, Kate. I will. Now, come on."

"No. I'm sewin' dresses for the ladies. I won't need to be with men anymore if I don't want to." He glanced at her, and she paled. "Not that you aren't good, Cash. I just want to try life a different way to see if I can."

"And who gave you this idea?"

"Eden and Mary."

"Oh, oh," Reese and Sullivan said at the same time. They moved forward to collect their wives and children.

"Fine," Cash snapped. "Laurel, let's go."

"No."

Cash shook his head as if he had water in his ear. "What was that?"

"No. I'm gonna help Kate. And Lily's gonna help us both."

"This could get good," Nate murmured.

"Everything is your fault!" Cash pointed at Lily. "You're in town one day and you've reformed all the perfectly good fallen women. I knew you were trouble the minute you walked in the joint."

"Thank you."

"Hey, I'm not fallen," Laurel shouted. "I stand up better than Nate. Don't talk down to me, Cash. I did what I had to do. Right, Lily?"

Lily stared at Cash. "Right."

"And now I don't have to anymore. So quit

orderin' me around, Daniel Cash. I don't need
you, either.''

"That's it."

Cash's voice was so low and deadly, everyone
went silent. Lily stood her ground, but her face
paled when Cash started toward her, so Rico
stepped between them. Cash bumped into him,
snarled, then slammed his shoulder into Rico's
chest.

Instead of going for his knife, Rico grabbed
Cash's gun hand. "You don't want to do this,
Cash."

"You want to let go of my arm, kid, before you
lose your busy fingers."

"Fine. But you will leave Lily alone."

Hurt flashed in Cash's cold, dark eyes so fast,
Rico must have imagined it. "You afraid I'm gonna
damage her, kid?"

"I will not let you."

"You think your knives are faster than my gun?"

"Nothing and no one is faster than your gun.
But I can't just stand here and let you—"

"What?" Cash shouted, and tore himself from
Rico's grip. "What do you think I'm going to do?"
He looked at the others. "Do you think I'm going
to shoot a woman in cold blood just because she's
the biggest pain in the ass to hit town since Eden?"

No one answered.

"Shit. I'm leaving." He tromped up the stairs to
get his things.

Rico stood where he was until Nate walked past.
He caught his friend's sleeve. "You don't have to
go with him."

Though he'd been drinking steadily all day,
Nate's eyes were sober as a gravedigger's. "Yeah,

I do. If a friend isn't watching his back, an enemy will be."

"He's going to die one day, Nate. He's set on it."

"Hell, kid, we all die one day. If I die helping a friend, maybe my life will be worth something." He tugged free and followed Cash up the stairs.

Rico turned and bumped into Lily. She gave him an odd look he hadn't the energy to figure out, then backed out of his way.

"Reese, you've got to do something," Rico said.

"Nothing I can do. Maybe it's best if they leave for a while. Let off some steam. You know they always come back calmer than when they left."

"But, James, they're going off to fight with guns," Mary cried.

"That's what they do, honey. That's what we all did once."

Sullivan and Eden had their heads together, whispering furiously. "It's not my fault, Sin! We were just helping the girls. What's so wrong with them getting a worthwhile job? Maybe Cash and Nate should try it. It wouldn't even hurt Rico."

"You think I have no worthwhile job?" he asked.

Eden flushed as if she hadn't realized she'd spoken aloud, or perhaps Rico did not understand plain English. "Well, you don't."

"What do you suggest I do with my many talents?"

"I don't know. Something other than teach Carrie to sneak around and play poker."

"Carrie!" Mary exclaimed. "Did you find her?"

Reese scooped up Georgie, who was hanging on his knee and smearing cookie globs all over his pants. "Not yet."

"Oh, James, she's so little."

Putting his arm around his wife, Reese kissed the top of her head. "I know. We'll find her tomorrow."

"We'll find her tomorrow," Cash mimicked as he came down the stairs, Nate at his heels. "You make me sick. I can't stay here and watch the disintegration by females of what was once an unbeatable unit."

"You need to watch yourself, Cash, before you say anything you'll be sorry for."

"I'm only sorry I didn't do something before you and Sullivan succumbed to temptation."

"Temptation is the game of Satan," Nate announced.

"Shut up, Rev. I'm talkin' here. You two are going to be worthless if there's any kind of gunplay. You'll be worrying about your wives or your passel of kids or the next brat your sweetheart is going to squeeze out, and you'll get shot in the head or let me get shot."

Fiona started to cry, so Georgie joined her. The tension and the anger in the room had reached the little ones. The older children remained silent but watchful.

Cash made a disgusted sound. "You can't even have boys; you've gotta make girls and increase the wailing population. Then they dimple at the kid and he's just as bad as the two of you." Cash glared at Rico. "You chose a woman over me, and I don't take that kindly. As far as I'm concerned, this six has just become two. Let's go, Nate."

Cash stomped out the door. Nate hesitated, glancing at Reese. Reese jerked his head at the door, and Nate gave one slow nod before he followed. Moments later, the staccato rhythm of hoofbeats faded into the distance.

"That didn't go well at all," Eden observed. "Sin, how are you going to get them to come back?"

He leaned over and picked up Fiona, who had stopped crying as soon as the angry voices left. "I'm not."

"What?" Eden glanced frantically at the door as if she'd go after them herself. Sullivan, knowing what she was capable of, grabbed the bustle of her skirt and held on. "You can't let them go off like that."

"I just did. It's their choice, Eden. If they stuck around here, drinking, gambling, and getting more bored by the day, they were going to do something stupid. Then I'd just have to put them in jail."

"You wouldn't!"

"Of course I would."

"Then I would have to break them out somehow." Rico sighed. "And we would have chaos."

Reese snorted. "They'll be fine. Now, let's go home. I'm exhausted."

The two families went on their way. Rico glanced around. Yvonne was nowhere to be found. Kate and Laurel were engrossed once more in their sewing. Considering how much time they'd spent with Nate and Cash, they sure didn't seem concerned that the two were gone, which depressed Rico even more than the events of the day.

How many women in saloons across the West had fallen all over him and told him they loved him? For how many had he returned the favor? And how little had any of it meant to him or to them?

"Thank you." Lily stood at his side.

"Don't mention it."

"I appreciate your standing up for me. You didn't—"

"I said, 'Don't mention it,' " he snapped. "I'm not happy about what I did, and I certainly did not do it to help you."

"Why did you do it?"

"I don't know. Maybe to get you into bed."

She tilted her head and stared at him as if she had never seen him before. "I don't think so," she said slowly. "You're not a sex-as-gratitude kind of man. Too much pride for that."

"You know nothing about me. I am a sex-for-any-reason, any-season, kind of man."

"Hmm." Her finger tapped at her lips. If he hadn't been so tired and sad, Rico just might have been interested in the shape of those lips and the taste of that finger. "Maybe you are, and maybe that's not so bad."

She joined the girls, leaving Rico to stare after her in confusion. Had that been a compliment? And if so, what did it mean?

One day in town and the woman was driving him crazy. He had no idea what to say or do or how to behave around her. Lily Fortier was going to be far more trouble than she was worth.

"No one's that good," he muttered. "Not even me."

CHAPTER 7

Carrie stilled at the sound of footsteps on the stairs. She knew those steps as well as she knew her own. Rico was back.

She smiled at the thought of the man she adored beyond all others. To her, Rico was the tallest, the handsomest, the best. He had saved her from the bad cougar cat and made sure her granddad took better care of her than he had before Rico and the rest of the six came to Rock Creek.

She never told him how sometimes her granddad hit her when she was sneaky or pinched her when she wouldn't shut up about Rico. The bruises never showed, and even though her granddad was mean, he was her granddad, and she had nobody else.

"Big baby." She snuffled. "None of the Rock Creek Six would cry because their mean granddad dropped over dead when he was screamin' at 'em." Maybe because none of the six would let *anyone* scream at them.

Now she was hidin' to prove to Rico she was the sneakiest kid around. Then maybe he'd let her ride with him, stay with him. If he didn't, she had no idea what she would do.

Her granddad had always told her horrible stories of what happened to orphaned little girls. Carrie shuddered and huddled against the head of the bed. She didn't think there were people in the world who were actually that awful, but you never could tell.

All she wanted was to be with Rico. If she could just keep things the way they were for another eight years or so, her life would be fine. Because one day she was going to grow up, be as pretty as . . . as . . . as Mrs. Sullivan and as sweet as Mrs. Reese, then Rico would marry her and never look at another woman the way he looked at Lily Fortier.

"*Chérie*," Carrie muttered. "In a pig's ear!"

The door opened, and Carrie gasped when the piano player slipped into the room. How had he sneaked up on her? She'd heard Rico's footsteps, and Rico walked quieter than anyone. But she hadn't heard a whisper of this boy's approach.

He shut the door and stared at her with solemn eyes. She'd been slipping about the saloon all day, and no one had seen her, but she'd heard a lot. The kid's name was Johnny, and he was Lily's brother, though he looked nothing like her.

Oh, sure, he had dark hair and dark blue eyes, but Lily's skin was pale, her features fine. Johnny's skin was darker, like Rico's, and his features heavier, almost a man's, nearly as handsome as Rico, too. But the kid was spookier than Cash, and he talked a whole lot less.

"Whaddaya want?" she demanded.

He raised one brow, pointed first at the bag in

the corner, then at himself, and opened his palm in a graceful movement to encompass the room. He had the longest fingers she'd ever seen, and he used them to play that piano as if he'd invented the thing. Carrie knew little of music, but she could tell good when she heard it.

"This is your room?" He nodded. "Sorry. I didn't know." He shrugged. "Are you gonna tell on me?"

He just stared at her.

"You can't talk, can you?" He spread his hands in a gesture at once foreign and yet familiar— maybe yes, maybe no. "That's what I thought. So you won't be *telling* on me at all."

Johnny put his fingers to his mouth as if to whistle.

"Don't." He dropped his hand, tilted his head, and waited for her to explain.

"If I hide long enough, Rico will be impressed." He gave one slow nod. "And if everyone is scared that I'm lost or hurt or dead, they'll be sorry, and they'll let me stay with him."

Johnny looked skeptical. He came over and sat down on the bed. For some reason, she liked him. Maybe because he listened better than anyone she'd ever known.

Carrie smiled and scooted closer. "So if you let me stay here just a little longer, I promise I won't be a problem."

She peered into his eyes, but he was looking at her shoulder and not at her face. Carrie glanced to the side and discovered that her dress—the only one she owned, which was a size too big because Granddad always bought ready-made and there weren't too many sizes to choose from—had slipped off her shoulder.

The last bruise her granddad would ever make shone dark against Carrie's pale skin. Johnny lifted his gaze to hers, and fury heated his eyes. He jabbed a finger at her shoulder.

"M-my granddad." She dropped her head. "I was a problem."

Johnny put his finger to Carrie's chin and lifted her face. He shook his head emphatically. She wasn't a problem. Her smile blossomed.

"So I can stay here?"

Yes.

She let out a sigh of relief. "How come you're so nice?"

He hesitated, then slowly raised the sleeve of his shirt to reveal healed white scars along his forearm. The sight of them made Carrie mad.

She growled deep in her throat, furious that someone had done that to him. He jerked his arm away and tugged on the sleeve as if embarrassed.

Carrie grabbed his hand, held on tight, then pulled up the sleeve and rubbed the scars with her fingertips. "They tickle."

His eyes dark in the pale of his face, they reminded her of the bruise along her collarbone. "I'll be your friend," she whispered. "I bet you don't have too many."

No.

"That's okay. One good friend is better than a hundred acquaintances. That's what Rico says."

She slipped her hand into Johnny's and squeezed. For a minute he just stared at her as if she were the oddest creature on earth. His hand tightened, then released, and his lips curved into the sweetest smile she'd ever seen. Carrie's world became just a little bit brighter.

Johnny was the kind of friend you didn't make every damn day.

Several days after arriving in Rock Creek, Lily stood in Rico's room, waiting for him to return from his daily search for the little girl. She hoped they found Carrie today, because the sadness in Rico's eyes was starting to get to Lily, too.

She had no idea what was wrong with her. Ever since Rico had stepped between her and Cash, she'd been unable to think of anything else but him.

Or maybe her fascination had begun earlier, when Eden and Mary had discussed his decorative appeal, his lack of a job or any marketable skills, his incredible charisma with women of every age.

Each time she closed her eyes, she remembered his kiss. He'd been very skilled. He'd made her feel things she'd never felt before, things she hadn't believed possible. He was probably going to be the biggest mistake of her life. But then, what good was life without a few unforgettable mistakes?

Besides, she wasn't as dumb as her mama had been. She wouldn't convince herself she loved him or, God forbid, that he loved her. She would not wait around for Rico to return once he left her. She would not waste away dreaming of the day he'd marry her. She would not put a noose around her neck because of Rico Salvatore, or any man.

Without warning, Rico burst inside. "Carrie?" His gaze swept the room, coming to rest on Lily.

Lily took in his tired face, his haunted eyes. She'd seen hundreds of sad eyes. Why did Rico's make her want to do something, anything, to make him smile?

"You didn't find her."

Rico's black hair gray with dust, he had dirt across his nose, something Lily found both endearing and appealing.

"Are you lost again, *señorita?*" He tossed the hat in his hand onto the bed and began to remove his knives.

"No. I was waiting for you."

"Most ladies would not wait in a man's room."

"I'm not most ladies. I'm worried about the little girl."

"Not worried about me?"

She eyed the cache of knives he'd set on the nightstand. "You can take care of yourself."

"Obviously you cannot. If you don't want me to touch you, stay out of my room. If you don't want me to want you, keep away from me altogether."

"You have that big of a problem with women?" She tilted her head and studied him. "Oh, I forgot. You have a problem the size of Texas."

He didn't smile or laugh or joke, and that concerned her. From what she'd seen so far, Rico found little that wasn't funny in this world. For a woman without enough laughter in her life, that trait did not annoy Lily as it seemed to annoy others. Instead, it made her want to be with him all the more.

"Right now my only problem is Carrie," he answered, then opened the door. "Go away, Lily."

She crossed the room, but instead of leaving, she shut the door. "I wanted to apologize for what I did to you that first day. It was rude."

"Crude," he corrected.

"But got my message across."

"Clearly." He sat on the bed, and his shoulders drooped.

She stood in front of him, put her hands on his shoulders, pressed down, then smoothed out. His head came up, his nose level with her belly. She could feel his breath even through her clothes, burning hot against her skin. His muscles tensed beneath her fingers.

"Relax," she murmured. "Let me help you."

He glanced at her with a frown but didn't pull away. As she rubbed his shoulders and his neck, bit by bit his head tilted forward until he laid his temple along her stomach. The position was both innocent and arousing.

No one had ever put themselves in front of her before. No one had ever faced down a friend in her defense. No man had ever looked past her face, her body, or her voice. Maybe that was all Rico saw, too.

But if she wanted the same thing, what was the harm? She'd been thinking about this for days, and the thinking had put her so on edge, she could barely stand to touch him and not take him.

Once, just once, she wanted a man in her bed who could give her nothing but pleasure, who wanted nothing from her but the same.

And the more she saw of him, the more she learned of him, the more she believed the man for the job was Rico.

Little by little he relaxed beneath her fingers. Inch by inch he sank into her embrace. She wanted very much to put her hands on his smooth, warm flesh. She'd been dreaming of that for several nights—strange, erotic dreams such as she'd never imagined possible, especially for a woman like her.

Lily tried to slip her hands beneath the collar of Rico's shirt, but it was too tight.

"What are you doing?"

"I thought I could do a better job without your shirt in my way."

As he lifted his head, his lips brushed her stomach. The caress burned through every layer of material—intimate, exhilarating. Her indrawn breath, loud in the silence between them, and the sudden absence of warmth across her belly made her want to pull his head back where it had been and cradle him against her.

"You had only to ask." His cocky self-assurance had returned. Why she liked that so much, Lily couldn't say, but she was happy to hear a lilt in his voice and see a tiny sparkle in his eyes where before there had reigned only sadness.

Rico opened a few buttons down the front of his shirt and drew the garment over his head.

She'd been right. His flesh was bronzed, supple, magnificent. As he tossed the shirt aside, muscles rippled beneath the skin. When he leaned back, putting his hands on the bed so he could see her face, his stomach flexed, exposing dips and hollows she wanted to touch with her tongue. Not a trace of hair marred the perfection of his flesh.

"What in hell are you up to, Lily?"

Her gaze flicked to his. "Up to?"

"Not more than a few days past you kicked me in my ego, as you say, for kissing you."

"Not for the kiss, per se, but the offer it entailed."

"*Excusa.*" He dipped his head. "Now you are in my room, touching me, asking me to take off my shirt . . ."

"And you don't like it?"

Confusion filled his eyes. "I didn't say that. I just don't understand."

"I'm not sure I do, either."

She sat on the bed, then tentatively reached out and put her hand on him. A sharp intake of breath was his only reaction—until his heart began to beat faster and harder against her palm. So hot, so smooth, so alive—she wanted to place her mouth where her hand rested.

"Does it matter why?" she asked. "Can't a woman change her mind?"

He kissed her, a convincing kiss if she'd needed more convincing. He wasn't rough or demanding; instead, he became gentle, as if unsure, nibbling at her lips. She shivered as he licked the seam, delved within, then shuddered as he tasted every inch of her mouth.

She gave herself over to the joy of touching him, running her fingers along his chest and belly, thumbs across his nipples, knuckles along the ridge of his ribs; then she clasped his shoulders, hanging on as the world tilted and tipped when he pushed her back onto the bed and rose above her.

"No," she rasped, and he stilled, then started to withdraw.

She clutched at him. "Wait—"

"You said no. I understand what no means."

Impressed, Lily studied Rico's face, still so tired and drawn. At this point, most men would have ignored her words, but Rico stopped the instant she said no.

"I meant let me touch you." He frowned. She pushed on his shoulders, and he reclined on the bed. "I want to—" She broke off, and her cheeks flooded with heat. She didn't think she could articulate what she had only just begun to want.

"Hey," he whispered, and tugged on her hair, which had come loose from his roving hands. "Touch me. Any way you want."

Her embarrassment and uncertainty fled. He had that way about him, no doubt because he'd known countless women and had practiced what to say. But wasn't that one of the reasons she wanted him? A man like him would have no illusions beyond the moment, just as she had no illusions past today. They were alike, and that way no one would get hurt.

Instead of touching, she tasted. His indrawn breath tightened his stomach, defined the ridges that fascinated her. She ran her tongue along one, walked her lips to another, then opened her mouth and suckled at the place where his belly disappeared into his pants.

He cursed, and his hips shifted restlessly, but he didn't touch her—either to urge or deny. Her mouth curved against him. She licked all the way up his chest, then focused on the flat brown discs of his nipples, teasing them until they were hard.

His fist tangled in her hair and pulled her mouth to his. No more gentleness, only need and desperate hunger. Her heart pounded, her dress became far too tight, her skirt tangled about her legs, annoying her.

Without warning, she was tossed onto her back. A cool draft of air hit her legs seconds before his scalding hot palm touched the bare skin above her stockings; then his long fingers trailed up her thigh.

With his teeth he tugged her dress lower, allowed the swell of her breasts to spill from the neckline, dipped his tongue between them, then swept it beneath the material and across an already hardened nipple.

She moaned, tangled her fingers in his hair, and held on. His busy mouth closed over her breast, suckling her through the gown, the rasp of his tongue against the cloth, against her, a more arousing sensation than when he'd tasted her flesh to flesh.

His fingers as busy as his mouth, he stroked her thigh, swept a thumb over her aching center, made her arch, begging silently for something . . . She wasn't sure what.

Needing to feel his mouth against hers, she tugged on his hair, none too gently. But when he lifted his head, his eyes went from dazed to sharp, and he turned his head, listening to something in the distance.

Then Lily heard it, too—the cadence of a little girl's laughter.

Rico was off the bed and out the door before she could open her mouth. After struggling to her feet, Lily straightened her skirt and her bodice, shoved her hair from her face, and followed Rico into the hall.

Just in time to see him scowl, snarl, then kick in the door of Johnny's room.

"No, Rico, no!" The words made Lily reach back into the room and grab one of Rico's discarded knives before she raced after him.

Inside Johnny's room, Carrie sat on the bed. A jumble of cards at the center revealed an interrupted game. Rico held Johnny by the shirt, half on the bed and half off.

"How long has she been here?" He shook the boy. "Why have you kept her from me?"

"Put him down," Lily ordered.

He didn't even look at her. "Not until he answers me. I have been dragging all over this godforsaken country, looking for a little girl amid all that great big nothing. And every day my gut bubbles and boils because I'm scared she's dead and it is all my fault."

"But Rico—"

He ignored Carrie, staring into Johnny's face intently. "So I ride and I ride until I am asleep on that horse, but at night I can't sleep at all because I see *mi chica* and I have failed her. And when the darkest night comes, I see the ghosts of all those I have failed, and I see . . ." His voice trailed off, and his fingers tightened on Johnny's shirt. "And all the while you had her here!"

Lily gave an exasperated sigh and stepped across the room to poke Rico in the back with her fingernail. Even though her body still hummed with unrelieved tension and her mind swirled with possibilities unfinished and he was shaking Johnny like a dog with a bone, Lily didn't want to hurt him. But she kept the knife ready just in case he got too brave or insisted on being too stupid.

"He couldn't answer you if he wanted to. Now let him go before I put a hole in your pretty hide with one of the knives you leave so carelessly about."

Slowly, he turned his head to the side, and she wiggled the knife for him to see. Faster than a water snake on the bayou, he dropped Johnny and disarmed her.

"*Señorita,* do not play knife games with me. You will lose." He turned toward Johnny, knife flipped toward the boy.

Terror flashed through Johnny's eyes as the knife glinted in front of his face. Sudden and ungovernable fury spurted in Lily's mind, and she kicked Rico in the back of the knee, then stepped between him and Johnny. "If you go near him with a knife again, I'll make sure you're wearing it."

Rico stared at Lily, and Lily stared right back. She would not allow him to put fear in Johnny's eyes again. "*Madre gallina,* I believe you would. Very well." He placed the knife in his back pocket. "You find out what is going on here and why *mi chica* is in his room when I have been looking all over the earth for her."

"Maybe you ought to ask *mi chica* that." Lily jerked her head at Carrie, who inched toward the door.

"Do not move another step," Rico snapped. "You will come here and explain yourself."

Carrie threw a withering glare at Lily, who resisted the urge to laugh. She'd been glared at by better glarers than this child—namely, half of New Orleans society and all of Baton Rouge's. Little girls didn't scare her. Not much did anymore.

"I . . . um . . . well, you see—"

"I do not see. I have been looking for you everywhere. You scared me half to death. I had Timmons bury your grandpapa yesterday. We could wait no longer for you to be there."

Carrie shrugged. "I didn't want to be there. Funerals are sad."

"They're supposed to be. Have you been here all along?"

She nodded, unafraid. "And you didn't know, did ya? I sneaked real good, Rico." Her face eager, she obviously longed for his approval more than anything else. "Just like you taught me."

"You taught her that?" Lily asked. "Nice job."

Rico and Carrie turned nearly identical scowls her way. "Stay out of this, Lily."

"Yeah, stay out of this, *chérie,*" Carrie sneered.

Lily raised her brow. The little girl had taken quite a dislike to her. She let her gaze wander over

Rico's exquisite, naked back. Lily had a feeling she knew why.

Poor Rico, the object of every woman's desire. Lily snorted and received another set of glares.

Sitting on the bed, she took Johnny's hand, surprised to find him trembling. "What's the matter?" she whispered.

Johnny glanced at Rico. "You're afraid of him?"

The boy lifted one shoulder and ducked his head. Lily turned and contemplated Rico, who was scowling at Carrie as if he weren't sure what to say or do. Even without his shirt, he looked dangerous, and the way he'd disarmed her, then turned the knife on Johnny . . . No wonder the boy was frightened.

"I don't think he'd hurt you, sugar. Anyway, I wouldn't let him."

Lily brushed Johnny's overly long hair from his face, and his dark blue eyes met hers. He smiled, and Lily's heart tumbled toward her belly. Why did his fear make her want to fight every dragon in his path? Just as he seemed to want to fight every ogre in hers.

"Carrie Brown," Rico said sternly. "You are in big trouble. We will go and see Sullivan right now."

"The sheriff? I didn't do nothin' wrong!" she shouted, and darted for the door.

Rico caught Carrie before she made it through, scooped her up, and tossed her over his shoulder. She started to kick and scream and curse.

"Did you teach her that, too?" Lily called over the din.

"Not me. Her grandpapa. Stop that, Carrie, or I will paddle your behind."

Out of the corner of Lily's eye she caught movement. Johnny rushed forward and yanked Carrie from Rico's arms. The element of surprise was on his side, and he was able to shove her behind him before Rico recovered from the assault.

"Get out of my way, piano boy."

Johnny belligerently stood his ground. Lily joined him. "He thinks you're going to hurt her."

The shock on Rico's face proved his innocence of such an intention as nothing else would. "Hurt her? I-I couldn't. Why would he think that?"

"Maybe the knife you held on him? Or perhaps the spanking you threatened her with."

Understanding dawned in his eyes. "I talk big. But I wouldn't hurt a child—not Carrie or Johnny."

Johnny put his chin up, pointed at his chest, and shook his head. Carrie stepped around him and slipped her hand into his. "He's not a child, Rico. He's almost a grown-up. He's been taking care of me."

Rico scowled. "When did you two become friends?"

Carrie glanced at Johnny, and something passed between them that made Lily frown. What secret had they shared that made them best friends even though they'd just met?

"Since I hid in his room and he caught me," Carrie answered.

"That wasn't very sneaky or very smart."

She kicked the floor. "Can't be perfect. Ended up I did the right thing. Johnny helped me."

"Johnny should have kept out of it. He might think he's old enough to care of you, but boys his age are not responsible. They think of other things and forget what they're supposed to be doing. They can't be trusted."

"Johnny isn't like that."

"They're all like that."

Rico sighed, and the exhaustion that had lined his face for days deepened. He went down on one knee. Without hesitation, Carrie slipped away from Johnny and went to him.

"Why didn't you come to me, *chica*? I thought we were pals forevermore."

"We are." She lifted her tiny hands to his cheeks and put her nose right up to his. "I love you, Rico. I want to be with you every damn day."

He winced. "Do not swear." Carrie gave an impatient growl that had Lily fighting a smile. "It is kind of hard to be together, *mi chica*, when you hide yourself away."

"But now that you found me, you won't ever let me go. You were so worried, you won't ever send me away. I can live with you always. Right?"

Rico's expression was gentle, and when he rubbed his nose against hers, Carrie giggled.

The two of them were so cute, Lily ought to be gagging. Instead, she gave into the smile. Johnny, however, appeared a little green.

"Right?" Carrie prodded, hope in her voice, heart in her eyes.

He rubbed his hand over her hair, winked, then opened his mouth, no doubt to agree, but the word that spun about the room was "Wrong."

Everyone turned to stare at the man who filled the open doorway.

CHAPTER 8

Rico got to his feet and faced Sullivan. Carrie's hand slid into his. Johnny moved closer to Lily. Lily inched closer to Rico, all four of them lining up against the intruder, an interesting development Rico had no time to ponder at the moment.

"What are you doing here?" Rico demanded.

"Someone sent for the sheriff when all the banging and the screaming started. I see the lost girl has turned up, and amazingly, she's with you."

"I didn't have her."

"Hmm." Sullivan didn't sound convinced. "Well, she can't stay with you."

"You told me she has no living relatives."

"That doesn't mean I'm gonna let a child live with you, Rico. You can barely take care of yourself."

"I don't need no one to take care of me," Carrie stated. "I'll take care of him."

"That's for sure," Sullivan muttered.

Carrie gazed at Rico with complete confidence and adoration. In her eyes, he was all-powerful. In her eyes, he would save her from all that was frightening in the world. But to Sullivan, Rico wasn't up to the task. When had his oldest friend become one of the bad guys?

"Carrie, why don't you go downstairs and help Kate and Laurel with the curtains?" he asked.

"Nope. Stayin' with you."

Rico glanced at Lily in mute appeal, but the boy took Carrie's hand, and she followed him out of the room without further argument. Lily stood behind Rico as if she had every right to be there. To be honest, he felt better with her nearby. Lily's instinctive movement toward him when Sullivan had surprised them all gave Rico a sense of worth such as he'd never had before and needed desperately right now.

"Thanks for the vote of confidence, *amigo*," Rico said.

For a minute, Sullivan appeared guilty, until he glanced at Lily, then around the clean but spare room. "Rico, you live in a saloon. You think the Reverend Clancy will allow a nine-year-old girl to live here?"

"You're the sheriff. If you say she stays, that blowhard Clancy will mumble, but he won't shout."

"Reese won't like it, either."

"He's not the boss of me, or you, anymore."

"Funny, but he seems to think he is."

"He knows how I feel about Carrie."

"I'm not debating that you care about her, more than I've ever seen you care about anyone. I'm not debating that she loves you. I'm debating what's best for her, and living in a saloon with an unemployed"—he threw up his hands—"whatever you are isn't it."

Fear bubbled in Rico's chest. He'd just found Carrie, and now Sullivan was going to drag her away. He'd spent the past several days in a panic, promising God and every angel that he would take care of her if only she was returned safely. And now his promise would be broken because he was irresponsible and worthless. Just like the last time.

"He isn't unemployed." Both Rico and Sullivan turned to Lily. "He works for me."

Rico raised his eyebrows but kept his mouth shut.

"As what?" Sullivan asked, his tone revealing he didn't believe a word of it.

"My saloon manager."

"Really? And what does that mean?"

Rico could tell what Sullivan thought it meant, and he was embarrassed that his friend thought him good enough for only one thing. Not that he wasn't very good at that one thing, but he'd never had to take money for it before. He had a feeling that taking money for it now would not get him Carrie. If it would, he'd agree in a heartbeat.

"It means he keeps out the riffraff," Lily stated. "He's very handy that way."

"I have no doubt he's handy. But a job here still doesn't mean he can keep Carrie. I'm sorry, kid. Really I am."

Rico went toe-to-toe with Sullivan. "You are not sending her to an orphanage. I'll shoot you myself before I'll let you do that."

"You and what great big gun? You couldn't hit me if you tried."

"I'll sneak up on you and stick you in your sleep."

Sullivan's long, sarcastic sneer gave his opinion

of that idea. He had taught Rico everything he knew about sneaking.

"Relax, Rico. You won't have to do me in. Tonight she'll stay with us. Tomorrow I'll see if there's a family in town who will take her."

"If not?"

"Then I'll check the surrounding ranches and the closest towns."

"I don't like it."

"I don't care."

Fifteen minutes later, Sullivan left with Carrie. Kicking and screaming, she rode his shoulder out the door. Even Rico's gentle conversation with her about what was best had done little good. Carrie knew what was best for Carrie—and that was Rico.

Hearing her cry twisted Rico's stomach tighter than a cinch on a winter-grazed horse. He felt as ill as Johnny looked. The boy hadn't enjoyed Carrie's tears, either, which made Rico forgive him a bit for hiding her. As her shouts faded, Johnny strode to the piano and began to play "Weeping Sad and Lonely."

From what Rico had observed of the boy so far, music was his way of communicating, since he had no other. The child sure could make you want to weep or whistle, depending on the tune he played. Right now Rico wanted to kick and scream and cry awhile himself.

Yvonne had disappeared into her room behind the bar as soon as Carrie started crying. She didn't seem to be very comfortable around children.

At least there were no customers tonight. Lily had posted a notice saying there would be a gala reopening that weekend. With all the hustle and bustle that went on in the saloon these days, the few regulars had opted to stay away until things settled down again.

Laurel and Kate, after a cursory glance at the screeching Carrie, continued to sew and decorate without speaking to anyone but each other. They had found their element with fabric, scissors, and thread. Whereas before they had both seemed a bit dim, now that they plied a trade at which they excelled, the two appeared as bright as anyone else.

Rico was glad they were happy. He only hoped the grand venture Lily envisioned would work.

Lily stared at him with an unfathomable expression. He had no idea what was the matter with her. Why had she come to his room and practically seduced him? Not saying that he hadn't enjoyed it, but the woman made no sense.

Had he suddenly become irresistible in the past few days? Ego the size of Texas or not, he didn't think so. In fact, after hearing from one and all how worthless he was, Rico figured Lily would order him out of her place instead of offering him a job. That is, if the offer was even real.

Right now he just wanted to sleep. Leaving Johnny to a rendition of "Do They Miss Me at Home," he nodded to Lily and retreated upstairs.

But instead of lying down, he sat at the window and stared across the street toward the hotel where Carrie slept. He hadn't felt this bad since he was fourteen and still lived at home in San Antone.

A soft tap on his door preceded its opening. "Rico?" Lily murmured. "You okay?"

When he didn't answer because he didn't know, she crossed the room and laid her hands on his shoulders. How could such a simple act feel so good? He wanted her to touch him, just like that, until his stomach stopped roiling and his head stopped spinning.

Leaning down, her face even with his, she followed the direction of his gaze. "She'll be all right."

He shrugged, and her fingers slid along his shirt. He'd put the thing on to take Carrie downstairs, and now he wished he'd taken it back off so he could feel her fingers on his skin.

A shiver raced down his back. There was something between them that had never been between him and any other woman, and he wasn't exactly sure what it was.

"Maybe," he answered.

"Sullivan's a good man. And Eden is a mother if ever I saw one."

"*Sí*. She is."

"So why are you so upset about a child who isn't even yours?"

"It does not matter if she's mine by blood, she is in my heart. Has been since the first day I saw her. I'd do anything for Carrie. Yet the men I've ridden with for years, men whose lives I've saved, think I'm too incompetent to care for a child."

"Are you?"

He glanced back out the window. Sadness filled his heart, along with the truth. "Yes."

Lily touched his face gently, as if she understood, as if she didn't care. Needing whatever comfort he could get right now, Rico rubbed his cheek along her palm. His unshaven chin rasped against her wrist, and she started, then caught her breath.

At the sound of arousal, he lifted his gaze and caught the heat in her eyes. Her hand hovered in the air between them, and he closed his fingers about her wrist, then drew it closer and closer to his lips, pressing an openmouthed kiss to the pulse that leaped there.

His tongue laved the throbbing vein, the ebb and flow of her blood trapped beneath the skin; life filled his mouth, and the salt and summer scent of Lily filled his nose. Consumed by her, tempted, entranced, a flutter of uncertainty made him lift his mouth and pull away. Still needing some kind of connection in the dark, lonely night, he laced his fingers between hers, and she held on.

Though he should take what she offered and let the questions be damned, Rico found that he could not.

"Tell me, *querida*, why you did not want me the first time I kissed you."

Lily shrugged. "You wanted nothing from me but sex. You barely even knew my name."

True enough. Still . . . "And now that I know your name?"

"You want nothing from me but sex."

"And this is different from the first time I touched you, why?"

"I know you better. I've been watching you, listening to the others. I want you just as you are."

He narrowed his eyes. Certain he was not going to like the answer to his next question, he asked anyway. "*How* am I?"

"Decorative, irresponsible, unemployed, and—"

He stood, pulling his hand from hers and moving far enough away that he could not smell her skin, even though he could still taste her flavor on his lips. She studied him, wary, uncertain.

"And what, Lily?"

Her brow lifted at the ice in his tone. "An excellent lover?"

"Is that a question?"

"I'd like to discover the answer."

"But why, *querida*? Why would you want to take a pretty, worthless bum to your bed? No one is that good."

"I bet you are."

"You flatter me." Funny, he didn't feel flattered; he felt a bit dirty.

"Is it working?"

"No. I thought you offered me a job. Was that just for show?"

She shook her head. "The offer is real."

"Ah, then I would not be unemployed. One less mark on my sterling character." He bowed his head in a gesture he'd often seen his father use with the help. "Unfortunately, I must decline your offer."

A frown creased Lily's flawless brow. "What's the matter with you? I offer you a job; I offer you what you want, me, and you act like I've called you dirt and spit on your shoe."

"Haven't you?"

"I don't recall that."

"Think about it again. I am no male courtesan, *señorita*. Just as I insulted you when I offered to pay, you insult me with the offer of work and your bed."

Understanding dawned in her eyes. "That's not what I meant."

"Nevertheless, it is what I hear."

"Clean out your ears, then."

"It is not necessary. What is between a man and a woman is supposed to be something beautiful— a gift, a promise, a time away from sadness and care, a way to feel better about oneself, not worse."

She nodded, eager. "Yes, that's what I meant."

"But the way you see me makes me sad. It makes me lonely even as your breath touches my skin and your body calls to mine. That's not how it should be. You reveal me as less than I ever wished to be, even though I know you see me exactly as I am."

Rico couldn't believe he was about to do what he was about to do. "Go away, Lily. Let me be alone with my decorative, irresponsible, unemployed self."

He turned away and gazed out the window at the hotel just as the lights went out. Darkness spread across the street and through his heart.

The door clicked shut behind him, and the loneliness he'd asked for was all he had to keep him company throughout the night.

Several days passed. Three Queens improved with each one. The girls hung curtains. Lily planned the program. Yvonne readied the bar and did the cooking. Rico built a stage, while Johnny continued to play sad songs unless Carrie was near.

Luckily, Carrie was near a lot. The child slipped her keepers' watch day in and day out to sneak about and follow Rico. According to Eden, Sullivan was having no luck finding a family for her. If she'd been a boy, any one of the surrounding ranchers would have taken her in to work. As it was, a foul-mouthed, sneaky nine-year-old girl who preferred to run around in bare feet and boys' clothes was not high on the list of anyone's needs in or around Rock Creek.

When she began to skip school, Eden and Sullivan sent her to live with the schoolmaster. From what Lily had heard, no one messed with Reese—except, it appeared, Carrie.

Rico ignored Lily daily. She shouldn't have cared, but every time he turned his back, she hurt.

Before Lily had come to Rock Creek and met Rico, emotions were not for her. Now she couldn't seem to stop feeling, stop wanting, stop needing.

She slept fitfully. Lonely and sad and somewhat sick of herself, when she did manage to drift off, images of Rico, without his shirt or anything else, made her hot and itchy, mindful that what she dreamed would never be.

A few days before her planned gala opening, Lily awoke later than usual to the sound of Johnny tinkering on the piano. What she needed was to get back to work. Readying Three Queens for the opening was not what she considered work. She was out of sorts because she hadn't sung each night. She thrived on the attention of the crowd. That was the only reason she was lonely, not because a knife-wielding pretty boy had turned his back on her.

She stomped downstairs, following the scent of coffee. Yvonne was worth every penny Lily would ever pay her by virtue of the coffee alone. The woman's second greatest virtue was her ability to keep quiet and go away until she was needed. After a single glance at Lily's face, Yvonne handed over a full cup and disappeared.

Lily sat at an empty table and brooded. No man had ever turned her down before. Not that she'd offered herself to any man, ever, but that was beside the point.

But for a man like Rico to refuse no-strings-attached sex with a woman he'd tried to buy only a few days before made Lily wonder if he possessed more character than she'd given him credit for.

He'd turned down both her and the job. While the former taunted an ego she hadn't known she possessed, the latter threatened her dream. How was she going to find another riffraff manager in a town like Rock Creek? How was she going to face Rico every day knowing she'd thrown herself at him and he'd tossed her right back?

Some of her mama's long-ago tears were starting to make sense, and that would not do at all.

She was no good at this man-woman nonsense. In her life, men took, women gave, and you lived with it, however little you liked it.

Fool. Idiot. Amateur.

Did she feel better now? Not really. No wonder Rico had told her no. She'd called him worse names and expected him to kiss her.

Johnny started to play "John Brown's Body." Lily got up and strode across the room.

"That's it." She put her hands over his and caused a horrible sound that made him cringe and look at her in reproach. "Sorry." She removed her hands. "I can't stand any more sad songs. It's too early in the day for that."

He shrugged and began to play "Dixie" an octave higher and several beats faster than it was written.

"Funny guy."

Johnny's fingers faltered to a stop as Lily spun about to face the speaker. A tall man filled the entrance to the saloon, one elbow perched upon each swinging door. The shadow of his hat and the downward tilt of his head, combined with the overcast early-morning light, did not allow Lily to see his face. Which only made her certain he had come to drag her back to hell.

The gun at his side looked like a professional's, well used and well loved, and when he came toward them, his loose-hipped grace reminded Lily of a stalking wildcat. A shiver sped down her spine. He was dangerous—always had been, always would be.

Lily had hoped, since no one had found them right away, that they were safe. She should have known R.W. would hire a man such as this one to find them.

Johnny suddenly stood beside her, tugging on Lily's arm, trying to pull her behind him. She wouldn't go. If their visitor had come from R.W., she would deal with him. She would not let him touch Johnny, and she would not go back to the life she'd led before. One taste of freedom had been all it took to show her that she'd lived in a prison for far too long.

Lily wished she hadn't become so cavalier about her knives. But in this town, with Rico hanging about, she hadn't felt the need to strap on the steel for several days. Now she had nothing with which to defend herself and Johnny.

Then the man thumbed up the brim of his hat, and she recognized him. Relief made her dizzy, and she leaned on Johnny a bit. "It's you," she stammered. "Th-the schoolteacher. Reese."

His golden eyebrows shot up toward his black hat. "You didn't recognize me?"

Guilt made people see all sorts of things that weren't there. Lily shook off the dizziness and the errant thoughts. Johnny moved away, but he didn't go far.

"No, I didn't. Not dressed like . . ." She made a helpless gesture with her hands.

He looked down at his clothes. "A bounty hunter?"

Lily winced. He caught the response, and his cagey green gaze sharpened. He might not be the enemy, but he was too observant by half. She schooled her face into an expression appropriate for polite chitchat, something she was very good at.

"With all the excitement, we didn't get a chance to meet properly the other day." She held out her hand. "Lily Fortier."

"James Reese." He took her hand, then studied her face with just a bit too much intelligence for her liking. "You can just call me Reese. Everyone does."

No matter how she tried, Lily could not reconcile the image of a scholarly book learner with this man in front of her now.

"Everyone calls you Reese except the children," she observed. "And Mary."

At the sound of his wife's name, a gentle look came over Reese's face, altering his watchful countenance immeasurably. "Once Mary called me that, too. But when we got married, she said she wasn't calling her husband by his last name, like an outlaw bandit, even if he insists upon dressing like one." He shrugged. "She doesn't particularly care for my fondness for black. Says I wear it to scare all the children into submission."

"Does it work?"

He winked. "Only with certain children."

Lily found herself charmed by him, as she'd been charmed by his wife and daughter. But he had come here for a reason, and until she knew what that reason was, she didn't dare allow herself to relax. "Is there anything I can help you with today?"

"Hope so. Is this Johnny? Your brother?"

Was that sarcasm on the word "brother"? Or merely the inflection of his voice—southern, deep, maybe Georgia. Lily gave herself a mental shake.

She was being silly. No one in this town would have reason to doubt their story, least of all this man, whom she'd barely met.

"Yes, this is Johnny. Why do you want to know?"

He gave her another odd look, and Lily felt as if she'd stepped into a hole she hadn't seen coming. Being too suspicious, too defensive, would make her look guilty—something she couldn't afford.

"I'm the schoolteacher," he said slowly. "I've come to take him to school."

"Johnny doesn't talk, Reese."

"So I heard. All the more reason for him to learn all that he can to get by in this world."

"I won't have him tormented over something he can't help or change."

"Do I look like the kind of man who allows tormenting to go on in my class?"

She bit her lip. "Perhaps not."

"Believe me, Miss Fortier, nothing goes on in my school that I don't want to go on there. Can Johnny write?"

"Only his name."

"Does he read?"

"Not that I know of."

Reese's gaze sharpened. "How long has your brother been like this?"

Lily realized her mistake. If Johnny was her brother, she'd know if he had learned to read. She'd know how long he'd been silent. She hesitated long enough for the stillness to stretch from thoughtful toward guilty.

Johnny moved forward, held up a single hand, then flattened his fingers, tilting them from side to side.

"Five years?" Reese looked at Lily. "Give or take?"

"Sounds about right."

"Did you lose the rest of your family in the war?"

She looked down. Reese must have taken that as a yes, for he put a large, gentle hand on her shoulder. "Everyone's been scarred by the war. Sometimes I wonder if there'll ever be a day when someone or something doesn't remind me of it."

He stared into space, and the peace that had filled his eyes at the mention of his wife fled. Memories flickered; ghosts of the South, no doubt. Everyone who'd worn the gray had them. Some were able to live with them better than others, though no one ever forgot.

Reese closed his eyes a moment, and when he opened them, the amiable schoolmaster had replaced the haunted soldier. "If Johnny once spoke, it'll be a lot easier to teach him to read and write."

Lily glanced at Johnny and caught the expression of longing in his eyes before he saw her looking at him and his face went carefully blank.

Lies multiplied until they took over your life. If they stuck with the lie that Johnny could not speak at all, he could learn as he wished to and not be tormented. Since they'd come here and Johnny had been accepted as a mute, he was less tense, he smiled more, he appeared happier. Perhaps prolonged silence would even cure his horrible stutter.

Though Lily was beginning to feel at home in Rock Creek and wished she could be completely truthful with her new friends, to keep Johnny safe, she would lie to an angel.

Lily laid a hand on the boy's arm. "You'd like to read, wouldn't you?" He shrugged. "And write?"

Another shrug. "I'd like you to go if it would make you happy, sugar."

His head came up, hope filled his eyes, and Lily knew she would have to let him go. "That's settled, then."

Reese nodded, then rubbed his hands together. "Now, one other problem." Lily and Johnny froze. "Have either of you seen Carrie."

She let out a long breath, which was echoed by Johnny. "Not since Sullivan carried her out of here kicking and screaming again yesterday."

Reese sighed. "I'd hoped she was here. Rico is going to have one big fit. We lost her again."

"If you can't keep her where she belongs and Sullivan can't, either, what good are you?"

He looked sheepish. "You don't know Carrie."

"I'm beginning to." And Lily was starting to like the courageous little girl more than she had any right to. "I'll wake Rico."

"Thanks. I'll get acquainted with your brother."

Lily paused on the first step and shot a look at Johnny. Not that he'd blab anything secret; still, she wanted him to be careful.

In Lily's mind R.W. owed her a lot more than a run-down saloon in a tiny Texas town for all the years she'd sung for her supper and . . . Well, she wasn't going to think of what she'd done to keep a roof over her head. And he owed Johnny more than a roll of dirty money. But R.W. wouldn't see it her way.

The boy didn't look at her, but Reese did, and that made Lily turn about and hurry upstairs. His curious gaze burned the middle of her back. The man was too smart and too observant for Lily's peace of mind. He knew she'd been warning

Johnny about something. Reese didn't trust her, and she didn't trust him.

At the top of the stairs, out of sight of those below, she paused and leaned her hot forehead against the cool wall as she tried to calm herself.

What did she have to fear from the schoolteacher? She should be more worried about Sinclair Sullivan. He would be the one contacted in the event someone connected Betty Lillian with Lily Fortier, although she really didn't see how that could happen.

New Orleans was always a madhouse at carnival, and the night she'd run had been no different. She doubted there was anyone talented enough to trace her to Rock Creek. Besides, R.W. was a cheap bastard. It would take more money than he was willing to spend to find her here. She had to believe that or she'd be jumping at shadows for the rest of her life, and that was no way to live.

Lily straightened, smoothing her skirt and her tightly bound hair. Just feeling the bun at her nape and the no-nonsense fabric of her skirt made Lily felt better. Things were different here. She was different. She'd just had a fright, is all.

For some reason, Reese and his sharp eyes had cut through to the fear she'd been suppressing. She hadn't killed anyone; she'd just run away from a bad situation. R.W. did not own her. Even if he thought he did.

She stopped in front of Rico's room and listened intently, but she heard not a sound that would indicate he was awake. So she tapped on the door and waited. Still she heard nothing.

She hated to wake him. He'd seemed exhausted last night—make that every night since they'd taken Carrie away the first time—exhausted from the inside out.

But he'd want to hear about Carrie. He'd drag himself out of bed and onto a horse as fast as he could, then race out into the hot sun to search for her.

Lily opened his door. "Rico," she whispered. "Reese is here and—"

The sight that greeted Lily froze the rest of the words in her throat. She could do nothing but hover in the doorway, half in the room, half out, staring at the picture on the bed.

Despite the stubble darkening his chin, Rico looked very young, very innocent, undeniably beautiful, as he slept. His dark hair stuck up, stark against the white pillow, which had made an endearing crease along his cheek.

He still wore his clothes, though he'd managed to remove his boots and his socks. The sight of his long, pale, bare feet peaking from beneath his dusty jeans only made him seem nearly as young as the little girl curled up to his chest.

The longing for something she could never have, didn't dare want, pierced her, sudden and unexpected. A man, a child, a home—dreams like those did not come true for a woman like her.

There would only be men, herself, and places like Three Queens for always. She'd known that for years, and she'd gotten used to the truth.

So why did the sight of this child—and that man—make all she'd once longed for in girlish, foolish dreams rise up and hurt her again more deeply than their absence had ever hurt her before?

CHAPTER 9

Rico awoke slowly, aware even before he opened his eyes that he was not alone. Though he might have begun life as the pampered only son of a wealthy rancher, leaving that life at the age of four- teen had molded him into a far different man than he would have become back in San Antonio.

Years of living on the edge, first alone, next with Sullivan, then the others, during the war and after had honed Rico's survival skills to razor sharpness.

He cracked one eye and peered down at the warm bundle burrowed against his side. Funny how a few short years of living safely in Rock Creek had softened him to the point that little girls could sneak into his room without waking him. If that kept up, he was going to die young.

"Psst!"

The hissing whisper made him tense and reach for the knife in a sheath that wasn't on his hip, where it belonged.

He was not only going to die young but soon.

Slowly, he turned his head, expecting to see the barrel of a gun pointed at his nose. People did not sneak into the room of a man like him just to see if they could.

The sight of Lily, bent over his bed and frowning at Carrie, made Rico go light-headed with relief. Dying he could live with. Dying in front of Carrie was another matter altogether.

Lily had an odd expression on her face—near to longing. Her gaze on Carrie, her serious eyes had gone dreamy, as if she wanted to reach out and brush Carrie's fine brown hair away from her face but was afraid.

Such a gesture would not be like Lily at all, but then, neither was any trace of fear. She was the most fearless and least needy woman he'd ever met. Maybe that was why he could not stop thinking about her even when he knew that he should.

She caught him looking at her and straightened. The gentleness in her expression disappeared. "What's she doing here?"

"Sleeping. As I was until you woke me. How did you get in here?"

"Easily. Do you ever lock the door, Rico?"

"There was never any need."

"Your ego is going to get you killed one day."

"Perhaps," he said flippantly, even though she was right.

With both Cash and Nate gone, Jed, too, testy folk from their years as hired guns after the war might take it upon themselves to come to town and settle scores with half the group instead of all. When the six were together, they became an entity few wanted to tangle with. But separated? Anything could happen. He needed to remember that and prepare accordingly.

Maybe he should just get out of town. Word was starting to spread that the six lived in Rock Creek. If he took a trip, he'd be safer, but then he'd be leaving Reese and Sullivan alone, with their families as well as the town to worry about. He couldn't leave them or Carrie or even Lily anymore.

The sound of footsteps on the stairs, then in the hall, made Rico tense, consider jumping up, jostling Carrie, and meeting his captain in the hall. Utter a lie, hide the child, keep her safe in any way that he could. But the sight of her pale face and slack mouth, the evidence of exhaustion in the dark rings beneath her eyes, made him stay right where he was, so that when Reese stepped into the room, Rico had to face him flat on his back with the evidence in his arms.

The disappointment on his friend's face hurt more than the angry words. "Dammit, Rico, what is she doing here? You're asking for a jail cell when Sullivan finds out you've kidnapped her."

"Hush, *mi capitán*. Do not wake her."

"I don't think a cyclone would do that," Lily observed. "Poor thing must be exhausted."

"Probably from sneaking out another window. Was that your idea, kid?"

Despair filled Rico's heart. No matter what he did, he would always be a kid to this man. Even when he'd done nothing, he was accused of everything. At least at home he'd *done* everything and been accused of nothing less.

"Maybe you should ask him if he's guilty before you fashion a noose." Lily's voice was tight with annoyance.

"Never mind, Lily," Rico said tiredly.

"I do mind." She put her hands on her hips and faced Reese down as few men had the courage to do. "He was sleeping when I came in here, and he was as surprised to see her as I was. She admitted she hid in the first place to scare everyone enough to let her stay with Rico."

Reese's eyes sharpened. "Manipulative."

Lily shrugged. "Clever. The child is alone. She's doing what she has to do to feel safe. If Rico makes her feel safe, why don't you let her stay with him? He's not as big of a moron as y'all seem to think."

"Gracias," Rico muttered.

Lily lifted a brow. "Think nothing of it."

"There'll be trouble," Reese said. "Certain folks aren't going to like it if she stays here."

Rico's heart lightened. Reese spoke as if he meant to let Carrie stay. Why Rico wanted the responsibility of a child, he couldn't say. Maybe to try and erase the mistakes of his past with a fresh new future?

"From what I hear, on your say-so, everyone will like it," Lily said. "Or at least keep quiet."

"You give me a lot of credit, Miss Fortier."

"Not me, the people of this town. Whatever you did, whatever you do, they seem to look at you as the leader. So lead. Do the right thing for that little girl."

Reese looked at Carrie, who slept on, oblivious to her life being discussed all around her. He raised his gaze to Rico's. Rico tightened his arm around Carrie, afraid if he let her go this time, she'd be gone forever.

As if in spite of himself, Reese nodded. But immediately after, he fixed Rico with a look straight from those days when each one of their lives had depended on him. "Do *not* screw this up, kid."

"I will do my best."

"You will do it."

"*Sí, mi capitán.*"

Reese paused in the doorway. "She needs to be in school this afternoon."

"I will see to it."

"Good." He turned to Lily. "I'll be taking Johnny with me."

She hesitated only a moment before she nodded. "Fine, Captain."

Reese scowled. He still resisted the title from anyone but Rico. "I'm not the captain." He strode away.

Lily stared after him. "You could have fooled me."

"Me, too." Carrie sat up, then bounced on the bed. "Bossy, bossy, bossy."

"How long have you been awake?" Rico asked.

"Since 'Dammit, Rico, what is she doing here?' " Carrie grinned as she mimicked Reese's words.

"Do not swear," Rico said automatically.

"I didn't. Mr. Reese did. I can stay with you now, right? He said I could, and everyone listens to him."

Rico sat up. "For the time being."

She threw her arms about his neck and hugged him for all she was worth. Rico held her tight, breathing in the sweet, clean smell of an angel.

"She'll need a room of her own."

Carrie let go of him and scowled at Lily. She really didn't like her at all. "Do not. I can stay with Rico."

"There are plenty of rooms. Pick one."

"I can't afford the one I have, remember?" Rico sighed. He hadn't thought past keeping Carrie—

typical of him, and he had to stop. For both their sakes, he needed to start thinking ahead.

He couldn't go traveling about anymore, picking up odd jobs, helping Cash or Jed or Nate. He would have to stay here. And what was he going to do in Rock Creek? It wasn't exactly a thriving center of commerce.

"My offer still stands." Lily gave an impatient huff at his blank stare. "The manager position? Keep out the riffraff, remember? Think you can handle that?"

"Rico's the best. He can do anything."

Carrie patted him on the head like a good dog. Rico sighed, hoping she never found out any different.

"So I hear." Amusement tinged Lily's voice.

Rico cut a glance at her. What did that mean?

She sobered almost instantly to do business. "Room and board for you both and a salary once Three Queens starts making a profit."

Still he hesitated, until Lily said the one thing that gave him hope. "I need you for this, Rico. You're the only man in town who can handle it."

Though he knew she probably said the last just to get herself a manager, still the words of confidence made the lump that had been in his stomach since they'd taken Carrie away shift and grow smaller.

He glanced at the little girl who believed in him with all her heart, then at the woman who had thought him as worthless as the rest of the world but no longer seemed to. If he took her offer, would he be sorry? Would he disappoint them both as he'd disappointed everyone else who had ever loved him?

If he didn't take the job, Carrie would suffer, and that he could not allow. He'd make a deal with the Devil himself to give Carrie the life she deserved.

"Deal?" Lily asked, and held out her hand.

Rico placed his hand in Lily's. "Deal."

Though her skin was soft, her fingers were strong, and when they closed about his, a ripple of awareness passed over Rico.

Make that a deal with the Devil *herself*.

Carrie couldn't believe her luck. Mr. Reese had said she could stay with Rico, and when he said something, it happened. She'd learned that quick enough once he'd begun teaching instead of Miss McKendrick; make that Mrs. Reese.

While his wife might have let Carrie miss a day of school before she came looking for her, Carrie had tried the same on Mr. Reese and discovered he was not amused. The quivering lip and tear-filled eyes that had worked so well on the Mrs. didn't make Mr. Reese so much as blink. She could not smile and wheedle and cuddle up to his knee as she did with Rico, either. Just the thought of trying it scared her to death, and Carrie wasn't scared of much.

Except bein' alone or bein' sent away from Rico for always. But now she could stay with him, and some of the fright that had caused her to act so badly since her granddad dropped dead began to fade.

The only thing that made her nervous was Miss Fortier and the way Rico looked at her—as if he wanted to cuddle up to her knee and beg her to let him stay right there forever. She'd never seen Rico look at anyone the way he looked at Lily Fortier. Which made Carrie hate her, even though she knew that hating was wrong and would get her sent to hell quicker than her granddad had gone there.

"Carrie, come along and pick a room," Miss Fortier called from the hall.

Though she wanted to say something naughty or at the very least stick out her tongue and refuse, Carrie did not think it smart to press her luck any more than she already had.

She glanced at Rico, who, despite their early-morning victory, didn't look all that happy or that well.

"Maybe I should stay with you." Carrie put her hand to Rico's forehead.

He smiled and rolled off the bed. "I am all right, *chica*. Go with Lily now. I will get your things from Mary and apologize to her for your rude leave-taking."

Carrie hung her head. "I'm sorry I ran away from Mrs. Reese. She's a nice lady."

"Then why did you do it?"

She looked directly into his eyes and told the truth. "She isn't you."

Rico continued to stare at her, almost as if he were going to say something; then Miss Fortier appeared in the doorway, and his gaze went from Carrie to her. He got that annoying, dazed look again that made Carrie want to kick him in the shins until he stopped.

What was so special about her?

"How about the room right next door?"

"Where's your room, Miss Fortier?" Carrie asked, not very nicely.

"Since we'll be living under the same roof, you may as well call me Lily. My room is on the other side of the hall."

"Good."

"Carrie," Rico warned.

"What did I say?" She turned innocent eyes on Rico.

He wasn't fooled, but he didn't say so—one of the things she adored about him. Rico knew she was a very good wheedler because he was one, too.

"Run along with Lily."

Because he asked it of her, she did, even though she didn't like it.

She liked it less when she reached her room and Lily said, "I'll have Yvonne fill the tub in the kitchen. We'll get you washed for school, and I'll braid your hair."

"Not hardly." Carrie put her hands on her hips and scowled.

Lily merely laughed. "And you'll start wearing dresses and shoes."

"What for?"

"Because that's what little girls do."

"Not this little girl."

Lily glanced over her shoulder, then stepped into the room and shut the door. "Listen, *fille*, you're going to do what I tell you."

"And if'n I don't."

"You won't be here long."

"You gonna toss me out?"

"I won't have to. If you continue to run around like a heathen—dirty, barefoot, and dressing like a boy—they'll use that to take you away from Rico."

Lily sounded so certain, Carrie's heart started to thud a little faster. "It never mattered before."

"That's because you were living with family. A lot can be forgiven family."

Carrie pondered that for a moment, remembering all that had happened while she lived with her granddad and how little had been done about it.

"Why should you care if I stay or if I go?" she asked Lily.

"Personally, *chérie*, I don't care. But Rico does."

"And why do you care about him?"

Carrie held her breath, afraid Lily would say she loved him. Rico needed someone to love him more than anyone she'd ever seen. But she wanted to be the one who loved him the most.

"I'm not sure." Lily frowned. "I think he needs you, or at least he needs to take care of you. I saw his face when they took you away, and I'll do whatever I have to do to make sure he never looks like that again."

Although Carrie liked hearing that Rico needed her and she was even secretly happy he'd been sad when they took her away, she didn't like the rest of Lily's words. Lily might not love him yet, but Carrie had a feeling she just might soon. What was not to love about Rico?

"So are you going to take that bath, let me do your hair, and pretend to be a sweet little girl?" Lily asked.

"Sure," Carrie promised even as she plotted ways to get rid of Lily right quick.

Still somewhat stunned at the twists and turns his so-called life had taken in the past few days, Rico made his way toward Reese and Mary's house, which stood behind the school.

He'd wanted a purpose. Looked like he had one—raising Carrie as best he could. He had a bad feeling his best was not going to be good enough. *Again.*

The children were outside for lunch. A cursory

glance found Johnny surrounded by boys smaller than he, but there were a whole lot of them.

Rico faltered to a stop. He hoped the children were just getting to know Johnny. But the tone of the voices that carried on the wind were catcalls and not welcoming murmurs.

One of the Sutton monsters kicked dirt on Johnny's shoe. The other one shoved him from behind. Pretty soon all the boys were jostling Johnny between them, like an insane game of tug-of-war. Rico started over, but before he took two steps, Reese came outside.

Everyone froze. Reese didn't even speak. One glare and all the bad boys drifted off, leaving Johnny alone. After a murmured conversation, Johnny went off, too, and Reese came toward Rico, who still hovered uncertainly at the edge of the schoolyard.

"Those Sutton twins are the spawn of Satan," Rico commented.

"Nope, just the spawn of Sutton. They might be bullies, but they're nothing if they aren't together. Johnny's new, and he's bigger, so they think they have to put him in his place."

"Which is?"

Reese cast a sharp look at Rico. "Whatever he makes it. Though he doesn't seem to care much what they say or do to him, he's going to have to take a stand or they'll never leave him alone."

"You think he will?"

"Not sure." Reese stared at Johnny, who sat on the steps and ate the lunch Yvonne had made him. "He's a bright kid. A whole lot brighter than I'd have thought from the way Lily talked."

"What do you mean?"

"She said he couldn't read or write, that he hadn't spoken in over five years."

"She's his sister, she ought to know."

"I suspect so."

Rico stared at Reese as Reese stared at Johnny. "What else do you suspect?" he asked.

"Not sure," he repeated. "But something's not right. I see the way the wind blows with you and her, and I don't want you hurt."

Not wanting to admit that the wind had knocked him over and stomped on him, Rico fell back on his usual flippancy.

"Me?" He put his hand over his heart. "Hurt by a woman? *Capitán*, you know me better than that."

"Do I? Sometimes I wonder. At any rate, I think there's more to Lily and Johnny than Lily and Johnny are saying."

"Does it matter? We all got our secrets. That should be the motto of the great state of Texas: Got a Secret? Come Hide It Here."

Reese turned his too observant gaze on Rico, and Rico fought not to squirm like one of the children. "You never shared any secrets with me, kid. Makes me wonder just what it is you're hiding."

Since Rico's secret would lose him Carrie, he shrugged and didn't answer, and since one of the rules of their friendship had always been *Don't ask*, Reese didn't.

"Sooner or later Johnny is going to have to stand up for himself," Reese murmured. "That's the only way he'll ever grow up. He'll have to face his past, whatever it is, if he wants a future—here or any-where else."

Rico wasn't foolish enough to believe they were talking about Johnny anymore.

CHAPTER 10

The gala grand opening of Three Queens occurred on a Saturday night. Considering how little money they'd had to spend on improvements, her place looked mighty fine to Lily's eyes.

Her place.

Lily leaned over the railing on the second floor and took in the entire first level. She couldn't remember the last time she'd used those words. Maybe she never had.

The shack where she'd lived, or rather existed, with her mother had not been her place. Lily had not let it be. Then the parade of other dwellings, some little more than boards in the wind, while she'd endured wherever and however she could, had not been hers, either. Certainly not any of the saloons she'd lived in with R.W. had been hers.

Betty Lillian might have existed before coming to Rock Creek. Now Lily Fortier planned to live.

Excitement made her heart flutter and her stom-

ach dance. New name, new life, fresh chance—
and she was going to make the most of every single
one.

She'd had a whole slew of new experiences, too,
since coming to Rock Creek. *Her* employees. *Her*
friends. *Her* brother—even if he wasn't.

Then there were the new and confusing relation
ships. Carrie, who wasn't hers, but rather Rico's.
And Rico—who was no one's, except maybe Carrie's.

Lily watched him as he checked everything one
last time. He'd taken to the management job as if
he'd been born to it. When she'd hired him, she'd
figured he would be the muscle, or maybe the knife
or the gun. Whatever it took to keep groping hands
off her ankles while she sang. But Rico had been
indispensable in readying the place, showing an
amazing aptitude for organization and detail that
had always been beyond Lily and did not seem like
Rico at all.

She doubted he'd believe her, but she couldn't
have made this opening occur with the grace and
verve she desired if Rico hadn't helped her.

He glanced up as if he'd felt her watching him.
He did that a lot. Probably because she watched
him a lot. She couldn't help herself. She wanted
him.

Their eyes locked. His dipped lower, and she
could almost feel the heat of his gaze first on her
neck, then across the sliver of skin revealed by the
neckline of her loose robe. She couldn't wait until
he got a look at her in the dress Kate had made.

Her entire body went liquid at the thought of
Rico's staring at her in that dress, then maybe later
helping her out of it. . . .

But he turned away without a word or a smile

and continued to work, reminding her that what she continued to dream would not happen. She believed he wanted her still, but she'd insulted him, beyond redemption, it seemed, and she had no idea how to change that.

Seduction, perhaps, but that was as beyond her understanding as an explanation for why she kept mooning over a man who obviously wanted nothing to do with her beyond employment. Lily wasn't used to men being indifferent to her.

"Rico!" Carrie ran in, and he caught her in mid-leap, spinning the child about as they both laughed.

She was filthy again, had no doubt been making mud pies in her bright yellow dress. Lily smiled. Even though Carrie could barely keep her distaste from her face and voice whenever she spoke to Lily, Lily found herself drawn to the brave little girl as she'd never been drawn to another child before, as she'd never let herself be drawn.

In that direction lay danger, because children were not for her, so she'd better not start dreaming of any.

"*Muchacha,* look at you." Rico set Carrie on the floor and tweaked her nose. The child's giggle made Lily's chest ache. *Damn.*

"You had best jump in the bath Yvonne has for you, then get into your brand-new dress."

"Another dress. Yuck!"

"But you will look beautiful. For me, *sí?*"

She sighed as if he'd asked her to take the weight of the world upon her small shoulders. "*Sí.*"

As Rico watched her trudge toward the kitchen, the love on his face shone so deep and so true, he appeared more beautiful than ever before.

Lily was starting to like him as well as want him,

and she did not know what to do about that. So she fled while she still could.

After making her way to her room, she wrestled her waist-length, wavy black hair into an elegant twist that would display her neck, shoulders, and tastefully bared cleavage to the best advantage in the ivory silk dress Kate had made for her.

Kate and Laurel had proved brilliant dressmakers, and it was only a matter of time until they opened their own business and left Lily to find new help. But she wouldn't be sad, only glad she'd been able to help two other women as she'd never been helped.

With her hair done, Lily stepped into her stockings and affixed them to her garters—one specially altered to hold a derringer. Then she strapped her knife to the retractable sheath, setting both aside to attach to her wrist after she was completely dressed.

Her ivory gloves would cover the sheath, though if she had to use the knife, the gloves would be ruined. But with Rico and Johnny about, Lily doubted she'd need the weapon. Still, she'd been faced with countless rooms filled with men, and she knew better than to depend on anyone but herself when things got nasty.

Lily reached for the dress, and her fingers encountered something cold, smooth, and mobile.

With a sharply indrawn breath, she yanked her hand back and stared in surprise at the coiled black-and-white snake on the bed. A milk snake! Large but harmless, thank God.

Now that Lily knew what the cold, moving object in her bed was, her heart slowed to a normal pace. She opened her door, shouted, "Rico!" and picked up the snake, one hand at the head, another below the coils, then stepped into the hall just as Rico pounded up the stairs.

The look on his face was completely inappropriate to the sight of her with a snake in her grasp. His eyes heated, and he stared at her as if he wanted to push her against the wall and finish what they'd started several times before.

Only then did she realize she stood in her corset, stockings, and garters alone. While Lily was gratified to learn he didn't despise her so much that he no longer wanted her, she really did need to get rid of the snake.

"You want to take this?" she asked, holding the snake up higher and moving it about to gain his attention.

He shook his head, blinked a few times, then scowled. "Where did that come from?"

"The river, most likely. I found it on my bed."

He strode forward and took the snake from her hands. His movement revealed Carrie at the top of the steps, scowling, fit for murder, and Lily knew how the snake had gotten into her room. Her lips twitched. She'd lived in a house where large, deadly cottonmouths lounged as if they owned the place. It would take more than a lethargic milk snake to get rid of her.

"How did this get in your room?" Rico asked.

Carrie's eyes widened. Lily shrugged. "I have no idea. Just get rid of it."

"I thought women didn't like snakes," Carrie said.

Rico narrowed his eyes upon her, but Carrie stared back with complete innocence.

"I'm not most women," Lily pointed out.

"I'll say," Rico muttered, and hurried down the stairs.

Lily and Carrie stared at each other down the length of the hall.

"How come you didn't scream and cry?"

"When I was a little girl, a snake like that would have been supper." Carrie turned an interesting shade of green. "It'll take more than that to get rid of me, *chérie.*"

Carrie lowered her head in acknowledgment. Lily did the same.

This meant war.

"Madre de Dios, the woman is trying to kill me." Rico practically ran out of the saloon and headed for the river.

After a frantic day of last-minute preparations that had followed several days of backbreaking building and lifting, Rico could honestly say he'd never worked harder in his life.

Folks on the street might look at him oddly for carrying a snake, but they greeted him by name. Rock Creek was more of a home than any other place had ever been.

Moving over the hills and down to the water, he tossed the snake into the shade that hovered about the river's bend. Damn, he was hot, even though the sun slid toward sleep and shadows spread across the river like the fingers of a mythical giant.

Rico knelt and stuck his hands into the water, letting the spring-cool liquid lap at his wrists and calm his runaway heart.

He'd decided Lily was not for him. Now that he worked for her, how could he ever make love to her and not feel bought and paid for? Silly, perhaps, but he had little to be proud of in his life—at least he'd never sold his greatest gift for money.

With a curse, Rico ducked his head beneath the water. As soon as he closed his eyes, he saw the image of Lily as he'd seen her last—white corset, stockings, garters nearly the same shade as her porcelain skin, hair pinned up so primly, he'd itched to yank it free and bury his face in the soft curls, her cheeks flushed rose, her lips smirking as no other woman's would with a great black-and-white snake in her hands.

He threw his head back, spraying droplets of water all over his shirt. He needed to return to Three Queens and change clothes for the big night. Instead, he sat on the damp earth at the edge of the river and watched the sun die.

She'd offered herself to him, and he'd turned her down. *Idiota!* Maybe if he'd taken her, he wouldn't still want her with a need that hummed in his blood every time he heard her voice or smelled that haunting scent, a combination of white spring trees and red summer flowers.

But if he took Lily as he wanted, as she wanted, would the crushing despair that came from knowing she thought him no more than a decorative ornament, no better than a bauble to be worn on her exquisite throat or hung from her lovely ears, ever leave him? Would he become what she thought he was with no hope of ever becoming more?

And when had he started to wish he could be someone better? When Carrie had looked at him and told him she loved him? When a child's simple faith had made him want to become something better than what he was?

Or had this restlessness begun when a woman made him wonder if he'd ever be more than his father had predicted?

A worthless, useless, pretty-as-a-picture embarrassment to the name of Salvatore.

Lily was ready an hour before Three Queens was set to open. She was so nervous, she could not eat. She knew better than to drink. So she paced.

"Everything will be fine," Yvonne assured her. "This place is finer than anything anyone's ever seen in these parts."

"You mean it's too much?"

Lily's panicked gaze flittered about the room. They'd cleaned the tables, mended the walls, scrubbed the floor. The curtains, lace and velvet, were nothing special, but very different from what had been there before. Namely nothing. Would the folks in and about Rock Creek be intimidated?

"I didn't say it was too much." Yvonne began to polish faster than usual. She was nervous, too. "I said the place is fine. Sit down, Lily."

"I can't."

"Then don't. But get away from me."

One thing Lily liked about Yvonne, she always knew where she stood with the woman. Right now Yvonne wanted to smack her stupid.

The girls appeared in brand-new dresses they'd made for themselves. Kate wore pink, and Laurel wore blue. Their grins went from ear to ear. They'd never had new clothes, and they'd never worn anything that didn't reveal more of them than it hid.

Lily had made sure they were covered adequately to befit their jobs as servers and nothing else. More had changed in this saloon than the name, and Lily would make certain everyone knew that.

Johnny clattered down the stairs wearing a brand-new starched white shirt and black trousers held up by red suspenders. He looked older for the clothes, but with his hair still wet and slicked back, he looked too young to be playing piano in a saloon.

Lily experienced a twinge. He should be going to school and fooling with his friends at the river, spooning with girls and attending church socials. Instead, he would play piano until well after midnight and sleep through church tomorrow.

Pausing in front of her, he took Lily's hands, holding them wide open so he could look her over with a critically tilted eye.

"Well?" she asked. "Will I do?"

His dark, solemn gaze met hers, and he wiggled his eyebrows, then grinned. Lily laughed and ran her fingers through his hair.

"If things go very well, maybe I can hire another piano player," she ventured.

His grin faded, and he looked crushed. "Not that you aren't the best there ever was, Johnny, but you should be a kid for a while."

"He's not a kid." Lily glanced in the direction of the indignant voice.

Carrie stood with her hands on her hips, lip belligerently stuck out in Johnny's defense. Even with the scowl, she looked adorable.

Kate had used the leftover material from Lily's dress to fashion another for Carrie. Not so fancy, of course, but perfect for a child—high neck, puffy sleeves, full skirt, and gloves. Carrie looked like a little doll—if you ignored the rat's nest in her hair and the smudge of mud in her ear.

"School's out soon," Carrie continued. "Then he can play piano at night, and I'll help him with his reading in the day."

"You have this all worked out between you?"

"Course. You can't take away the music, Lily. It's his favorite thing. How would you feel if a big, fat, ugly lady told you you couldn't sing?"

Lily narrowed her eyes on Carrie. The little tyrant just scrunched up her nose and glared. "A big, fat, ugly lady?"

"Yeah, they're all over the place."

"I can imagine. Well, I guess I wouldn't like it at all." She took Johnny's hand. "We'll just leave things as they are, then. I wouldn't want to sing to anyone's music but yours, *chéri.*"

Johnny's smile made her nervousness flee. His serenity always had that effect on Lily.

"Lily, the place looks wonderful!" Eden and Mary, dressed in their Sunday best, stood in the doorway, beaming at her as if she'd just done the most clever thing imaginable instead of refurbishing the town saloon.

Their husbands crowded in behind them, appearing uncomfortable despite the fact that they'd been in the place at least a hundred times before.

They glanced at each other, then warily about the room, their eyes flicking from the shiny lanterns glowing merrily at intervals along the wall to the sparkling clean glasses and full crystal bottles behind the bar.

"Oh, brother," Sullivan murmured. "Cash . . ."

"Isn't going to like this," Reese finished.

"It's a good thing he is gone, then, *si?*"

Lily jumped at the sound of Rico's voice directly behind her.

The sight of him rendered her speechless. Had she called him decorative? He was downright poetic.

The starched white of his shirt sparkled against his olive skin, black hair, and ebony eyes. The black vest and tight black pants emphasized his lean, muscular build. But what really made it difficult for Lily to breathe was the way he'd rolled up his cuffs to bare his tanned, sinewy forearms and left open the top three buttons of his shirt to reveal the smooth, supple chest she enjoyed looking at far too much.

"The place is Lily's," he said. "She won it with three queens, fair and square. Cash has nothing to say about it."

Fair? she thought. *Maybe. But square?*

Well, that was neither here nor there now. As long as R.W. never found her, fair and square didn't count for beans and barley.

"*Señorita.*" Rico bowed. "It is time for you to prepare to go onstage."

He held out his arm. Sullivan snorted, but Reese shot him a look that stifled any further comment. Then Reese turned a contemplative gaze on Rico, who merely inclined his head formally and led Lily away.

"Oh, brother," Sullivan said again.

"You got that right," Reese murmured.

CHAPTER 11

In the small curtained room to the rear of the stage, Lily waited. The familiar sounds of a gathering crowd filtered through the air. But how big of a crowd?

Opening night could make or break a place like this. She had no doubt she could eke out a living for herself and Johnny by running a saloon and gambling establishment, but she wanted so much more for them both. As Carrie had said, how would she feel if she could not sing?

So awful she did not want to think about it for long.

Singing was a part of her, just as the piano was a part of Johnny. Singing was the one thing she did better than any other, the one thing that made her special in a world that didn't see her as special at all.

"It is time, *señorita*."

Rico's soft, lightly accented voice caused her

breath to catch nearly as much as the sight of him so near when she had not heard his approach. "You never call me Lily anymore."

He lifted one shoulder, the movement pulling the material of his shirt tight, allowing her to see the darker shade of his skin beneath the white cotton. "It does not seem appropriate when you are my boss."

"And when Reese was your boss you called him *señor?*"

Rico's teeth flashed, strong and straight and white. "I called him *mi capitán.*"

"Even though he wasn't."

"He was; he simply chose not to admit it."

"And I am neither young nor a lady."

"You may not think so, but I do." He waved his hand briskly. "Now come along; your public is waiting." Lily hung back. "You are not afraid? *La señorita* who battles snakes in her unmentionables."

She gave a reluctant smile. "It wasn't much of a battle."

"Still, you amazed Carrie." He fixed her with a dark, unfathomable gaze. "You amazed me."

"I did?" Was that her voice, breathless, as if she'd just been kissed senseless or perhaps ravished in the back room?

"You do." He held out his hand. "Come along and amaze them all."

Rico's strong fingers closed over hers, and he drew her toward him. When she was so close her skirt brushed his shiny black boots, he whispered, "Lily."

The sound of her name caused a shiver and made her want him all over again. But even as his eyes promised uncertain delights, his body inched away from hers. She followed him the few short steps to where a curtain separated the back of the stage from the front.

"Ready?" he asked.

She took a deep breath, and it caught in her throat. He gave her a look of concern. "Are you always this nervous?"

"Only when the rest of my life depends on something."

"Ah, true enough." He leaned closer, and she froze as he kissed her gently on the forehead. "For luck, *sí?*"

"*Sí,*" she repeated.

Rico opened the curtain and drew her with him into a room so filled with people, there was barely space left to stand. Lily's eyes widened until she thought they might pop out and roll around on the stage.

She glanced at Rico, who merely winked and urged her forward. The crowd began to clap. She found her friends in the front row. Yvonne, arms folded, face solemn, nodded to her from behind the bar. Then Johnny began to play "I Dream of Jeanie with the Light Brown Hair," and without conscious thought Lily gave herself over to the music that had always saved her before.

And it saved her now. Within moments she became caught in the melody, and the audience must have, too, since they grew quiet. She'd captured them with the words, the tune, her voice, a certain magic.

Together she and Johnny lured them in, made them theirs. Not a person in the crowd wasn't snared in the web they spun. They gave something to everyone, from ballads to ditties, songs sung long before the war and beyond, and when she finished, Lily knew she'd sung the best she ever had. Perhaps because she'd sung in her place, her way.

Complete silence blanketed the room as the last note died away. Lily held her breath. Had she been the only one enthralled by what she'd done?

Then the room erupted with applause, stamping feet, and whistles. Her friends jumped up and cheered. Kate and Laurel set down trays filled with drinks to clap and grin. Thank God she *had* been as good as she'd thought.

Lily let the breath whistle past her lips, bowed, swept her hand toward Johnny, and hit Rico in the stomach.

His gut was as hard as his boot, so he didn't double over. He didn't even react. For a moment, she wondered why he was there, until he moved past her to stand at the edge of the stage and glare at the men who crowded close, vying for her attention. One snarl from him and they all backed away.

Decorative *and* functional—how convenient.

Lily went to stand at his side. "How did this happen?"

Rico's gaze slid toward her, then back to the crowd. "You're amazing. What did you think would happen?"

His words caused a warm glow throughout Lily's body. She'd been told the same thing before, by people who were in the entertainment business. Why did this man's praise make her feel as if his were the only words that mattered?

Giving in to impulse, she took his hand, and when he let her, she smiled. "I meant, where did all these people come from? I don't think there are this many folks in the entire town."

"There aren't." His shrug appeared sheepish. "I rode out to the ranches, then sent word to the nearest towns. Ranbourne even put an article in their paper. I kept a copy for you. People around here don't get much chance to enjoy a night like this."

"Encore!" The shout swept around the room, growing louder as each voice took up the word.

"Encore, Lily, encore." Rico backed away, tugging on his hand, but she held on.

"You did that for me?"

Something unfathomable flickered in his dark, dark eyes. "*Haría cualquier cosa para ti,*" he whispered, then disappeared behind the stage curtain.

Lily had no idea what he'd said and no time now to ask, even though she wanted to very much.

In a daze of delight she crossed to the piano. Johnny raised his eyebrow. What did she want to sing?

"Whatever you want." She could barely think past the joy and the excitement. The audience settled as she reached for the glass of water atop the piano.

She took a deep draft to soothe her throat. The taste of vinegar filled her mouth, burned her nose, and made her eyes water. But with the crowd staring at her, she could not spray the noxious liquid all over the floor.

One face amid the multitude caught her eye. Carrie, her chin perched on her arms as she leaned on the edge of the stage, smirked while her eyes danced with devilish delight.

Lily forced herself to swallow the mouthful. She refused to choke. Instead, she breathed in through her burning nose and out through her tingling mouth until her eyes quit watering.

Then she went on with the show, singing even better than before, seeing the disgust on Carrie's face was nearly as much fun as listening to the applause she received for the encore.

The night was an unmitigated success. Lily couldn't remember the last time she'd been able to sing without fending off gropers and ignoring hecklers. But with Rico on the stage and Reese and Sullivan right in front, no one dared touch her, and no one uttered an unkind word.

After her last song, Rico returned. This time Carrie hopped on the stage and hugged his waist. Johnny went off to find water that wasn't vinegar, and Lily confronted her enemy.

"I've never had water that soothed my throat so well," she began. "I think I could have sung another hour after drinking that."

Rico gave her a strange look. "Never heard that our well was so fine; I'm glad you like it."

Carrie's face revealed every thought in her little head. She expected Lily to tattle on her. But that wasn't how things were done between worthy adversaries. Instead, Lily smiled, winked, and moved on. Let the little terror wonder when she'd strike and how—or even if. That's how things were done between women.

"I'll just say good night to Eden and Mary," Lily said.

"I'll put Carrie to bed and be right back down."

"No! I wanna play poker. Johnny taught me how to kick some ass in cards."

Rico put his hand to his forehead and rubbed. "Carrie, you've got to stop cursing."

Confusion filled her innocent brown eyes. "What did I say?"

"We'll discuss it upstairs." He took her hand

and pulled her steadily away, even as she hung back.

"Aw, sh—"

"Hey!" Rico snapped.

"Shucks," she finished.

Half an hour later, Lily said good-bye to the last well-wisher and slipped toward her dressing room for a drink of real water and a moment of pure silence before she joined one of the games and dealt poker far into the night.

Lily kicked off her ivory slippers. After reclining on one chair, she propped her feet on another. Tentatively, she sipped the glass of water on the table, found it uncontaminated, and let her head fall back as she closed her eyes for just a minute.

Footfalls in the hallway were followed by the swish of the curtain across her door. She'd figured Rico would find her once he made certain Carrie was asleep. "I'll be right out," she murmured.

"When the hell did you get to town, pretty lady?"

Her eyes flew open. She had never seen the man who filled the doorway. She would remember someone that tall and wide and . . . and . . . scruffy. There was no other word for it.

Beneath all that hair and beard he might be handsome. Maybe. She wasn't going to stick around to find out.

Lily got slowly to her feet, careful not to make any sudden moves. This man looked as if he'd just come out of the wilderness after living there most of his life.

"Who are you?" she asked, stalling.

"I asked you first." He stepped inside, making the room grow smaller because of his size, seeming to take the air, since Lily couldn't breathe very well once he loomed close enough to touch.

"I'm Lily." Her thumb brushed her thigh, where the derringer lay. Damn thing was useless unless this man gave her time to lift her skirt and yank it free. While lifting her skirt might be just what he had in mind, she didn't think she'd oblige.

"Lily," he repeated. "Nice name."

"Glad you like it." She stepped sideways as he advanced, hoping to work her way toward the door and escape, though in her experience, if he'd meant to grab her, he would have already. Still the mere size of the man made Lily nervous.

Behind the flounce of her skirt, Lily prepared to ruin an exquisite set of gloves if she had to palm her knife. She really hoped she wouldn't have to.

"I think I like *you*."

He took one giant step in her direction, and Lily twisted her wrist. The knife shot through the material and filled her hand with steel.

She lifted her arm and waved the knife back and forth. "Ah, ah, ah. Go away like a good boy."

He didn't even look at the knife. Lily's unease spread. She didn't think her blade would do much damage to that body unless she stuck him just right, and she didn't believe she had it in her to kill him—at least not for this. He grinned. "But I'm *not* a good boy."

"Aren't you afraid of the knife?"

He gave a snort of derision. "That's not a knife."

A whoosh filled the air, and a Bowie knife stuck in the floor between the man's boots. He lowered his gaze to the waving handle, then raised his eyes to hers. "That's a knife." He didn't even look toward the door. "Hello, kid. I should have known she was yours."

Rico stepped between Lily and the stranger, who obviously wasn't a stranger to him. Just having Rico near made Lily's heart stop thundering—at least in fear.

Bending down, Rico pulled his knife from the floor, then pointed the handle at the man. "You better get out of here before I take better aim next time."

"You mean you missed?"

"I never miss."

"With a knife."

"What else is there?"

The two of them grinned like fools, then slapped each other on the back. "Welcome home, Jed," Rico said; then he turned to Lily. "This is Eden's brother, Jedidiah Rourke."

Lily gaped. "Eden's *brother*?"

She couldn't reconcile this overgrown bear of a man with the sweet and dainty Eden.

Jed scratched his beard and looked embarrassed. She almost expected him to shuffle his feet and say, "Aw, shucks."

"I, uh, hope I didn't scare you. I was just foolin'."

"Lily?" Rico laughed. "She does not scare that easy."

"Were you gonna stick me with that hairpin?" Jed indicated the knife she still held in her hand.

Lily looked at her shredded glove. "I still might. You owe me a pair of gloves, Mr. Rourke."

"Just Jed, and you're right. I'll take care of that as soon as I get to a town where they make 'em."

"Things have changed, *amigo.* You can buy gloves in Rock Creek now. Kate and Laurel turned out to be seamstresses."

"I bet Cash loves that."

"He's gone," Lily put in. "He wasn't too happy when I turned up owning the saloon."

"Bet not. Did he threaten to shoot you?"

"Not in so many words."

Jed grunted, then glanced at Rico. "Nate?"

"Gone with Cash."

"Where?"

"Last we heard, Fort Worth. I'm sure if they move on, we'll hear something else soon."

"We always do," he growled. "Where can a thirsty man get a drink around here?"

Rico looked so pleased to see his friend, and since the man *was* Eden's brother, he couldn't be all bad, so Lily unbuckled her knife, tossed it onto the table, and led the way to the bar.

Countless voices greeted Jed. He'd obviously been here in the past and was well liked. When Yvonne grinned and hurried to place a bottle and glass on the bar before Jed even got there, Lily decided to give him a second chance. Her own second chance was going so well.

"On the house," she murmured to Yvonne. The two men were so engrossed in their discussion, she didn't think they noticed when she slipped away to deal poker until midnight and beyond.

"I can't believe this place." Jed sipped his second whiskey and stared at the saloon some more. "It's so . . ."

"Clean?" Rico murmured, his gaze on Lily.

She was taking her table for all that they had, and even as each man lost, he laughed and begged to be taken some more.

"I was going to say full."

"It's amazing what clearing out the dirt, patching up the bullet holes, and lighting a few lamps will do for a place."

"Not to mention the addition of a beautiful

woman wearing a revealing dress and dealing poker."

Rico switched his gaze to Jed. "You ought to hear her sing. You'll forget all about her dress."

"I somehow doubt that."

"Well, why don't you try?"

Jed grinned. "Don't worry, kid, I won't poach. Though she seems a little old for you—or maybe she's just mature."

"She isn't anything to me except my boss."

"And how did that happen? You needed money, you could have come and helped me with that small-time silver-mine skirmish in Nevada. Could have even used your help when I hired my gun to that Mexican village just past the border. Hell, if you were desperate, you could have gone with Nate and Cash."

"Not anymore. Carrle is living with me now."

"What happened to Brown?"

"Dead." Before Jed could accuse him of the crime, Rico held up his hand. "He dropped dead while having a screaming fit. You know how he was."

Jed nodded. Everyone in Rock Creek knew how Brown was. "Bound to happen sooner or later with that man's temper. Things sure have changed while I've been away. You're workin' for a woman, and all the other boys are either married or off tryin' to die. Maybe I should stick around a while."

"I know you, Jed. Your idea of a while is a week. You can't stay in one place for long before your feet are itching to be in another."

"So I like new places, just like you like new women." He raised a brow at Lily. "Or at least you used to."

"I like *women*." Rico sipped his drink and

thought about that. "Perhaps because they like me. I know most enjoy my face or have heard of my skills."

Jed lifted his eyebrow. "Skills? Is that what they call it these days?"

Rico ignored Jed's sarcasm, hesitating, uncertain how to confide such a mystery to his friend. "No matter how many women I bed, the need for another and another has never left me."

His eyes went to Lily. *Until now.*

From the moment Rico had first been touched, kissed, and loved by a female, he had worked at the craft of pleasing them. Women were so soft, so sweet smelling, and when they held him in their arms in the darkest of the night, he felt as if he were special, at least for that bit of time.

So he'd developed two exceptional skills—the knife and sex. One had kept him alive, the other had made his life worth living.

Or had it? Had he ever felt needed or loved for himself?

"You've got a restless . . ." Jed hesitated, glancing at Rico's new black trousers, then up to his face with a smirk. "Heart," he finished. "Like I got restless feet."

"What's the cure?"

"Not sure, kid." Lily's laughter trilled through the room, drawing the attention of every man. "Maybe the right woman would do it for us both."

"How do you know who the right woman is?"

"Unfortunately, I think the right woman is a myth. At least for men like us."

What a cheery thought. Rico didn't buy it. Reese had been the most haunted man Rico had ever seen. Not that he was a carnival clown now, but when Reese looked at Mary or Georgie, the love in his eyes outshone the shadows.

Sullivan was the same. The only place he'd ever belonged had been riding with the five men who had never cared if he was white, red, purple, or green. Now Sullivan belonged to Rock Creek almost as deeply as he belonged to Eden and their four kids.

Jed moved off to drink with some men from an outlying ranch where the six had bought horses in the past, leaving Rico alone with his deep, deep thoughts.

Would touching Lily erase the eternal restlessness in his soul? Did he want the kind of life Reese and Sullivan had? Or should he accept the fact that all he deserved was the wandering existence of Jed, if not the doomed fate of Nate and Cash?

Instead of drifting through life, finding momentary satisfaction with woman after woman, might touching the right woman save him from himself?

Rico finished his drink and crossed the room to stand at Lily's side. He put his hand on her shoulder. When she reached up without even looking at him and covered his hand with her own, the funny dance his stomach had been doing since the first time he kissed her turned into an all-out jig.

If she wasn't the right woman, Rico didn't know who was.

The trick would be convincing Lily of that.

CHAPTER 12

Three Queens closed at two A.M. Lily sent everyone to bed. Since tomorrow—make that today—was Sunday and the place would be shut until evening, any cleanup could wait until after they got some sleep.

Alone in the saloon, Lily began to blow out the lights. Funny, but she really wasn't tired at all.

Leaving just a few burning, she climbed on the stage and contemplated the empty room, remembering again what it had felt like to be at the center of the storm of adulation. She knew why she needed the attention. She'd had very little as a child. To her mother, only men had mattered, one after the other.

Once Lily was on her own, she received attention for her body and her face. At first she'd enjoyed it—until she realized how fleeting regard based on appearance was. But the appreciation she received because of her talent—devotion based on a worthwhile ability—was something that lasted. She'd quickly come to need the applause as much as she needed a place to live and food to eat.

Though Lily knew better than to dream, for a moment she did, anyway, and the dream was beautiful. Three Queens became everything she'd ever hoped to have—a prosperous business, a place to call home, a safe haven for always.

"Ba, ba, da, da . . ." Lily hummed to herself and began to waltz, swaying to imaginary music, twirling the full skirt of her new dress like a child. Faster and faster, around and around, until she became dizzy and began to laugh.

"You should laugh more often."

Lily stopped, but her head kept spinning, and when she stumbled a few steps, strong hands grasped, then steadied, her. The scent of summer wind and spring water calmed her thundering heart.

"Rico!" She should have known. No one else could sneak like him, except maybe Carrie. Lily wondered what the little imp had planned for her next. She had a lovely surprise in store for Carrie.

Even though the world had stopped tilting, Rico did not let her go. His hands gentled on her arms, and his thumbs stroked along her skin.

He was so good at knowing exactly where to touch, how hard or how soft, and how long. Lily held very still lest any movement on her part made him let her go. She did not want to be released. Not yet. Instead, she stared into his dark eyes, eyes that so often danced, even as deep down they cried.

"You should dance more often as well, *Lilita*."

The foreign twist at the end of her name rolled over Lily like water down a cliff. Her stomach fell just as far when he drew her closer than would ever be acceptable in polite society. But then, Lily had never lived in polite society, and if Rico had, those days were long past.

His mouth nuzzled her hair. "Sing," he whispered. "Something low and sad, just for me."

It wasn't easy to sing a cappella, and Lily hadn't done it since her last street corner, but she managed. Soft and sweet, the words of "My Old Kentucky Home" slid past her lips and swirled around them.

Together they moved, body to body, the skim of clothes against limbs another dance altogether, an erotic slip and slide that excited Lily in ways she'd never imagined.

The combination of song, dance, flickering lights, the darkest hour of the night, and the darkest man she'd ever known made this small moment in time as intense as any she'd ever experienced.

When the last notes of the song died away, Rico quit moving, but he held her still, the rise and fall of his chest beneath her cheek as soothing as the brush of lips on the top of her head, both a stark contrast to the evidence of his desire that he did nothing to hide.

"You were the most beautiful woman I'd ever seen tonight."

Lily sighed in disappointment. She would think that a man like him, whom everyone saw as mere decoration, would know how little beauty mattered in the scheme of life.

"The way your eyes lit up with each song, the way your mouth formed the words—your voice gave them meaning as your body swayed to the music. I could listen to you sing for the rest of my life and never get tired. You've got a gift for certain, and that gift is beautiful."

Lily lifted her head from Rico's chest and stared into his face. His lips tilted in question at the intensity of her gaze. "So when you say I'm beautiful, you mean my voice?"

"Any man with eyes can see you're stunning, Lily. But . . ." He shrugged. "Pretty does not mean so much to me. I have been loved too many times for this face alone, and in the end the love is as lasting as this face will be. What is in a person's heart is what counts. And in your heart, *Lilita*, is beautiful music."

Surprised to hear her innermost thoughts put to words, Lily lifted her hand and trailed her fingers down his cheek. The night stubble scraped her skin and made her shiver. She'd once dreamed of a man who could see the woman she wanted to be. Rico had seen the woman still trapped within her soul.

He captured her fingers against his face, then turned his mouth to press a burning kiss to the center of her palm.

"I'm sorry," she whispered.

His dark head tilted as his eyes met hers. "*Qué?*"

"That I said you were useless. You aren't. You're the best manager I've ever seen."

He shrugged off her praise as if embarrassed. "You do not need to apologize for what you believed as the truth. I had no skills past the knife and a certain flare as a lover. I have learned much from Yvonne, the girls, and you. Do not feel bad. You are not the only one who sees me as a child who cannot grow up."

She slipped her free hand behind his head and drew his mouth even closer. "I don't see you as a child. I never did."

"*Gracias*," he murmured right before his lips touched hers.

Whoever had taught him to kiss had done their job well. He gave, took, advanced, retreated, soft to hard, gentle atop rough. Seduction. Kissing Rico was addictive and could quickly become as necessary as breakfast, as right as anything Lily had ever known.

Her knees weak, she wished she could sink down onto the plank stage and pull him with her, but she wasn't so far gone as not to realize how dangerous that would be. As if he knew her weakness, his strong arms came about her back and pulled her close so she did not have to struggle to stay afoot anymore.

As his body had only moments ago, his tongue now danced with hers. He tasted of coffee and whiskey, shiny morning, dark of night.

Her skin tingled cool as her blood ran hot. Her breasts seemed to swell against the low-cut neckline of her gown, and her nipples hardened and scraped against her corset. Lower, deeper, her body softened and wept for his.

This from a single kiss that went on and on.

"Upstairs," she managed to gasp when they came up for air.

He leaned his forehead against hers and closed his eyes for a moment as if searching for control. The dark sweep of his lashes across his high cheekbones made him look young and innocent, as sweet as sin must be.

"*Lilita*, we should not."

"Should," she countered. "Now."

He laughed, a tight, pained sound. "You wish to kill me." His eyes opened, and humor shone in their depths. "I would die happy, *sí*?"

"I hope so." She sobered, then brushed his hair away from his face. He got a bewildered look, as if he did not know what to make of her gentleness. Her heart ached for the man who'd been used nearly as much as she had. "I hurt you before, and I didn't mean to. I want you. You want me. Can't we just have this?"

"What is this?" His face, so earnest and intense, begged for the truth, or as much truth as she could give.

"Don't touch me so I'll sing. I won't let you so I can eat."

"Ah, Lily."

"Shh." She put her fingers against his lips. "Promise?"

He linked their hands together. "*Sí.* Don't touch me because of this." He put a finger to his cheek. "I won't let you because I'm so lonely I could die of it. Promise?"

"*Oui,*" she whispered, and blinked away tears he would not appreciate. "Rico, I have never been with anyone because I wanted to be. I want to be with you."

A gentleness came over his face that touched her heart as much as the awe in his voice. "You honor me."

No one had ever looked at her like that before. For a moment, she let him; then she shook her head. "We owe each other nothing. We expect nothing from each other beyond this. I want to laugh and make love and live."

"I am very good at all three."

"Teach me to be, too. Teach me something good."

"You have come to the right man."

"I think I've known that for a while now."

His smile filled with pleasure. "Upstairs?"

The weight on her chest that was always there—the weight of survival, responsibility, of just herself—lifted. She felt a lightness of being that put a skip in her step as she kicked off her shoes and jumped off the stage.

"I'll race you," she threw over her shoulder, and hurried up the stairs.

To her room she ran. Her own terms, her own place. Despite her lead, he was right on her heels as she sped through the door.

Breathless, flushed, excited, she spun about at the foot of the bed. The door clicked shut. He grinned wickedly and flicked the lock.

Expecting him to come barreling across the room, tumble her back on the bed, and get down to business, she was surprised when he stayed right where he was, shrugging free of his black vest and letting the garment slide down his arms to the floor.

His long, dark fingers, stark against the white cotton, with seductive lassitude he unbuttoned his shirt, holding her gaze all the while.

A shrug of each lean, well-formed shoulder and the white shirt joined the black vest at his feet. Lily's heart had slowed from her run, but she still breathed as heavily as if she'd just gone up the stairs three times with her corset laced too tightly.

She'd thought this man dangerous with a knife? He was ever so much more dangerous with a shirt—make that without.

His bronzed skin glistened in the lamplight that flickered from the bedside table. Lily licked her lips, imagining what he might taste like. That she would soon know only made her all the more breathless.

Those nimble fingers moved to the buttons on his trousers. Popping free the first, then the second, he revealed that beneath the tight black material lay only him. Or perhaps lay was not the right word. The sight of his arousal straining beneath the confining buttons made her itch to set him free.

He drew one finger along his own length, then pointed at her. "Now you."

The whisper swirled about the room. She yanked her gaze to his face. "D-don't you want to undress me?"

His smile was as languid as his hands had been. "Half the fun, *Lilita*, is the watching."

True. But she did not think she could undress half as erotically as he had, and she did not want to disappoint him.

Her uncertainty must have shown on her face, for he made a *tsking* noise with his tongue. "It does not matter how you reveal yourself, only that you do. The first step in this act we have decided to undertake begins with trust. I trust you enough to show myself as I am. Trust me. I will not hurt you."

She stared into his eyes and saw both vulnerability and strength. With a nod she reached for the pins in her hair.

"Ah!" He held up his hand. "Leave the hair for me. As I have left something for you."

He winked, and she couldn't help but grin despite her nervousness. How could a woman like her, who had taken her first lover at the age of fifteen in order to survive, feel as if she'd never done this before? Perhaps because she had never done *this*.

Deftly she released the buttons on the back of her dress and pulled the ivory silk down her arms.

"Slowly," he breathed, just above a whisper. "No hurry tonight."

Once freed, the weight of the garment swished past her hips, pooling about her feet. She stepped over the pile and kicked it beneath the bed, something she'd never do on a normal night. But nothing about this night had been normal.

Only her corset, garters, and stockings remained. "No chemise?" She glanced at him, only to find his gaze riveted on her legs. "Such a rebel."

"It spoiled the line of the dress."

"I am so glad it did." He motioned for her to continue. "The stockings, *por favor*?"

Removing the derringer was always a trick. With him watching her so intently, she fumbled. His hands covered hers, making her start and look into the face so close to her own. How could he appear both gentle and intense at the same time.

"Let me," he murmured. "Before you blow off your pretty toe."

Easily, he released the weapon, then stepped back to let her continue. But when she bent to unroll the stockings, her corset sliced into her belly.

Her hiss of pain brought him instantly to her side. "What is it?"

"I can't bend in the corset."

He shook his head. "Such silly clothes women wear."

"You won't get an argument from me."

"Let me," he repeated.

Thinking he meant to release her corset strings, she began to turn. But he knelt in front of her, and as his fingers brushed her thigh, as his breath brushed her where she was pretty hot already, arousal ripped through Lily. She clutched his shoulders.

He looked up. "Perhaps slow is not the best idea tonight."

She could only shrug helplessly, uncertain of what she wanted or how she wanted it, because she could no longer think at all.

Smoothing his palms down first one leg, then the other, he tossed her stockings after the dress. But instead of gaining his feet, he put his mouth where his fingers had been—lips along her knee, a wet slide of tongue to the inside of her thigh, and then an openmouthed suckle where her leg joined her pelvis.

No one on earth had ever kissed her there.

"Can't breathe," she murmured, and the voice was not her own.

"Hush, *bambina*. Let me make it all right."

He removed her corset as if he removed them every day. Most likely he did, but she would not think of that now, could not think of anything but his mouth kissing her in all sorts of places she'd never been kissed before and loving each and every one.

Weak and dizzy, when he pushed her back on the bed, she went. She was completely naked, while he still wore his pants. But as she tugged at the waistband, he stilled her searching fingers. "Not yet. Fast for you, then slow for me."

She had no idea what he meant until his hot mouth closed on the peak of her breast and he drew in, tongue pushing on the underside, suckling, making her need—anything.

He was everywhere at once, mouth here, fingers there, the brush of his chin hard, the drift of his hair so soft. His teeth along her hipbone made her arch, and when he fastened his mouth there, where everything screamed for him, she stopped breathing.

She started again with a French curse, and he laughed against her skin. Something wonderful lay just beyond a peak she could see very clearly behind her closed eyelids.

When she would have thrashed, his large hands closed over her hips, and his smart mouth worked witchcraft, bringing her to a gasping, shuddering climax, taking her somewhere else she had never been before.

He slid up the bed and lay at her side, holding her hand as she came back from the fall. When she opened her eyes, he watched her, and she was surprised to discover she didn't mind.

"What was that?" she asked.

"What you asked for. Didn't you want me to teach you something good?"

"I think I missed part of the lesson."

He removed the remaining pins from her hair, brushing the rest of them off the bed. "Shall we run through it more slowly this time?"

She placed her fingers on the third button of his trousers. "If you can manage."

"I thought I was the best manager you'd ever seen. Let me show you just how useful I can be."

In answer, she freed buttons three, four, and five, then tossed his trousers to keep company with her dress.

Rico had never been nervous in a woman's company. Why now, when he'd gained entrance to a bed he'd wanted far longer than he'd wanted any other, did he now tremble? Because he'd been claiming incredible prowess and now he must produce? He had no one to blame but himself. Braggarts were often called upon to live up to their big mouths, or other parts, as the case might be.

Lily's hand closed around him, and he jumped. "Shh," she murmured against his chest. "Let me soothe that ego."

Incredibly, he laughed. She joined in, her chuckles spouting tiny bursts of air against his sensitive skin. Lifting her head, she gazed into his face, and the lightness in her eyes made him happy. He rarely saw anything but worry there.

"I've never laughed like this," she said.

"You should more often."

"I never thought sex was very funny."

"I suspect most men would not be too happy to have their lover laugh."

"You don't seem to mind."

"I do not think you are laughing at me."

"And if I was?"

He cupped his hand along her hip and rolled her body flush with his. "I would make you stop."

"Mmm." She arched her back, pressing his arousal to her stomach. "I don't feel like laughing so much anymore."

His smile was one of satisfaction as he lowered his mouth to hers. Why had he said they would go slow for him? He didn't think he could wait. Not after tasting her, touching her, hearing her laughter, experiencing her every response as if it were his own.

One of the reasons he was very good at sex was that he cared as much, if not more, about his partner's satisfaction as his own. To be honest, men needed very little in the way of stimulation to find release. Women were another matter. Discovering what caused a woman to writhe and beg beneath him made his own fulfillment that much deeper.

He wanted to make Lily's time with him memorable. From the way she'd behaved before, the surprise on her face, the wonder in her voice, she had never been with a man the way she was now with him. For Lily, men had never given, only taken. Men like those gave all the rest a very bad name.

Knowing he was the first to show her such magic made him gentler than usual, as if she were a virgin in body as well as soul. He would not take her inner innocence by rushing or blundering or thinking of himself when this was about her. He would be her first in a way no one else could ever be, and he wanted the memory to be as beautiful for her as it already was for him.

He always took a long, long time to ascertain each and every one of a woman's favorite, secret places. He would take even longer with Lily.

Releasing her, he spread her black hair like a fan across the white sheets.

She reached for him again, but he circled each of her wrists with his own, then pinned her arms next to her head.

"What are you doing?"

He glanced quickly into her face. She wasn't frightened, only confused. "I like to look as well as touch."

Using one hand to hold her wrists, he ran his other down the length of her body. Her sigh was deep and full of pleasure.

"So soft," he marveled. "So white and smooth. All curves and sweet-smelling skin."

His hand swept up her belly, cupped the weight of each breast, lifted one to his mouth for a taste, then another.

He learned her body all over again and did not release her hands until her breath was as ragged as her voice when she moaned his name. Her fingers fluttered over his back, tickling, teasing, until his own breathing harshened.

He'd been hard for an hour. Hell, he'd been hard for weeks. His control was excellent, but it was slipping.

He ached to bury himself deep within her body, hold himself there while her soft folds squeezed him tight, rubbed him harder, milked him dry. Instead, he brushed his swollen length against her, taunting them both with what was yet to come.

Rolling her atop him, he filled his hands with her breasts. Her hair curtained them, brushed against his chest, made him grit his teeth against the pulse in his groin. She was lost in the sensation. Her hands kneaded his shoulders; her body tightened along his. He grasped her hips and lifted her atop his length.

Her eyes flew open in shock. "Oh, my," she breathed.

She'd never done this, either? If he hadn't been focused on keeping himself in control until she found fulfillment, he might have taken time to curse the idiots of the world. When a woman rode a man, controlling the pace and the depth of their joining, it was one of the most pleasurable experiences to be found. He'd heard some men did not like to be dominated in that way, but he wasn't one of them.

He let her take command, do what she wished with him. Quickly, she found her rhythm; he made it his, then theirs.

He wanted to watch her face as she came apart

in his arms, so he twisted her hair around his wrist
to keep the riotous curls from obscuring his vision.

Her breath hitched; her pace became frenzied.
"Look at me," he ground out. She was lost; she
did not hear him. Clasping her hips, he stilled
her movements until slowly her eyes opened and
focused on him.

He raised his body, changing the angle, deepen-
ing the thrust, and she clasped his shoulders, face
to face, body to body, soul to soul, for a single
instant.

"Rico," she said, the word as sharp as a curse.

"Not yet," he muttered. "Wait." He thrust.
"Wait." Again he arched.

Her body convulsed. "Now," she demanded.

He could no longer stop himself from comple-
tion. As he emptied himself into her, the waves of
pleasure spurred hers on and on, so that when
they were both spent, they could do nothing but
tumble limply back on the bed, a tangle of limbs,
hair, and sheets.

Her fingers twined with his, and he turned his
head to find her looking at him. She smiled, and
his stomach fluttered.

"Thank you," she whispered.

He didn't want her gratitude. He wasn't sure
what he wanted anymore. "For what?"

"For showing me something better than good.
I'll never forget this. Or you."

She already spoke as if this were the last time.
He knew *that* wasn't what he wanted.

"You asked if we could just have this. We can.
For as long as you want."

"As long as *I* want?" Her lips curved, but the
smile didn't meet her eyes.

"*Sí.*"

She brushed the hair from his face with a tender gesture. "Ah, Rico, I know how this works. Men leave when a better offer comes along."

"Where would I go? What better offer can there be for a man like me than this town, this place, and a woman like you?"

She shrugged. "There's always something. I understand the way life is."

"You didn't understand the way sex was, and I taught you differently. If you give me a chance, I'll show you I'm not a man who leaves."

She didn't look convinced. "So what are you saying? You love me? You want to be together forever?"

Though her words were sarcastic and sharp, he thought he saw a shadow of hope deep in her eyes. He could have her right where he wanted her if he told her that he loved her. But he wasn't sure what love was, and he found that though he'd lied to countless women in his life, he could not lie to this one.

"I'm not sure if I love you, Lily."

She blinked as if he'd surprised her. She'd expected the lie. "Love is only a word, Rico. Something men use to get what they want. I've known that all my life. I appreciate that you didn't use the tired old word with me."

He didn't think he'd ever met a woman who didn't believe in love. Of course, he'd never met a woman who would pick up a snake in her corset, either.

They made quite a pair—her full of scorn and him so unsure.

"All I know is there's never been anyone like you. I've never felt what I did right here with you. And I don't want this to be all there is."

"*Chéri*, what else is there?"

"I don't know any more than you do. But I've got nowhere to go and nothing but time. Why don't we find out?"

She stared at him as if he'd lost his mind. Maybe he had. But he wasn't going to let her go until he discovered what "this" was. If the right woman had saved Reese and Sullivan, maybe Lily could save him. Perhaps he could even save her.

"What happens if we discover there's nothing more than this?"

"Then we become friends." Her gaze narrowed. "Or not."

"If either one of us wants out, we say so." He nodded. "No lies, no disappearing in the night. I hate that."

For a moment, Rico wondered who had disappeared in the night and if Lily might have believed in love before he had. "All right."

"And before dawn each day, we return to our own rooms."

He scowled. "Why?"

"Carrie."

Rico covered his face. He was a horrible guardian if Lily had to remind him of the child. He sighed. "*Sí.*"

She tugged his hand from his face. "I think we have another hour before dawn. Care to seal this bargain?"

In one quick movement he rolled her onto her back. "I think we might have just enough time."

CHAPTER 13

"Just enough," Lily whispered as Rico slipped out of her room—an interesting observation from a woman for whom sex had always been way too much.

Stretching languidly, she pulled the pillow on which he'd rested his head over her face and breathed deeply. The scent of Rico made her remember every inch she had kissed, every move that he'd made.

He had not been bragging about the things he was good at. Too bad for him that he could not bottle and sell the feeling she had now. He would be a millionaire.

Lily tossed the pillow aside, sitting up with a frown. She didn't think she'd appreciate his making any other woman feel this good. They had not discussed exclusive rights to each other. But the thought of Rico touching anyone else as he'd touched her last night, of his murmuring Spanish nonsense to another or looking into some stranger's eyes with the intensity he'd looked into hers, made Lily contemplate murder.

She'd always liked it when R.W. became infatuated with another woman for a while. That meant he left her alone. He always came back. Habit, she supposed. And she was always sorry when he did. Looking back on that life after experiencing the joy and laughter of last night made Lily sad.

So she searched for a happy thought. Mary and Eden had said Rico had never had a woman in this town, almost as if he were awaiting someone special.

Lily snorted. Now she sounded like her mother, and that would not do. The minute a woman started to believe she was special, that she was necessary, that she was loved, disaster wasn't too far behind.

She tossed aside the sheets. Naked, she strode to the mirror and stared at the stranger reflected there—swollen lips, dark circles beneath her eyes from a night without sleep, beard scrapes across her chin and neck. She'd be wearing her ugly, high-necked black gown today.

Though she'd rather wear something bright and pretty to match the mood she could not shake no matter how her dour conscience muttered, she didn't plan to let the world know what had happened last night. For the moment, it would remain between her and Rico alone.

What she'd like to do right now was sleep, and on any other day following a night like the last she would. But this morning Lily had a battle to win.

After washing, then dressing, she knelt and pulled a covered box from beneath her bed. Airholes punched in the top and the sides should have given her surprise adequate fresh air. Lily checked, anyway.

"Ah, *Monsieur Lézard*, you slept better than me, I see. Now it's time for you to do that favor we discussed at the river yesterday, *oui*? Later, I will take you home."

Lily reached into the box and picked up her prize, then slipped out the door and across the hall.

Carrie awoke slowly, glad she'd slept through the night again. Maybe her nightmares were gone forever.

The way she woke up crying embarrassed her, though no one ever heard. Even when she shivered and shook and cried some more beneath the covers, she never broke down and crawled into bed with Rico. She wouldn't even go to Johnny's room, though she knew he'd understand, because she didn't want either one of them to know what a complete baby she was.

But sometimes even Carrie had to admit that she was only nine and she missed her mama.

Though her daddy was dead from the war, her mama was out there somewhere. Sometimes Carrie thought that was worse than her being dead. Because Daddy hadn't left her on purpose. But Mama had.

Carrie sighed, shifted, and considered going back to sleep. But when something that wasn't her moved as well, her eyes snapped open, and she stared into the darkest, deadest gaze she'd ever seen.

The creature blinked. Carrie did not. Though her heart had given one painful thump at first sight, Carrie wasn't any more afraid of lizards than she was of snakes.

"Nice try, *chérie.*" Carrie smirked, palmed the lizard, and sat up. So that was the way Lily wanted to play this—trick upon trick until one of them surrendered. She'd wondered why Lily had not tattled to Rico about the snake or the vinegar. Carrie couldn't quite figure Lily out. But she would.

The lizard was calm and kind of cute, which gave Carrie an idea. Lily thought she was dealing with an amateur. She'd soon learn differently.

At breakfast a few hours later, Carrie ate flapjacks while her new pet rode her shoulder.

Yvonne had taken one look at the green-brown creature and hissed, "Out."

Carrie merely shook her head and kept eating. She'd already had a few run-ins with Yvonne, over washing behind her ears and such. Carrie had discovered that when you ignored her, Yvonne went away.

She went away this morning, too, but she returned with Rico, who smiled far too happily for a man who looked as though he hadn't slept at all. His smile dissolved like sugar in water at the sight of Carrie and her friend.

"*What* is that?"

"Gizzard." Carrie stuffed her mouth with flapjacks.

"Looks like a lizard."

She swallowed. "Gizzard, my new pet lizard."

Rico opened his mouth. Nothing came out, so he snapped it shut again. Then Lily showed up.

The silly smile Rico had worn when he'd come into the kitchen reappeared when he looked at Lily, who started smiling that way, too. Carrie half-expected them to hold hands and start singing.

"Shit," she muttered. She knew what smiles like those meant. "You had sex, didn't ya?"

Rico winced and scowled at Carrie, but at least he quit smiling like the village idiot. "*Chica,* you will quit swearing. And you will tell me where you got that—that—that—"

"Gizzard, the lizard."

Carrie turned a triumphant sneer toward Lily, expecting her to be horrified that Carrie had made a pet of her trick. Instead, Lily gazed at her with an expression Carrie had rarely seen on anyone's face—almost as if Lily thought she was something special. But that *couldn't* be.

"Take the creature right back where it came from," Rico ordered.

"But . . ." Lily raised her eyebrows in challenge. "Lily gave it to me."

Lily choked. Carrie grinned. *Gotcha.*

If Lily denied it, she'd be lying. If she admitted she'd put the lizard on Carrie while she slept, Carrie didn't think Rico would find it funny.

He turned to Lily. "Is that true?"

Carrie held her breath; a sudden hope that Lily would agree possessed her. Even though Lily's agreement would make this particular battle a draw, Carrie would get to keep Gizzard. She'd already grown quite fond of him.

Lily watched Carrie's face far too closely. Carrie tried to look as disinterested in the outcome of the conversation as Gizzard was in her flapjacks.

When Lily said, "*Oui,* I gave her the creature," Carrie wasn't sure if she'd succeeded or not.

"What for?"

Lily shrugged. "Every girl needs a pet." She strolled over to Rico and murmured, "I have you, *chéri.*"

The look on Rico's face annoyed Carrie no end. Men were such fools when it came to women. Or at least that's what her granddad had always said whenever he discussed her mother and his only son.

Carrie had to do something about Lily, and she needed to get serious about it now. As Rico and Lily whispered and cooed, her busy brain thought back on everything she'd overheard in the days she'd been lurking about the saloon. One tidbit might just do the trick.

"You've only got him because he let you, Lily."

"*Pardon moi?*"

Carrie rolled her eyes. That Frenchie crap was getting on her nerves. "Before Cash and Nate left, they made a bet on you and Rico."

"Carrie," Rico warned. "You shouldn't eavesdrop."

Carrie ignored his words and his narrowed eyes. Lily had stopped touching him and started looking at her. "Cash bet Rico could get you into bed in a week, but Nate said it would take three."

"What did Rico say?" Lily's voice was cool enough to make Carrie kind of nervous. But she'd never been one to give up when she wanted something, and she wanted Lily away from Rico.

"He said they should give him a month so he'd have a fair chance."

"A month?" She turned to Rico. "I'm flattered. I bet it never took you that long before."

He looked crushed, his eyes bruised, and Carrie wanted to take her hateful words back. She hadn't wanted to hurt *him*.

"Lily," he began, but she put up her hand.

Carrie held her breath and waited for the screaming and the shouting. Maybe even some kicking and punching. Instead, Lily stepped forward and put her fingers atop Rico's lips. Carrie stared. So did Rico.

"It doesn't matter. I don't care about them. I don't care about before. I don't care what brought you to me. I only care that you came."

He took her hand from his mouth but held on to her fingers. "It wasn't like it sounds."

"I don't care if it was. Forget it."

The wonder on his face caught at Carrie's heart. Rico needed someone to believe good of him no matter what. Carrie did, but her belief didn't seem to be enough.

Now Lily believed the best of him, too, and for some reason, that made Carrie hate her a whole lot less.

The two of them walked out of the kitchen without glancing at Carrie again. But the look on Rico's face won Lily the battle, and Carrie didn't even care.

Rico couldn't believe what had just happened. Any other woman, upon learning of such a bet, would have screamed, thrown things, resorted to physical violence. At the very least, fired him, kicked him out, never spoken to him again. It would not have mattered how many times he tried to explain that he had not made the bet, that for once he had only been there while others behaved like children.

Instead of any one of those things, Lily touched his lips and said she did not care. Rico wasn't sure what to make of that.

"Let's go for a walk," he said.

"Outside?"

"That is the usual place for such an activity."

"I thought you'd want to ..." She glanced upstairs, toward their rooms.

The longing on her face soothed his panicky stomach. She still wanted him despite what she'd heard. What they had shared had been more than he'd ever dreamed it could be. And he wanted her all over again.

Even wearing the horrible black dress she'd come to Rock Creek in, she was the most fascinating woman he'd ever known. Perhaps because beneath that nun's habit lay the body of a temptress. When she let down her tightly wrapped hair, the mass curled seductively, and when she whispered his name as she came apart in his arms, he felt as if he'd finally found a home.

But more than a night in her bed, more than a hundred nights, the gift of her trust was the most precious gift of all. No one trusted Rico. Or if they did, they were soon sorry.

"Rico?" She kissed his cheek. He could do nothing but stare at her in wonder. "Upstairs?"

For a moment, he considered racing her back to bed. He would sink into her softness, lose himself again and again, revel in the woman who was making him believe that perhaps he could love, after all.

"Not right now. Let's walk and talk."

She shook her head. "I don't understand you."

"That merely makes two of us."

He held out his arm. She placed her hand into the crook, and together they went onto the boardwalk. The church bell began to ring, signaling the end of the service.

"That sound brings back memories," he murmured.

"You go to church often?"

"Don't sound so shocked."

"I didn't mean—"

"Never mind. You are right. I do not go. Not because I do not believe but because of the man who is the preacher here."

Rev. Maurice Clancy stepped from the church. Since Lily and Rico were the only people on the boardwalk, his gaze shot to them, and his scowl covered the distance, dispensing disapproval of them both.

Rico couldn't resist. He stopped, swept off his hat, and bowed to the minister. Clancy's back straightened as if a red-hot branding iron had poked him in the butt. Then he turned his back.

"Not an openhearted man," Lily observed.

"I wouldn't say that. He has a reputation for being open to a whole lot of hearts."

"The reverend?"

Rico shrugged. "Gossip. He's married now."

Clancy's new, young wife emerged from the church ahead of the congregation. There was something strange about Sylvia. She certainly looked like no minister's wife Rico had ever seen, and she didn't behave like one, either—keeping to herself rather than befriending the women of the community, doing neither charity work nor visiting the sick. Sylvia and Clancy made quite a pair.

She knew Jed from way back, though how, she wouldn't say, and Jed wasn't talking. Yet she avoided Eden with the same fervor that she avoided every other woman in Rock Creek. Even Clancy's daughter, Jo, had hightailed it out of town so fast, everyone wondered.

Whenever Jed was in town, Sylvia found some

excuse to see him alone. Rico glanced at the hotel. He wondered if she even knew Jed was back and how long it would take before she waylaid him. Clancy had never liked any of the six—for a man of God he liked very little—but Rico figured he might soon like Jed least of all.

"So why does the church bell bring back memories?" Lily asked.

Rico scented the river on the midmorning air, stepped off the boardwalk, and helped Lily down after him. They continued their stroll toward the hills that led to the water.

"I'm sure someone's told you why we came here."

"Yvonne mentioned it."

"Yvonne? She wasn't here."

"You seem to have become the local legend."

Rico grunted. "Just did our job. We used to keep a lookout in the tower. Up there you can see for miles around Rock Creek. When El Diablo came, whoever was up there rang the bell."

"Then the rest of you would come running."

"It is what we do."

They reached the top of the hill and paused, looking down into the tiny valley that cradled the river. Here he had once rescued Carrie from a cougar. Rico could not come to this place without remembering the terror he had felt when he'd raced the big cat for possession of the child. Reese had saved them both that day with a single shot from his gun.

Each man had saved the others many times. They'd never kept score of the past or owed each other anything but loyalty in the here and now.

"If one of you rang the proverbial bell tomorrow, would Cash and Nate come running?"

He hadn't thought of that. In fact, he'd tried not to think of Nate and Cash at all, because then the guilt set in.

"I'm not sure," he admitted.

"They would come."

"For the others, yes, they would."

"You think that if you were in trouble they'd ignore the bell?"

He shrugged. "I can take care of myself. I do not need to ring any bell."

Even as he said it, sadness washed over him. The six of them had been together for ten years. They had come together to face hell. They had gone there and returned several times. Nothing had ever come between them until now. Because of him.

"So you need no one. What an ego." Lily's gentle smile lightened her words and his heart.

"Big as Texas," Rico agreed.

She came into his arms somewhat clumsily, as if she were not used to fond embraces. She probably wasn't. Rico wanted to teach her so much, almost as much as he wanted to learn from her. Her cheek against his chest, he pressed his lips to her hair.

"Why the ugly dress today?" he asked.

She laughed. The movement rubbed her breasts against him. He held very still, enjoying that for a while.

"The marks," she murmured.

"Marks?"

"From last night."

He put his hands on her shoulders, holding her away from him so he could see her face. "I hurt you? I marked you? *Idiota.*" He hit himself in the forehead with the flat of his hand.

She snatched his wrist before he could do it again. "Stop that. You didn't hurt me."

"You are certain?"

"I think I'd know." Her cheeks colored, and she looked down at her feet. Sometimes the combination of self-reliant woman of the world and this innocent girl who knew little of pleasure made Rico go hot and heavy with want when he least expected it. "I like the marks. They remind me of you."

His heart rolled over. Women said all sorts of nonsense to get him into their bed, even crazier things to keep him there. But no one had ever said anything so sweet, or so tempting, as that.

Rico lifted Lily's chin, and his mouth captured hers. With a soft cry, she fisted her hands in his shirt and pulled him closer. Their lips parted; their tongues mated. Her teeth scraped along his lip; then she laved the slight hurt. His body screamed to take her right there on the hill, so he pulled his mouth away before he waited too long and was unable to listen to any whisper of reason that might remain.

Eyes closed, her mouth followed his on the retreat, hands reaching for his face to bring him back. He caught her fingers in his own and kissed them gently until she opened her eyes.

She looked around the hill where they stood, then back toward town, where anyone could see them if they were so inclined, and blushed.

"Don't be embarrassed for wanting me," he said. "I want you ten times more than you could ever imagine."

"It's not the same. When people talk, it will be about me and not you."

"No one will talk. I will make certain of it."

"You have that much power here?"

"I have the power of our past, what we did for this place. I will use it to protect you if I must."

"Life is safe in Rock Creek because of what you did."

"What all of us did."

"Maybe you'll never need to ring the bell for help. Maybe you'll be safe here, too."

"Do not worry about me, Lily."

"I feel guilty. It was because of me that they left."

"They left because Cash has problems."

"What kind of problems?"

"I don't know. No one does. One of the bonds of our friendship is that we do not ask about our pasts. We've all got our secrets."

She lifted her head, and the intensity of her stare made him uneasy. "Do you?"

In an effort to erase the frown between her eyes, he answered lightly. "As many as you, *Lilita.*"

"That's what I was afraid of," she muttered.

"You have secrets?"

"**Does**n't every woman?"

Rico had no idea. He'd never stayed with a woman more than a day or two and rarely cared enough to learn more than their name. But he wanted to know everything about Lily—from the day she'd been born until the day her booted foot hit the dust of Rock Creek.

Yet old habits died hard. If he asked about her past, she would ask about his. And while he would gladly die for her, he could not bring himself to tell her the truth he had never shared with another living soul. Because his secret would make her hate him.

Now that he'd basked in her forgiving smile, he would do anything to keep her from knowing he had killed the little sister he adored.

CHAPTER 14

Simple pleasures could seduce faster than gold and diamonds. For a single night in her bed, Lily had been offered both a thousand times. Such suggestions had always left her cold.

But an hour in the sun, sitting between Rico's legs, her back against his chest as they watched the river wander past, tempted her to offer him a thousand nights and more.

He'd led her to a tiny cove between a grouping of large rocks. Though they were secluded within, the sun shone upon them with joyous fury.

Rico was quiet, too quiet for him, as he chewed on some secret he thought he should tell her. His long, clever fingers had loosened her hair, and as they lay in the sun, he worked at the tangles until the strands flowed freely over his thighs and his chest.

"I could care less what you've done."

His hand jerked, pulling her hair. She kept her

gaze on the water, hoping he would relax and tell her what he was hiding, even as she prayed he would not. "It is easy not to care when you do not know."

"Your friends don't care. Why should I? What you do now is what matters to me, Rico."

"Is that so? You were thinking something like this, perhaps?" He drew her head to the side and kissed her neck.

"You're trying to distract me."

"Is it working?" His tongue ran along the hollow beneath her jaw.

"Mmm, hmm."

"You taste of summer and sunshine. I want to taste you all over."

Her eyes closed against the bright daylight, she smiled.

"When you smile like that," he whispered, "I want to teach you everything that I know."

"I thought you already did."

"Not by half, *Lilita.*" His fingers plucked at the tight collar of her gown. "From now on you will buy dresses that have buttons in the front."

"Why?"

His hand brushed her cheek gently, and for some reason, perhaps the heat of the day, her eyes burned.

"Then, while we lazed by the river, I would release one button after another. As I kissed you here." He pressed his mouth to the corner of her eye. Why did that make her shiver? "I would slip my hand inside your dress and fondle your breasts until the peaks were as hard as I am."

He arched, and she felt him press into the small of her back. Why did that make her shudder?

His tongue traced her ear; his breath blew past

her cheek. The contrast made her nipples tighten and thrust against her chemise. As if he knew, his hand drifted over her bodice; his palm slid back and forth against her, barely touching her at all, yet she thought she might go mad from it.

"Turn around." His voice had gone from gentle to hoarse.

Her eyes popped open. "Now?"

"You said it only mattered to you what I did right here and now. I am happy to oblige, but it must be right here and now." He pressed against her again. "I will not make it back to the saloon this way."

She turned in his embrace, sliding along his arousal. His indrawn breath was one of pain. She reached out to touch him, and he grabbed her wrist.

"I do not think that would be a good idea." His face strained, she longed to wipe the lines away with her thumb. "Fast for me this time, *sí?*"

She glanced at the hills. "But—"

"No one comes to the river on a Sunday afternoon. Even if they did, we are secluded here, and I promise to be quick. You want me to teach you all I know. Let me teach you how to make love in the sun."

How he tempted her with just the words—let, love, sun, teach.

"Help me out of this dress."

He shook his head. "First lesson—remove as little clothing as possible, leaving what you have to hide every secret. Come here." He spread her skirts about them both, then released his trousers and filled her in a single thrust.

He promised fast, and he delivered. What she hadn't realized was that fast could also mean thorough. Until she'd met him, Lily had not realized a lot of things.

How sex could be thrilling and tender, both serious and funny. How you could care more about someone else than yourself. How the shadows that haunted another's eyes could make you forget shadows of your own. How a woman who had never wanted to feel suddenly couldn't stop.

Still deep within her, Rico cradled Lily against his chest. Another treat she'd never get enough of—the holding and the cuddling afterward.

The sun warmed her hair, heating the black dress until sweat dewed her face. Though Lily wanted to stay right where she was for a long, long while, she could not. "We should get back."

"Mmm," he murmured against her breast.

She smiled and threaded her fingers through his hair. To know that she could have as devastating an affect on him as he did on her made Lily feel stronger, but at the same time weaker. She should fight against anything that made her weak, but she just didn't have the strength to resist him any longer. Rico was going to hurt her. He wouldn't be able to help himself. But until then she was going to live in the here and now, just as she'd told him to do.

Lily began to stand, but Rico held on, wouldn't let her go. Thinking he meant to kiss her one last time, she moved her face near his.

His gaze met hers, so serious that she blinked. "We haven't talked about consequences."

For a moment, she thought he knew about R.W., and her face paled. His eyes went soft, and he drifted his fingertips along her chin. "I'd marry you, *Lilita*. If you needed me."

The realization that he meant a child as the consequence made her jump to her feet. Most men would find her secret, her shortcoming, her curse, a great gift. She didn't think Rico would. Just the way he looked at Carrie . . . He wanted children of his own, and that was something she would never be able to give him.

"What is the matter?" He straightened his clothes, then stood at her side.

She could tell him the truth and risk having him look at her like a pariah or remember that he wasn't going to stay with her forever—this was just for the here and now—so her secrets were none of his business. Just as his were none of hers.

"Nothing's the matter." She forced a smile and took his hand.

"Did you hear what I said?" He gazed into her face with such earnestness, she wanted to kiss him. But now wasn't the time.

"Yes. Thank you."

"Thank you? That's all you have to say?"

"Don't worry about it, Rico."

"How can I not? I cannot keep my hands from you. You are like a sickness I cannot heal."

"Sickness." Well, that was flattering. For a man with a gilded tongue, he needed to choose his words better. The tenderness she'd felt for him only a moment ago disintegrated bit by bit as he continued to talk.

"I burn for you. I have since the first day. I thought touching you, taking you, would make me burn less. Instead, I only burn more."

"You didn't *take* anything." Lily yanked her hand from his. "I gave."

"Give. Take. What is the difference?"

"Only a man wouldn't know."

"Why do you dislike men so much?"

"I wasn't disliking you until a minute ago."

"Why are we arguing? All I wanted to do was assure you that I wouldn't leave you if you needed me."

"And I said don't worry. I might not know much about the pleasure of this act we seem so fascinated with, but I do know how to prevent unpleasant problems. I know all about the bad side."

"No comprendo." He appeared genuinely puzzled. Well, at least he didn't know *everything.*

"I'm glad you don't understand. I'm glad you've never had to see what I've seen or do what I've done. Sometimes sex is about power and payment, lust and greed."

"You always call it sex, never love."

"Sex isn't love, Rico. Maybe sometimes it's more than sex, but don't confuse physical pleasure with everlasting love. There is no such thing."

"A mother's love is not everlasting?"

"Not in my experience."

"You are a hard woman."

"I've had to be. Do you know when I first gave myself to someone? I was fifteen. My mother killed herself over a man, and it wasn't my father. He ran off long before I was born."

"In the middle of the night?"

Lily gave him a sharp glance. Had she told him that? She couldn't remember, so she ignored the question and continued with her story. "My mother didn't care that I was alone; she only cared that some fool didn't love her. She left me with nothing but this face, a body, my voice. Have you ever been so hungry you'd eat anything? So cold you wished you could die? For a meal and a room, I gave my innocence. I've been giving it ever since."

"That was not giving."

"Exactly. So *pardon moi* if I see little love in this act you set such store by."

"But what is between us is not like that."

"It isn't love, either."

"How do you know?"

She knew better than to believe in love, so why did her heart sputter with hope at his question? "How could you love someone like me? I've had men just to survive."

"I've killed men to survive. Why does that make me better than you?"

Lily had no answer. Rico inched closer and tentatively reached out to draw her into his arms. She was so exhausted from the sun and the revelations that she let him. He stroked her back and kissed her hair the way she was starting to depend on.

"Do you know what I was doing when I was fourteen?"

She snorted. "I can imagine."

"Well, there was that. But for me this act I set such store by has always been one of joy. I am sorry it has not been that way for you. But I plan to change your opinion, if I haven't already."

"You can keep trying."

He chuckled and kissed her again. "When I was fourteen, I went to war."

She pulled back to stare at him in horror. "Fourteen? That's criminal."

He shrugged. "I was not the only one that young. I was big for my age. Tall. I had no fear of anyone or anything. At first."

"Then later?"

A shadow began in his eyes and spread over his face. For a moment, he looked as old as the river that gurgled and flowed behind them. Lily had seen that look a thousand times before—in every face of every man who had survived wearing the gray.

"Later, I learned that having no fear was perhaps the most fearsome thing of all."

She kissed him on the jaw. The shadows retreated from his face, though they still lingered in his eyes. He smiled at her, and her heart did a slow roll toward her stomach.

"*Pobrecita.* Forget your past and I will forget mine. We will have what we have. Sex. Love. Lust. Need. The word does not matter. Let me make you happy."

She tilted her head, surprised to discover the truth. "You do make me happy. Happier than I can ever remember being."

His smile reached his eyes, joy driving away the last shadow. "Then my hopes are fulfilled. We'd better get back."

She caught his hand. "Until tonight?"

He raised her wrist to his lips. "Your room or mine."

"Surprise me."

"*Lilita,* it is what I live for."

"Rico!" Carrie, with Gizzard still perched on her shoulder, waved to him from the porch.

He returned the greeting, stifling a smile. Lily and Carrie didn't fool him. They seemed to be playing some sort of female-dominance game. Rico did not plan to get in the middle of that, though he thought the pet lizard was a bit much.

He wasn't a squeamish man. Any man who had lived through the war, who had seen and done what he had, would not become weak-kneed about much.

But the sight of his little girl wearing that huge green lizard on her shoulder gave Rico a sick feeling in his belly. One he would have to learn to live with, because the expression on Carrie's face whenever she looked at that thing revealed her love for it. Gizzard, on the other hand, didn't seem to have many variations to his expression at all. Still, the lizard remained on her shoulder without a twitch. Maybe that was lizard love.

"The girls are packing to leave," Carrie called.

Rico glanced at Lily, but she was already on her way up the steps and through the swinging doors.

"What happened?" he asked Carrie.

"I didn't do anything."

Her automatic denial reminded Rico of . . . himself. "I didn't say you did."

"Oh." She frowned, obviously unused to adults believing her innocent just because she said so. Rico had the same problem. "They just came downstairs with their bags and started folding up their sewing stuff. Yvonne talked to them. They don't seem mad or anything."

Inside, Lily hugged first Kate, then Laurel. "You don't have to go," she said.

"We know," Kate said. The two girls exchanged excited smiles. "But if we're working here, we'd rather not live here, too. New life, new place."

"My sentiments exactly," Lily said.

"We'll work every night," Laurel continued. "But we've gotten so many dress orders, we don't have room upstairs to make them. And we can't keep using the tables down here now that you're open for business again. We rented a storefront on Main Street. It'll be our dress shop and our home."

"You let me know when I should look for new

waitresses. I'm sure your business will become so busy, you won't be able to work here anymore."

"Until we get ahead, we'll have to." Kate shuffled her feet, then threw her arms around Lily once more. "It's all because you gave us a chance. We'll never forget it."

Lily looked stunned. Before she could say anything, Kate and Laurel gathered their things and fled.

"They're right," Rico said. "They'd never have tried anything different if it wasn't for you."

"And Eden and Mary."

"Eden and Mary have been suggesting things to them, politely, of course, since they came to town. The girls never listened."

"Whyever not?"

"Would you listen to advice from them on how you should change your life?" Lily snorted. "That's what I thought."

"Nothing against Eden and Mary. They're wonderful. And I really don't know what their lives were like before they came here, but I highly doubt they resembled mine."

Rico thought back to when he and the others had come to Rock Creek. "It was Mary's idea to hire the six of us. She went to Dallas all by herself and hunted down Reese."

"She did?"

"She's got guts. Some people didn't take kindly to her managing things for them. But as she said, someone had to. Eden traveled all the way to Rock Creek from Georgia without telling Jed she was coming. She picked up Millie and Teddy along the way. Saved Sullivan from some rowdies a few towns over. She's got guts to spare as well."

Lily appeared thoughtful. "Well, that's more than I expected, but still not quite a past like mine."

"I thought we were forgetting the past."

"Do you really think we can?"

"For a moment, here and there."

"And I'm sure I know the moments you mean." Rico smiled. "I knew that you would."

"Would you two quit cooin' and moonin' at each other?"

Rico looked down into Carrie's annoyed face. Gizzard didn't look too happy, either. "Is there something you needed, *chica?*"

"What in hell do you feed a lizard."

Lily choked, a laugh, Rico was certain, and he shot her a glare. "Oh, yes, this is very funny. I must now be a lizard's uncle."

"You'll be the best one ever, Rico. Come on." Carrie tugged at his hand. "I bet Mr. Reese knows what to feed Gizzard. Don't ya think, huh?"

"Most definitely." He patted her hand. "Wait on the porch. I'll be right there."

Carrie scrunched her face tight. "Quit kissin' on Lily. Didn't your mama ever tell you women have bugs."

"My mama died when I was very young."

Her face fell. "I'm sorry."

"So was I. Now wait on the porch like a good girl."

Carrie did as he asked, feet dragging, lizard tail limp down her back. Gizzard seemed to take her feelings for his own.

"I'm sorry, too." Lily placed her hand on his arm. "You never mentioned your parents."

And he didn't plan to now. "I'd better take Carrie and that thing over to Reese's. I would hate to discover lizards get mean with hunger."

"I doubt there's much mean in Gizzard."

"You're probably right." He moved out of her reach. "Do you want to rent out the girls' rooms. I could tell Eden to send any extra travelers this way and put up a sign at the stage office."

"No." She shook her head. "I don't want any strangers here. Not with the children."

"I hadn't thought of that." Rico rubbed his temples. He needed to start thinking like a father, and he wasn't sure that he could.

"It'll just be me and you, Johnny and Carrie. With Yvonne downstairs."

"We will be just one big, happy family."

"Maybe. I never had a family."

Rico had a family, but he couldn't recall their ever being happy.

Sunday was a good day. No school, which sat fine with Carrie, and since the saloon was quiet, Rico spent all afternoon with her.

After Mr. Reese told them to catch bugs for Gizzard, they went down to the river and did just that, splashing around and laughing. Life was almost as it used to be before Lily showed up.

Back at Three Queens, Johnny let Carrie sit on his piano bench while he played. When she got tired, he let her lean her head against his arm and rest. Johnny was nearly as wonderful as Rico, even if he did gaze at Lily with a stupid smile, just like every other man.

Carrie awoke in her bed Monday morning with a fuzzy memory of Rico carrying her upstairs as Johnny played "Free at Last." A sad song, but she liked it because now that she was away from Granddad, she was free, too. Funny, but Johnny played that song a lot, almost as if he liked it for the same reasons. But why would Johnny suddenly feel free?

Carrie liked falling asleep to piano music. She never dreamed bad things then. Even better was when Rico tucked her in, kissed her head, and wished her good night, almost like a daddy. Maybe. She couldn't remember her daddy at all.

On Monday morning, Carrie dawdled as much as she could get away with. But whereas her granddad would say, "Git to school, daughter of a whore," and then go back to bed, Rico stood right by her, urging her along gently until she went out the front door.

In the end, when the school bell rang signaling the children to come inside, Carrie stood halfway between Three Queens and the schoolyard.

She glanced over her shoulder to where Rico watched from the porch, holding Gizzard the way he hated, like a sack of flour slung over one arm. Carrie gave Rico a long, lonely look, but he pointed his finger at the school.

"Go on now, *chica*. You promised."

Because she had, Carrie continued, though she dragged her feet and hung her head as if headed for her doom. Part of the agreement that allowed her to stay with Rico was that she went to school every day and did not disappear anymore. Carrie really didn't like school. She didn't like anything that kept her away from Rico, and now Gizzard as well.

The morning was just as boring as it always was. Mr. Reese tried, but Carrie would rather learn about guns and outlaws than recite psalms and cipher.

When the lunch bell rang, Carrie was the first one out the door. She didn't have too many friends, mainly because she didn't know how to make any. In the past, she'd skipped school so much, everyone had made friends without her. Millie, Teddy, and Rafe Sullivan were nice enough, but those three kind of hung together in a pack.

The bratty Sutton twins were her age, but Carrie wished they'd drop into a deep, dark hole and the earth would swallow them forever. They'd been picking on Johnny since the day he arrived at school, and sooner or later Carrie was going to have to do something.

Johnny appeared at the door, and Carrie brightened. "Johnny!" she called. "I've got your lunch."

Although he was a lot older than she, Johnny was her friend. Maybe he'd eat lunch with her; then she wouldn't be so lonely.

He looked up at the sound of her voice, and a smile tilted his lips. Raising his hand, he started down the steps. Just then, the Sutton twins appeared behind him. They whispered, grinned evilly, and shoved Johnny right in the middle of the back.

He landed in the dirt at Carrie's feet. When he lifted his head, a flush of embarrassment darkened his already-dark complexion. Carrie's hands curled into fists.

"Whatcha gonna do about that, Fortier?" Frank sneered. "Gonna *tell* on me?"

"Now you know he can't tell no one nothin'," Jack said. "He's a dummy."

"Not half as dumb as you two," Carrie shouted. "You don't have one brain put together."

Carrie started forward, ready to bloody their noses, as she'd done a few times before. She'd get into trouble, probably sent home with another note. But at least this time her granddad wouldn't slap her and add to the bruises the twins had already caused.

Suddenly, Johnny was there, taking her hand, pulling her back. She glanced at him with a scowl, and he shook his head.

"See?" Jack announced. "He's not only dumb, he's chicken."

"Is not!" She pulled her hand from Johnny's and barreled forward. Johnny grabbed her skirt and yanked her back. "Stop that!" she told him.

He picked up the lunch pail she'd dropped, pointed to a shady spot beneath a nearby tree, and rubbed his stomach.

"You're hungry?"

She glanced at the Sutton twins, who sneered and giggled, then back at Johnny. She really wanted to bust their snotty noses, but she also wanted to sit in the shade with her friend and share lunch.

Johnny smiled at her, jerked his head toward the tree, then held out his hand as if she were a woman and not a little girl. She was just about to take it when Frank shoved between them, knocked the pail onto the ground, and squished the contents into the dirt beneath his boot.

"Gonna *tell* on me now, dummy?"

The rest of the kids smelled a fight and gathered in a circle. The Sullivans hung back, looking as nervous as Carrie felt, and she recalled how Teddy had been picked on when he first came to Rock Creek, too. The Suttons were bullies. Beating up on the new kid was what they did whenever Mr. Reese wasn't looking.

Carrie glanced at the school, hoping Mr. Reese would come out and put a stop to the twins' tormenting of Johnny. She thought she saw a shadow at the window, but when he didn't come outside, she figured it was just a reflection of the clouds and the sun. She could run inside and tattle, but then she'd have to leave Johnny alone, and you just didn't do that to a friend.

Johnny bent and started to pick up what was left of their lunch. Frank put a foot on his shoulder and knocked him back into the dirt. Carrie hurried forward. But Johnny stopped her with a single look.

Standing, he towered over the twins. But there were two of them, and they were solid and mean. Carrie held her breath, prepared to wade in and help. Then Johnny turned his back and held out his hand to her again. She couldn't believe he meant to let them get away with that.

But his eyes implored her to take his offer, so she did. As they walked toward the shade tree, she recalled the scars on his arm and the sadness in his eyes all the time. Maybe being hurt himself made Johnny unable to hurt anyone else, even if they deserved it.

They were halfway to the tree when something hit Carrie in the back and she fell to the ground. Sputtering and coughing as she ate dirt, Carrie felt a rush of air past her ear, and when she rolled over, she discovered Johnny shaking Frank like a dog with an old towel. Things looked almost fair until Jack grabbed Johnny's arm and held him as Frank punched Johnny in the gut.

With a war whoop, Carrie jumped on Jack's back and evened things up her way.

CHAPTER 15

Three Queens didn't get much business during the day. People drifted in and out. Rarely more than two or three occupied the place at one time.

Lily and Yvonne had set up a schedule by which either Lily, Yvonne, or Rico ran the bar each day. That way the other two would be off. On the day the stage came through, two of them would work.

Lily stood behind the bar, eyeing Virgil Wyndham, an unpleasant, potbellied man who seemed to come to town every week for no discernible reason other than to drink, smoke, and gamble. Why such behavior in a gambler should surprise her, Lily had no idea. Why he annoyed her so much, she could not figure out, either. So he looked down her dress whenever he ordered a drink. She'd gotten used to that years ago and considered it part of the territory.

But since coming to Rock Creek, since knowing

Rico, who never looked at her like that, leers had become more personal than professional.

Her second customer sat in the corner. A stranger, he also made her nervous, because while she never caught him watching her, she knew somehow that he was.

"You seem uncomfortable, *querida.*"

She jumped, and Rico caught the bottle as it slipped from her hand. He set it on the bar. "How many times do I have to tell you not to do that?" she snapped.

"What?"

"Sneak up on me."

"I did not mean to. You were engrossed in watching the man in the corner. Should I be jealous? Must I kill him?"

Lily slid her gaze toward Rico. His grin would have negated the words if it weren't for that flicker of violence in his dark eyes, which always surprised her. Although he was nothing but gentle, there was always an undercurrent of tension, a barely suppressed savagery, that made Lily's stomach dance with uncertain knowledge.

"He's handsome enough, I suppose." She took in the stranger's long, tall body, his wind-roughened hands and sun-bleached hair. "But not at all my type."

"What is your type?"

She turned. Their noses brushed. "You," she whispered, and kissed him quickly.

"Then he lives."

The saloon doors slammed inward with uncommon force. Rico had a knife in his hand so fast that Lily had no idea where he'd gotten it. Perhaps from the same place she'd gotten hers. They both pocketed their weapons when they recognized Reese.

"What are you doing here in the middle of the day?" Rico asked.

Reese stood aside to admit Carrie and Johnny.

At the sight of them, Lily let out a cry and hurried from behind the bar. Rico just vaulted the thing altogether. He reached Carrie seconds before she reached Johnny.

"What have you done to her?" Rico touched a bloody scrape across Carrie's cheek, then examined several bruises already darkening her arms.

Johnny had a black eye, and he held his forearm against his stomach.

"Your hand?" Lily asked.

He shook his head and placed his palm against his belly. At the slight touch, he winced.

Fury shot through Lily so strong and deep, she felt as if her head might explode. She turned on Reese. "Who touched him?"

He blinked at the expression on her face, glanced at Rico, obviously didn't like what he saw there, either, and took a single step back. "The Sutton twins—"

"We *kicked* their ass!" Carrie shouted.

"Stop swearing," Lily ordered, advancing on Reese.

"You let those devil children loose?" Rico growled, penning Reese in from the other side.

Reese looked at Lily, at Rico, then held up his hands. "Whoa."

"Whoa, yourself. Where are these children's parents?"

"Now I don't think that's a good idea, Lily."

"I don't care what you think, *Reese*. No one touches my child."

"Thought he was your brother."

"Whatever. He's a child in my care, and I thought he was safe in yours."

Reese's gaze went past them to the children. He motioned for Rico and Lily to join him near the bar, out of their hearing. Without even knowing when she had reached for him, Lily found her hand holding tightly to Rico's.

"I told you, Rico, that Johnny would have to stand up for himself sooner or later."

"So he did. How did Carrie get hurt?"

"He *didn't* stand up for himself. He let those Sutton twins shove him into the dirt, trip him, stomp on his lunch. It didn't matter, he just walked away. But one of them touched her, and then all hell broke loose."

"He wouldn't defend himself, but he'd defend her?"

Lily glanced at Johnny, who watched the adults solemnly while Carrie leaned against him and chattered. Lily winked at him, and his concerned expression faded.

"I am still not seeing how Carrie got hurt."

"One of the Suttons hit Johnny, and she jumped on him."

"Good for her," Lily murmured.

"You approve?"

"Carrie loves who she loves, deeply and without question. She defends them with everything she has. Sounds to me like two bullies against one silent, gentle boy needed a bit of evening out."

"And where were you, *mi capitán*?"

Reese cleared his throat. "Inside. I went right out when Carrie got involved."

"But you watched while the Suttons tormented Johnny?" Lily resisted the childish urge to kick him in the knee. "You told me there was nothing that went on in your school you didn't know about."

"There isn't. They've been picking on Johnny from the beginning. The only way to stop it completely was for him to stand up to them. I can't be there for him every minute."

"I can try. Right now I'm going to make sure those brats never touch him again. Where do the Suttons live?"

"I know," Rico said.

"Yvonne!" Lily shouted. When the bartender appeared, Lily pushed the children in her direction. "Could you do a little doctoring, please? We'll be right back."

Yvonne's eyes widened at the sight of the bumps and bruises, but little rattled her. She herded the children toward her room without question.

Which was why Lily had called her. She wasn't sure if she could keep her hands from shaking with anger or her lips from trembling at every gasp of pain. If this panic-stricken feeling was any indication of how she dealt with minor injuries in children, it was lucky she would never have any of her own.

"Three Queens is closed," she announced.

The creepy, handsome stranger had disappeared during the excitement. Only Wyndham remained, and he downed his drink, then slipped out the door.

"Let's go." Lily took Rico's hand again.

Reese stepped in front of them. "Your knives?"

Lily laughed. "You think we're going to use knives in this discussion?"

"The last time Rico had a discussion with Sutton, he used his knife to make him eat pie. I don't want to be responsible for what he makes Sutton eat this time around.''

''This is no longer your business, *mi capitán*. You brought the children home. You told us what happened. Now it is my business. Mine and Lily's. Move aside.''

''I'll just go with you.''

''No. I do not need your help. I do not need you to make certain I do the right thing. Or to stand behind me and make certain Sutton does. Carrie is mine. Johnny is Lily's. And I think Carrie and Johnny have somehow become each other's.''

Reese contemplated Rico for a long moment; then he turned his sharp green gaze on Lily. She tilted her chin and met that suspicious stare head-on, until his eyes dropped to their joined hands.

A smile spread across his face. ''Looks to me like you have the start of a family here, Rico.''

Family?

Lily waited for Rico to laugh and deny they were anything of the kind. Four lonely people with pasts murkier than a creek in a summer drought did not a family make. Rico pulled his hand from hers, and she braced herself for the pain of his denial.

Instead, he put his arm around her shoulders and tugged Lily close to his side. ''Looks to me like I do, too.''

The meeting with Rose and Baxter Sutton went better than Rico expected. He walked in, grabbed Baxter by the shirt, shook him a little, and told him how things were going to be. ''You will control your demons, Baxter.''

''Gurgel, glunk,'' Baxter agreed.

''You're cutting off his air!'' Rose cried.

She attempted to run forward and help her husband, but Lily stepped in front of her. "Ah, ah, ah." She waved her finger in Rose's face. "If you'd controlled your demons, none of this would be happening."

Rico loosened his hold a bit. He didn't want Baxter to pass out and miss all the fun. "Not another mark on Carrie, not a single scratch on Johnny, or I'll be back."

He let Baxter go. The man tumbled to the ground. Rose rushed over and helped him up. Rico never could figure out what Rose saw in the man. Maybe love wasn't so much blind as dumb.

"I don't know why you're having such a fit," Baxter said. "No one else in town ever does."

"That's because they don't want their credit cut off."

"I never did that."

"Because no one has ever complained."

"If you're going to get picky, that girl's mouth needs a good wash with soap."

"We are working on her language."

"And that boy don't belong in school."

"*Pardon moi?*" Lily's voice was deceptively quiet. She sashayed up to Sutton, pulled her knife from her pocket, and examined the blade. "I thought you said my brother didn't belong in school, but that could not be. Because in this country every child belongs, *oui?* Even demon seed."

Lily tilted the silver right, then left, until it caught the sunlight from the window and flashed a reflection into Baxter's eyes. The man flinched. "Yeah, you're right. Free country."

Rico fought not to smirk. She was magnificent.

He took her arm. She pocketed the knife. As they left together, Rico saw the man who had been watching Lily in the saloon all day slip out the back door of Sutton's store. That guy was beginning to get on his nerves.

Monday night in Rock Creek might as well have been Ash Wednesday anywhere. Three Queens was deader than El Diablo. The children had gone to bed. Lily and Yvonne, too. Jed walked in about ten, but he left well before midnight. When he stayed at Eden's, he made certain he never went home drunk.

"Don't want my little sister to think I'm a worthless big brother," he would say.

Rico could understand that.

The saloon was empty long before Rico closed up. Turning out the last light, he glanced around the place. Funny, but it felt like home.

Shaking his head, he trudged upstairs. At Carrie's room he stopped, hesitated, then opened the door. She lay asleep, freshly washed and dressed in a white nightgown Lily had insisted she must have, even though the child had probably never slept in anything but underclothes in her life. Still, Rico had to admit she looked adorable in the garment.

He stood at her bed and fought the lump in his throat. How had he come to love her more than life itself? He'd battle any monster, slay any dragon, give everything he had, so she would never be hurt again.

The scrape across her cheek shone stark against the sleep-pale shade of her face. He leaned over, kissed the hurt, and in her sleep she murmured, "Rico."

He left quickly lest he wake her. Passing Johnny's room, Rico noticed the door ajar. Meaning only to close it tightly, he glanced inside to make sure the boy was asleep. He wasn't.

Golden lamplight filled the room, illuminating Johnny standing shirtless, his back to the door. Despite the tawny shade of his skin, a livid bruise marred the flesh just under his ribs, extending from the back around to his front. The sight of it made Rico angry all over again.

"Are you all right?" Though he spoke softly so as not to startle the boy, Johnny jumped, turned, and the gaze that flew to Rico's was far too frightened for the situation.

Johnny grabbed for his shirt, but it was too late. Rico could see the scars that marred both his arms, all the way up to his shoulders.

"Madre de Dios." Rico shut the door behind him.

Johnny's dark blue eyes loomed huge in his suddenly stark face. The paleness of his skin only made his black eye look worse. As he fumbled with his shirt, the movements drew more attention to the marks on his arms. No wonder the kid had been so scared whenever Rico held a knife.

"Who did that to you?"

Johnny finished putting on his shirt, then shook his head frantically. Rico grabbed his wrist and shoved up the sleeve. "I know what these are." Johnny's mouth moved, but as usual, no sound came out. "I want to know who did this and where I can find them."

Johnny spread his hands wide and shrugged. *Why?*

"Because I'm going to kill him."

The kid's gentle smile made Rico feel almost foolish. "Why is that funny? If Lily saw—"

Johnny grabbed Rico's hands in a crushing grip and shook his head some more. Rico wondered if all that head shaking was keeping the kid from talking. He might just be tossing his brains around too much.

"Lily doesn't know, does she?"

No.

"They must be pretty recent, then, if your sister hasn't seen them."

Yes.

"Because if she did see them, she'd do murder, wouldn't she?"

Yes.

"You don't want me to tell her."

Johnny's entreating gaze said it all.

"Why not?"

The boy opened his mouth, then shut it again. He covered his face as if embarrassed.

"You don't need to be embarrassed. Whoever did that to you is the one who should be embarrassed."

Johnny lowered his hands. He pointed at the scars on his arm, then to Rico, then next door to Lily's room, then slashed his hand across his neck.

"I won't tell, kid."

Johnny put his palm over his heart.

"I promise." Rico turned to leave but paused with his hand on the door. "And one other thing." He glanced at Johnny. "No one's ever going to hurt you like that again. Not while you live with me."

Johnny stared at him for a long, long time, as if taking Rico's measure. The boy had never trusted him, and Rico could understand why. A man with a knife had hurt him. Rico was surprised Johnny had even been able to look at him.

Rico held Johnny's gaze moment to moment. He'd meant what he said. No one was going to touch this boy as long as Rico was around. Just the thought of someone hurting Johnny in any way made Rico want to slice them up and feed the pieces to the buzzards.

At last Johnny gave a single, slow nod. A warm feeling trickled through Rico at the evidence of the boy's trust. He'd said he would protect him, and Johnny believed it. Rico didn't deserve that, but he would earn it. This time he wouldn't shirk a single responsibility. Those in his care would be safe from every harm—or he would die making certain that they were.

Closing the door behind him, Rico checked on his last charge. Lily would no doubt spit and sputter that she could take care of herself, and she probably could. Her self-sufficiency was one of the things that had drawn him to her. But Rico wouldn't rest peacefully until everyone was tucked safely in their beds. This late-night walk through Three Queens could become a habit.

Rico cracked Lily's door, then opened it wider at the sight of an empty bed.

"Looking for someone?"

He discovered her peeking at him from his room and grinned. Since he could only see Lily's head, Rico had a feeling the rest of her was naked. "I was looking for a woman." He crossed to his room.

"Any particular type?"

"You'll do." He dove forward, grabbing her around the waist—which *was* quite naked—kicking the door shut, and twirling her about as she laughed. Tangling her legs with his, she tipped them onto the bed and pulled his mouth close for a long, searching kiss.

When Rico lifted his head, Lily smiled and began to play with his hair. Why he liked that so much, he couldn't quite figure, but she seemed to enjoy running her fingers through the strands, too.

"What took you so long? I've been waiting forever."

Her smiling face, her flushed cheeks, the sparkle of her eyes, and the laughter in her voice pulled at his heart. She was so beautiful, so right, and she was his. Rico didn't ever want to let her go.

He kissed her brow, then laid his head on her shoulder. "Me, too," he whispered. "Forever."

At his serious tone, her fingers stilled in his hair. "You all right?"

He thought back on so many years of sadness and strife, war and pain. Friendship but no home. Existence with no love. Loneliness so deep he ached with it always, and now, suddenly, the loneliness was gone.

"I am now," he said.

"Me, too."

Lily couldn't sleep. Rico didn't seem to have that problem. He sprawled across the bed, one leg thrown over hers, his hand cupping her hip as his breath brushed her breast.

The moon poured in through the window and turned his dark hair silver. She brushed her fingers through the soft strands, and he murmured her name in his sleep, then cuddled closer.

Lily's eyes burned, and her throat went thick. She really liked him. That was the only word for it—intense like. Nothing to worry about. Rico liked her, too.

Each time they had sex, the act became more fervent. When he pushed deep inside her and pulsed to the beat of her heart, the feeling of closeness remained with her for hours. When he looked into her eyes as he gasped out her name, she felt as if she could see into his soul and he could see into hers.

Just because afterward she had a harder and harder time leaving him, just because she couldn't imagine *ever* leaving him for good, she didn't need to worry. What she needed to do was enjoy the here and now.

So why did she have an awful feeling that disaster lay just around the corner? Because she'd never been this happy in her life, so it followed that something would come to ruin it soon. Silly thoughts, she was certain, but Lily had them just the same.

Gently, she slid from Rico's embrace. He shifted, held on tighter, and murmured, "Don't go, *Lilita.*"

Her heart tumbled to her stomach. She picked up his hand and kissed the palm. "I have to, *chéri.* What if Carrie has a bad dream and comes to your room?"

He didn't answer. He was already asleep again.

To tell the truth, the little girl had not climbed into Rico's bed since coming to live at Three Queens, but sometimes she looked tired in the morning, and Rico said she dreamed of things she would not say. The thought of the brave little girl being tormented by nightmares tugged at Lily in ways she could not understand.

Lily found her nightdress, and as the long white cotton settled around her body, she took one last look at Rico. He'd scooted into the warm nest where her body had been and pressed his face into her pillow. She passed a hand over his hair one last time, then let herself out into the hall.

Her fingers on the door to her room, she paused as a muffled cry split the night. *Carrie.*

Lily hesitated. Should she get Rico and tell him the child dreamed or let the little girl decide on her own if she wanted company? Another cry, sharper and more heart-wrenching than the first, had Lily crossing the distance and slipping into the child's room herself.

Carrie had thrashed her covers onto the floor. Her nightgown twisted about her legs, binding her; she continued to fight the confinement. Her hair was dark with sweat, and her pale face shined slick.

Uncertain what to do, Lily hovered by the door. Then Carrie sobbed, "Mama? Why did you leave me alone?"

Lily's breath caught at the agony in the child's voice. In an instant she was back in the bayou, her mother gone, she herself alone. Unable to leave now, Lily crossed the room and gently returned the covers to Carrie's bed.

She had few soft memories of her mother. There had been too many nights alone, too many broken promises, too many men more important than her, but Lily did remember her mother singing to her when she was ill, and she recalled how soothing that small gesture had been to a child.

Lily sat on the bed and quietly hummed a non-sensical tune. Carrie stopped thrashing, though she continued to moan at intervals.

So Lily sang a lullaby, and as she did, Carrie became calmer. By the time the song was finished, the child lay still. When the last note died away, her eyes opened, and she gazed curiously at Lily.

Lily braced herself for an onslaught. "Sing another." Carrie inched closer. "Please."

How could she refuse such a sweet request for an encore?

In the middle of the second song, Carrie crawled into Lily's lap. Lily faltered mid-note but managed to finish.

"How come you're being so nice?" Carrie asked, her sweaty head dampening the bodice of Lily's nightdress.

Tentatively, Lily ran her fingers through Carrie's hair, the way Rico always liked her to. The child sighed with contentment and cuddled closer. Lily's heart started to beat far too fast.

"Because you're letting me," she answered.

"I had a dream."

"Mmm, hmm."

"My mama left, you know. She didn't love me much."

Lily's mother hadn't loved her much, either. An affinity for Carrie, the need to make everything all right for the child, overcame Lily's usual reticence with children.

"I'm sure that's not true. I'm sure your mother loved you."

"If she loved me, she wouldn't have left me behind. She'd have taken me with her."

"Maybe. I certainly wouldn't have left you."

Carrie stiffened. "You wouldn't?"

"No. If I had a little girl, I'd never let her out of my sight."

Carrie pondered on that awhile. They sat in companionable silence, Carrie warm and heavy against her breast, her sweet child's breath brushing Lily's neck.

"Lily?" Carrie turned her head so she could see Lily's face. "How come you didn't tell Rico about the snake or the vinegar?"

Lily resisted a near-irresistible urge to kiss Carrie's damp brow. "That was just between us women."

A smile spread all over her face. "Really? Us women?"

"*Oui*. Men don't understand such things."

"That's for sure." She rolled her eyes as if she were nineteen instead of nine, then laid her head back against Lily's chest. "Lily?"

"Mmm?"

"You aren't big and fat and ugly."

Lily allowed a smile of her own to escape into the darkness. "*Merci*."

"Can you sing to me some more?"

"That would be my pleasure."

CHAPTER 16

Rico awoke alone. That was not unusual, though he couldn't say he liked it. He and Lily had agreed to keep up a fiction of separate bedrooms for the sake of the children in their care.

Since Carrie already knew what was going on and Johnny didn't seem the slow sort, Rico figured their sneaking about was unnecessary, and Lily's continued insistence on it made Rico wonder how many times she'd found her mother with a man. Memories like that would explain many things about Lily.

So, to pacify her, he always made sure the door was locked behind them—just in case Carrie wandered over from her room. He didn't relish waking up in bed with Lily to find Carrie staring at him with angry eyes.

And Carrie would be angry, because she seemed to have a vendetta against Lily. He wasn't sure what

to do about that except let them work things out
on their own.

Dressed and washed, Rico stepped into the hall.
Hearing voices from Carrie's room, he paused outside the half-open door to listen.

"*Chérie,* you cannot continue to swear like a mule
skinner. It's very unpleasant in a sweet-faced child
like yourself."

"I don't care."

"Have you ever seen Rico's face when you
curse?"

"Yeah." The sigh that followed the word was
long and world-weary. "He feels bad. Why? It's not
his fault."

Rico tilted his head. The two spoke civilly, almost
as if they had become friends. *Interesting.*

"People seem to believe the worst of him. I can't
understand why. He's afraid you'll be taken away
again if he can't raise you right."

"There's not a damn thing wrong with me."

Rico closed his eyes. What *was* he going to do
with her? He had no idea how to be a father. All
he knew how to do was love her.

"I never said there was anything wrong with you.
But there are times when a woman must do what
she must do in order to have what she wants."

Rico opened his eyes and leaned closer until he
could see the two of them on the bed. Both in white
nightgowns, their heads close together—light to
dark—they made a picture so innocent, sweet, and
beautifully right, Rico's eyes burned.

"What do I have to do?"

"Don't swear."

"But sometimes, Lily, only a cuss word will do."

"I agree." Rico frowned. She did? Since when?

"But there is a way to curse and sound very refined."

"How?"

"If you promise to swear less, I will teach you to curse in French. You will sound 'oh, so genteel,' and no one will have the slightest idea what you're saying."

"Can you?

"Of course. I learned to swear in French from one of the highest-paid—" Lily coughed. "Um, a woman I knew. She was from Paris. She knew all the best curse words. And the French have some we don't even know in English."

"Really?" Carrie breathed, her face alight with awe.

"Really."

Rico backed away quietly. Sometime during the night the two had made peace. Why and how, he did not care. It seemed Carrie needed a woman's touch, and as long as she'd gotten it, he was happy.

Rico left them to their cussing lesson. Halfway through his first cup of coffee, the saloon doors swung open to admit Reese, Sullivan, and Jed, which could only mean trouble.

Reese motioned for Rico to sit when he would have stood. The three joined him at the table, and Reese got right to the point. "There's a man in town asking questions about Lily."

"Talked to each one of us," Jed put in.

"And a few other folks, too," said Sullivan.

"What kind of questions?"

"Where she's from."

"How long she's been here and how she came to own the saloon."

"If she's partial to knives."

Rico frowned. "Partial to knives? What does that mean?"

Jed shrugged. "He asked each one of us that, and to be truthful, kid, we all had a story to tell about a knife and Lily."

"But you didn't tell it." Rico peered at each of his friends in turn.

"Of course not," Reese said. "I think she's hiding something. This just proves it. But we know better than to answer questions just because some stranger comes to town asking them."

"Who is this guy?"

"He was in here when I brought the children home the other day."

"Wyndham?"

"No, the guy in the corner. Blond hair, lawman's eyes."

Rico remembered. "He was watching Lily."

"I noticed that, too. But then a lot of men watch Lily."

"And they always will. Where did our curious friend go?"

Reese raised his gaze from Rico to look at the door behind him. Slowly, Rico turned. He stood to meet the tall, young man. The others rose and formed a line behind him.

"Name's Noah Russell."

Rico nodded but did not introduce himself. Russell had been asking questions. He already knew the name of everyone in the room.

"I'm with the Pinkerton Detective Agency."

No one spoke. If Rico had learned one thing from his friends, it was to keep quiet as long as he could. Let Russell tell all that he knew first; then Rico would know what he was dealing with. If you kept quiet long enough, they always spilled everything, and Noah Russell did not prove an exception to this rule.

"I was hired by a widow in New Orleans to find the murderer of her husband, Randolph Ward. Recognize the name?"

Rico shook his head and waited some more. Russell did not disappoint.

"Carpetbagger. But a dead one, found with a neat slice in his heart. His mistress, one Betty Lillian, disappeared that same night."

Rico lifted one shoulder, then lowered it.

"You don't know this woman? She was a singer of some renown in the American section of New Orleans. Seems her piano player disappeared that same night. Kid by the name of Jean Baptiste. He—"

A crash had all five men whirling toward the sound, hands reaching for their guns. Johnny stood in the doorway to the kitchen, his face as pale as the shards of crockery at his feet. He raised wide, terrified eyes first to Rico, then to the stairs.

Rico followed Johnny's gaze. Lily stood on the steps looking as beautiful as he'd ever seen her—no doubt because he might lose her in another instant.

Lily had expected disaster, but not quite so soon. One look at Johnny's face and she knew their secret had been spilled. He rushed over and grabbed her hands. His mouth was moving frantically, but Lily scowled, shook her head, and he went silent. If Johnny talked now, it would only make things worse, only prove them liars. He tried to pull her back upstairs, but there was no point in running anymore.

"What frightened him?" she demanded. Then her gaze fell on the stranger who'd watched her yesterday. "Who are you?"

"Russell, ma'am. Pinkerton Detective Agency."

Keeping her eyes on the detective, she turned Johnny about. "Go upstairs. Now."

Johnny shook his head, but she gave him a ferocious glare, and he went, dragging his feet on every step. Right before he disappeared, he glanced down the stairs toward Rico. Whatever Rico did made Johnny relax and go quietly. Thank God for that. She had to think, and with Johnny so frightened, all she wanted to do was hold him, as she'd held Carrie all night long.

Lily descended the stairs and crossed the room to stand next to Rico. He tried to take her hand, but she pulled away, hiding it in the folds of her skirt. Until she knew exactly what R.W. was up to sending a Pinkerton detective after them, she would need all her faculties. Whenever she touched Rico, she lost a little bit of her mind.

"What do you want, Mr. Russell?" Best to take the offense. This was, after all, her place.

"Do you know a man named Randolph Ward?"

"R.W.?" She thought quickly. No reason to lie. She had nothing to hide. "Certainly."

"You're Betty Lillian."

She hesitated a moment too long, so there was really no reason to answer at all. "I was."

One of Rico's friends cursed, which made her uneasy. What difference did her name make to the ownership of Three Queens?

"Why did you change your name? Hiding something?"

"New name, new life. I'm not the only one who changes their name and comes to Texas."

"But most of those people are on the run. What were you running from, Miss Lillian?"

"Miss Fortier," she corrected, then shrugged. "R.W. would have tried to stop me from leaving. He thought I owed him my life. I believed differently. When this place came into my possession, I left. Simple as that. If he feels I owe him for Three Queens, we can work something out. There was no reason to hire a detective."

Russell frowned. "You stole this place?"

"I won it fair and square in a poker game. I did nothing wrong."

"Except stick your ever-present knife into Randolph Ward's heart."

Dizziness rushed over Lily, but she fought back the weakness. "No. He was alive when I left him."

"That's what they all say, lady." Russell moved forward as if to take her arm.

Rico stepped in his way. "I do not think so, *amigo.*"

"I have orders to take her back to New Orleans for trial."

"No."

The man reached for his pocket, and in an instant three guns were trained on him, with a knife to his neck. Lily was impressed. She hadn't even seen Rico draw his blade. The fact that he had, for her, made her throat tight and achy. For all he knew, she was a cold-blooded murderess, yet he defended her without question.

"I was just going to get the court papers." To his credit, Russell didn't look scared. Rico lifted the knife from the man's throat but held the weapon ready and kept himself between Lily and the detective. "Sheriff?" Russell handed a piece of parchment to Sullivan.

He glanced at it, frowned, then handed the paper to Reese. Jed sidled over and read it, too. All three stared at her. Why did that make her feel guilty? She had not done it.

The curious lack of emotion she'd always displayed before coming to Rock Creek crept over her. She should feel regret for the death of a man she'd known for a very long time. But she didn't.

"Why is a Pinkerton detective on this case?" Sullivan asked. "Looks like something for a U.S. marshal."

"I was hired by the widow. She didn't think the regular law enforcement agency was taking the case seriously enough."

"Widow? R.W. was married?"

"Come now, Miss *Fortier*." Russell put a sarcastic twist on her new name, "You'd been the man's mistress for years and you didn't know he had a wife?"

Lily winced and cut a glance toward Rico. He stared at her, unconcerned. She *had* told him about her past—but not every detail.

"He never mentioned a wife in all our years together."

"Until perhaps that last night. Is that why you killed him?"

"I didn't kill him. What do I have to do to make you believe me?"

"That's not for me to decide. It's for the judge. And I *am* taking you back. Your friends can't ignore the law."

Jed snorted. Reese laughed out loud. Even Sullivan's lips twitched. Rico was the only one who didn't look amused. He caressed his knife as he had caressed her body only hours before; then he raised his dark gaze to the detective, and she did not like what she saw there.

"I'll go," Lily blurted out.

Rico's eyes returned to her, and he slowly shook his head. "You will not."

"Rico," Sullivan said. "She has to. The warrant is real."

"This is Texas. People disappear every damn day."

"She won't disappear," Russell said. "Now that I've found her, I'm not letting Betty Lillian out of my sight."

Turning his blade so the morning light hit the silver and made it sparkle, Rico smiled at last. The expression made Lily shiver. "I was not talking about her."

"That sounds like a threat." The detective looked at the other men. "You heard him threaten me."

"Nope," Jed said.

"Not me," Reese agreed.

"Sheriff?"

"Didn't hear a word," Sullivan said.

"I see. I heard about y'all even before I came here. The Rock Creek Six, but you look about two short. I thought you were some of the good guys."

Reese rubbed his forehead and sighed. "Me, too. Maybe she should go back, Rico. Just to get everything straightened out."

"No," Rico said.

At the same time, Lily said, "Yes."

"Lily, let me handle this," Rico insisted.

"I'm not going to let you kill someone for me."

"Who said anything about killing?"

Lily raised her eyebrow, and after a short battle of wills, Rico looked away. "I don't want to look over my shoulder forever. I'll go back. I'll get it settled." She touched his arm, and he looked into her face. "I didn't do it."

"I know you didn't."

"You believe me?"

"There was never any question."

Lily stared at him. He meant it. She didn't know what to say.

Russell muttered something about "love" and "blind."

"You have something you wish to share with us?" Rico asked.

"Nope." He turned to Sullivan. "Sheriff, I have to send a few wires and get some supplies. We'll leave tomorrow. Could you lock her up until then?"

Lily blinked. He meant to put her in jail?

"She's not guilty until a judge says she is. I'm not locking her up."

Sullivan walked out. Rico appeared as if he were holding back a laugh. *Now* he thought everything was funny. Lily wished she could find humor in this situation. Although she'd sworn never to return to New Orleans, here she was volunteering. But if R.W. was dead, what could it hurt?

For a minute the detective looked nonplussed at Sullivan's defection. "Well, I guess you can't get far. If you run off, I'll just chase you again."

"Everything I have is here. If I leave it, I'll have nothing. I said I'd go with you. Why would I run off now?"

"Why did you run off before?"

"I didn't. I came here to start a new life."

"But you went to some trouble to disappear, didn't you? Changed your name. Traveled with the kid as cover."

"I did not use Johnny. He came on his own, and he's not going back. He stays here."

"I'm not interested in him."

"I am. His place is here."

"Fine by me." Russell contemplated Lily as if he weren't quite sure what to make of her. "Leaving in the middle of Mardi Gras nearly worked."

"If it was such a good idea, how did you find me?"

"Wasn't easy. Someone heard Ward arguing with a customer about a saloon he'd lost to you for three queens."

Lily winced. She couldn't believe Scruffy Texas had gone whining to R.W. If someone hadn't killed him, R.W. would have caught her before she left. If she didn't know better, *she'd* think she'd killed R.W., too.

"Next morning, Ward turns up dead, and you're gone. Things got easier once I found out about the boy. Would have taken me quite a while to trace down all the women leaving New Orleans that day."

"How long before you'd have given up."

"Never. One thing I don't do is quit. That's why I'm the best, and that's why Mrs. Ward hired me."

"Modest, too," Jed mumbled, but he looked intrigued.

"Truth is truth." He headed for the door. "I'll be back soon."

"I can hardly wait," Lily said.

Russell paused. "You and I will leave at dawn."

"Wrong," Rico put in.

Lily sighed. "I thought this was decided."

"*Sí.* But I am going, too."

"I don't think so." She knew exactly what he planned to do as soon as they were out in the desert—kill himself a Pinkerton detective. She wasn't going to let him do that for her.

"He can come if he likes," Russell said. "I'd welcome the extra gun."

"Gun," Jed barked. "That's funny."

Rico glared at him, but Jed just smirked.

"If I say you can't come, you'll only trail us."

"Of course."

"So I'd rather have you where I can see you." Russell thumbed his hat and left.

Reese and Jed exchanged a glance Lily couldn't interpret and followed the man. As soon as they were alone, Rico crossed the room and pulled her into his arms.

She hadn't realized how much she needed to be there until the familiar thunder of his heart beat against her cheek and the scent of him—crisp cotton and musky man—surrounded her. She hadn't realized how deeply she feared he would hate her, that he would believe the lawman instead of the liar, until relief nearly staggered her. He held her no differently in this moment than any of the moments that had gone before.

"I'm sorry," she whispered.

"For what?" He kissed her hair.

"My name isn't Lily. And Johnny isn't my brother. His name isn't even Johnny."

"To me you are Lily. And I'm sure Johnny doesn't care what you call him. He loves you as much as any brother could." Rico released her, and for the first time in Lily's life, she clung to someone. "Here he comes now, *querida*, and I think he needs you more than I do. Chin up." He kissed her eyebrow and turned her about. "Be that woman who kicked me in my ego. Be strong for the boy."

Johnny stood at the foot of the stairs; the fear on his face tore at her heart. She held open her arms, and he stumbled into them. "Everything will be all right, *ange*. I will keep you safe; I swear."

Carrie was right behind him. She gave Lily a look that was far too old for her face, then patted Johnny on the back, touched Lily's hand, and launched herself into Rico's arms.

Over the heads of Johnny and Carrie, Rico's and Lily's eyes met. They had much to talk about, but not right now. Right now was for their children.

CHAPTER 17

Calming Johnny took a while. His heart fluttered against Lily's breast, and in his eyes lurked a depth of panic that disturbed her. He had never liked R.W. The man had possessed a mean streak a mile wide, and Johnny was a gentle soul, easily hurt by harsh words and loud voices. Whenever the boy had stuttered, R.W. had shouted, causing Johnny's affliction to worsen to the point of silence. Only then had R.W. left him alone.

"It'll be all right," Lily murmured against his temple. He shook his head and would not let her go. Lily rubbed the length of his back. He'd grown since they'd come here. A big boy, he would become a very large man. "I won't let anyone take you back there. I promise." She put her mouth by his ear. "But you must stay quiet now. If anyone discovers our lie about you, they won't believe anything we say anymore."

Lily was insistent, and eventually Johnny nodded

his agreement. But the shadow in his eyes remained.

Calming Carrie took even longer. She did not want to be separated from Rico, and she let everyone know it loud and clear. But no matter how hard Carrie begged, no matter what she threatened, Rico refused to let her go to New Orleans. In the end, Johnny separated himself from Lily with a quick hug, took Carrie's hand, and led her off to school in mid-tirade.

Then Russell returned, and the way he hovered about made Lily more nervous than the first time she'd performed in front of a crowd of a hundred. His lawman's gaze pressed on her heavier than a roomful of critics.

Within an hour, news spread that a Pinkerton detective was taking Lily away. Gawkers arrived, and business became brisk. Lily ended up serving while both Rico and Yvonne worked the bar.

Eden and Mary ran in, pledged eternal friendship, and swore to watch over the children. Lily couldn't get over it. She'd thought everyone would convict her on the say-so of a stranger. Once again, she'd underestimated Mary and Eden.

When Carrie came home from school and heard she was staying with Mary, she threw a huge French cursing fit in the middle of the saloon.

"You taught her that?" Rico raised his voice to be heard above the din. "Nice job."

"Doesn't she sound so much more refined than when she walked around saying 'damn' all the time?"

"Not really," Rico muttered.

"If you shut up," Yvonne snapped, "you can stay here with me. And the piano lover, too."

Lily frowned. So did Rico. But Carrie stopped

shouting and threw her arms around Yvonne's waist. "Thank you, thank you, thank you!"

Holding up her hands as if in surrender, Yvonne stared in surprise at the child attached to her. "Stop dribbling on me and go help Johnny with his homework."

" 'Kay!" Carrie skipped off, dragging Johnny along behind her.

"Are you sure, Yvonne?" Rico asked.

Yvonne didn't look sure, but she nodded, anyway. "She was just settling in. Why drag her back where she doesn't want to go? Besides, Johnny is going to have to play funeral dirges until you come home or life just won't be the same."

Lily put her hand on Yvonne's shoulder. "I appreciate what you're doing. It'll help to know they're safe with you."

Yvonne shrugged Lily off. "Just get your butt back here and don't leave me alone with that hellion too long." She stalked toward the stockroom.

Lily watched her with a sad smile. Yvonne tried so hard to be tough, but she couldn't quite pull it off. In the beginning, she'd avoided the children, but they seemed to have grown on her. Both Carrie and Johnny had a way of slipping beneath any wall a person might erect against their charm and worming their way directly into one's heart.

Rico put his arm around Lily's shoulders, then tugged her close so she could lean against him. "I'll miss Yvonne," Lily murmured.

"You'll be back."

"What are you two whispering about?"

Rico scowled at Russell, who had crept up on them. "How deep your shallow grave is going to be."

Russell laughed, unconcerned. "I'll be back here

at dawn. Be ready to leave." The cocky bastard left whistling.

For the first time since Cash had ridden out of town, Lily wished him back. Russell would have annoyed Cash plenty.

The rest of the night passed in a whirl of drinks, cards, smoke, and people. Kate and Laurel rushed in as soon as they heard. They prattled their sympathy at Lily until she began to look drawn and pale. Rico stepped in and set them to work.

When they closed at last, Lily appeared so tired, Rico considered carrying her up the stairs, but he didn't think he'd make it, either. Instead, they helped each other. It was becoming a habit.

Rico paused outside Lily's room. "You should sleep in your own bed tonight. Get some rest."

Lily shook her head and led him into his room, then closed the door and locked it. "I want to sleep with you. All night. I need to wake up in the morning with you in my arms and see your face as soon as I open my eyes."

The neediness in Lily's voice, on her face, disturbed Rico. Lily had never needed anyone, least of all him, and while he didn't mind being needed, he didn't want her frightened, either.

"I can think of nothing better than waking up to the dawn and you. Let's get to bed. The trail will be long and tiring for both of us."

She searched his face. "Why are you going, Rico?"

"To protect you."

"From what? The truth?"

He stepped closer and cupped her cheek. "Do you think the truth will set you free, *Lilita*?"

"Of course."

"Sometimes things do not happen that way. Sometimes the wrong person dies no matter their innocence."

She frowned. "What are you saying?"

"I'm saying I do not trust anyone with your life but me."

"Neither do I," she whispered, and put her hand up to capture his against her face.

Doubt flickered through Rico. Maybe Lily shouldn't trust him so completely. But the fact that she did made Rico feel more capable than he'd ever felt before. She made him feel strong and whole and alive. He should tell her the truth, but then she just might hate him.

"I want to tell you about R.W.," she said.

"He doesn't matter."

Lily drew him over to sit beside her on the bed. "He does matter, since it's because of him we have to leave Rock Creek. I told you I'd had men to survive. He was one of them. Well, there were really only two. The first lost me in a card game to R.W. about seven years ago."

"Someone bet you on the turn of a card?"

She shrugged. "Life was better with R.W. More secure, at any rate. But even though he made me successful, I still wanted out. I didn't like being reminded every day where I came from and what I owed him. I was supposed to give him everything I won when I dealt poker. I kept Three Queens. I guess that means I *did* steal the place."

"In my book, whatever a person wins at cards is theirs."

"I like your book." She squeezed his hand. "I ran because I knew he'd never let me go. But I didn't kill him."

"I don't care if you did."

She started. "What?"

"If you killed him, you had a very good reason."

"You don't care?"

"Why should I? I've done far worse things in my life than you could ever dream of, *Lilita.*"

"I somehow doubt that."

He was going to tell her, though he'd sworn never to tell another living soul. He couldn't let her continue to believe he was worth trusting. He would protect her with his life, but she had to understand that sometimes even that wasn't enough.

"I had a sister once," he blurted out. "The last time I saw Anna, she was the same age as Carrie the first day I met her. Anna used to look at me exactly as Carrie does now."

"As if the sun and the moon set on you and nothing you do could ever be wrong enough for her?"

"*Sí*. But Anna learned differently. I hope to God Carrie never does."

"You don't have to tell me this, Rico. I know you. You're a gentle, funny, and passionate man. Nothing you've ever done can change who you are to me now. Nothing you've ever done will make Carrie not love you."

He grabbed her by the arms and yanked her close. "I killed my sister!"

"You did not!" she scoffed, complete disbelief in her eyes.

Rico released her and jumped to his feet. "Why do you always defend me?"

"Because you won't."

"I am not worth your protection."

"And I'm not worth yours."

"That is a matter of opinion." She smiled serenely as she began to unbutton her dress. "What are you doing?"

"Getting ready for bed."

"You don't want to sleep with a man like me."

She paused, and her hands dropped into her lap. "Why don't you tell me exactly what happened. Then I'll let you know what I want." She patted the bed in invitation.

Rico was too agitated to sit. Now that he'd started to remember, everything came rushing back.

"Anna was six, and I was fourteen. Our *madre* died when Anna was born. Our father had little use for either one of us. He thought me a worthless son. I did not care for cattle. I paid little attention to my studies. The more he called me worthless, the harder I tried to live up to his opinion."

"His opinion was as worthless as he said you were."

Rico smiled. She wouldn't give up. But he wasn't through with the story yet.

"So I was worthless and Anna but a girl. We had only each other. She followed me like a puppy. I loved her. But one day I wanted to be alone. I'd had enough of my little sister, so I snuck off and left Anna behind. I crossed our river, and I spent the day far off, where I was not supposed to go, practicing with my precious knives. When I returned to the water, I heard wailing and shouting from the other side. Anna had tried to follow me, and she drowned in the shallows."

Rico could still see her little body on the opposite bank, still see his father's anguished face and hear him shout, "Where is her worthless brother? I want him to see what he has done."

Lily touched his arm. Rico stared down at her,

for a moment not realizing who she was or where he was. He'd been back in San Antonio. He'd been fourteen again, horrified at what his selfish irresponsibility had wrought.

"Then what happened?" she whispered.

"I ran."

Lily blinked. "What?"

"I left that moment, and I never went back. I couldn't stand to see Anna buried. I went east, joined the army, and you know the rest."

"What happened to Anna was an accident, Rico."

"No. An accident is unavoidable. Anna would still be alive if I'd watched over her as I was supposed to, as I'd promised. If I'd been less selfish, less childish—"

"You *were* a child, and children are, for the most part, selfish."

Frustration ripped through Rico. Lily refused to hear what he was saying. "The last thing I said to her was 'Go away and leave me alone.' So she did. I've been alone ever since."

"You're not alone anymore."

"Listen to me!" Rico shouted, but his voice shook. "I *want* to protect you. But I just might fail. That's what I do."

"You've never failed me."

"Yet."

Incredibly, she laughed and put her arms around him. "Come to bed, Rico. I know you won't fail me there."

"You're crazy."

"I will be as soon as you touch me."

He didn't touch her; he stared at her, unable to believe that he'd told her his darkest secret and she didn't care. What had he ever done to deserve a single moment in her company?

He touched her cheek, gently, reverently, and her laughing eyes sobered. "What?" she whispered. "What's the matter now?"

"Russell said love is blind." Hope flickered in her eyes, igniting the same within him. "He's wrong."

The spark of hope died, but Lily put on a brave smile. "We always agreed that what we had between us wasn't love."

"*You* said that. I never agreed." Rico spent a moment looking at her, attempting to arrange his thoughts, trying to find the words that would give her his heart and his soul. "Love isn't blind, because I can see quite clearly how I feel, and I can see quite clearly why. You're the strongest, most giving and trusting woman I've ever met, and I'd be a fool not to love you."

She snorted. "You are a fool."

"I might be worthless and useless, but I've never been stupid. I know love when I see it. Love is you."

She pulled away, her movements odd and jerky. "You don't have to tell me that. I've given you all that I have."

"What are you talking about?"

"Men use the word love to get what they want from women. I've seen it happen a thousand times before."

"Some men use the word because it's true."

She made an exasperated sound as she faced him. "Rico, do you know how many men have told me they loved me?"

"*I* never told you." He grabbed her by the arms and shook her once. "I never told *anyone* and meant it."

The distrust that had filled her eyes faded. "Kiss me," she begged. "Show me."

Lily wouldn't believe the words. He couldn't blame her. She'd spent a lifetime hearing the word love bandied about as a bribe or a joke. She needed him to show her; he could oblige.

El haría cualquier cosa para ella.

Rico gentled his hands on Lily's arms, rubbed them up and down, then leaned over to kiss her as she came up on her toes to kiss him. As their mouths met, matched, mated, he finished unbuttoning her bodice and slipped his fingers inside, across the slope of her breast to her waist. Then he turned his mind to kissing—nibbling, tasting, tormenting her lips and tongue until the fullness of her breast weighting the back of his hand rose and fell ever so much faster.

Removing her dress, then her undergarments, he followed them to the ground, kneeling to remove her shoes and stockings, then putting his mouth to her belly, rubbing his cheek along the soft curve, tasting the spike of her hip and the dip that led him lower still.

When her knees weakened, he tumbled her onto his bed. She reached for him, but he would not come.

"I am showing you, *Lilita*. Leave me be."

Needing to feel flesh against flesh, he lost his clothes and worshiped every inch of her skin with his mouth, his hands, himself.

He drove her up, coaxed her down, made her curse, then made her come. At the first harsh intake of breath that signaled her release, he sheathed himself within her, held himself still as her tremors made him shudder with a need to

plunge and plunder, fought the end because he
wanted this to be their beginning.

Watching her face, he touched her cheek. What
was between them, he'd never known before, knew
instinctively that he would never know again. He
had lost count of the number of women he'd plea-
sured, but he would forever remember his last—
his love.

When he could no longer do anything but give
in, he pulled her tightly against him and showed
her in the way she'd asked him to that he loved
her now and always would. As he pulsed deep inside her and she tightened around him, he understood why people would die for love. Sex was special.
But sex with love . . . There were no words to explain
the completeness of a single shining moment.

He kissed her gently, upon all the spots that
made her shiver, until their bodies cooled and their
hearts calmed. Tangled together, all skin and limbs
and sheets, he pressed his fingers to where her
heart lived, and when she opened her eyes, he
murmured, "What do you feel right here, right
now, *Lilita*?"

"Peace."

"Yes," he agreed. "Such as I have never known.
What we have here between us, what we have with
Johnny and Carrie—I think that's what a family
might be like." He remained silent for a moment,
trying to put into words what he'd always been
missing but never known until now. "Love no matter what."

Skepticism shadowed her face. Before she could
deny or refute him, he hurried on, trying to convince her as well as himself. "You said it yourself.
Carrie loves me. Always. And I love her the same.

She can do nothing that would make me not love her. Don't you love Johnny the same way?"

Lily's brow creased. "Yes. But there's a difference between love for children and love between a man and a woman. I've never seen that kind of love work."

"What about Mary and Reese? Eden and Sullivan?"

Uncertainty flickered in her eyes before she doused it. "Who knows if they'll last?"

"I know. Reese threw himself in the path of a bullet for Mary. He almost died. She carried Georgie, alone and unmarried, until he came back for her. She never stopped waiting for him. I don't think she ever would have."

More memories came tumbling from his mouth as he tried to convince her that love could last between the right woman and the right man. "Jed wanted better than a half-breed scout for his baby sister. But Eden wanted Sullivan, and she meant to have him—the world be damned. I want what they have, and I mean to have it with you. *Haría cualquier cosa para tí.*"

"You keep saying that. What does it mean?"

Rico rolled onto his back, carrying her with him. Her hair curtained their faces. "I would do anything for you," he whispered.

Lily laughed and tumbled off of him. "You're insane."

"Maybe. I heard the right woman can save a man." Coming up on his elbow, Rico reached for Lily's hand, then kissed her knuckles. The laughter left her face, and she stared at him almost as if she were afraid. "Save me, Lily."

"There's nothing wrong with you," she snapped.

"Ah, *querida,* that is why I need you so badly.

Only you would hear my darkest secret and say it doesn't matter. Only you would know me as I am and say there's nothing wrong with me."

Hope flickered once again in her eyes. Lily saw the dream, and she wanted it as well. But she'd been hurt too many times, lied to again and again.

Rico pulled her into his arms, smoothed her hair, whispered nonsense as she drifted toward sleep.

This was going to take some time. Anything worth having always did.

CHAPTER 18

Before the sun completely burst over the eastern horizon, Lily and Rico said their good-byes. Carrie was mutinous, Johnny silent as usual but still agitated. He couldn't stop pacing and wringing his hands.

"They'll be fine as soon as you go," Yvonne assured them. "Kids always are."

Lily tried to smile, but her heart was breaking. She didn't want to leave Johnny; she couldn't bear to leave Carrie. Heck, she didn't even want to leave Kate and Laurel.

When had Rock Creek become home? The moment she'd started to care about the people in it.

"Time to go," Russell announced.

At his words, Carrie threw herself around Rico's waist and started wailing. He picked her up and walked a short distance away, murmuring into her ear.

Lily's throat went thick at the sight. He was a Pied Piper for children. Even Johnny loved him now, and that only made things more complicated. Because even if she could believe Rico loved her, she couldn't give him what he wanted. She wasn't like Mary and Eden, and she never would be. Even if she loved him, and she wasn't saying she did, she'd never tell him so, because a life with her would be no life at all. He'd shared his deepest secret, but she couldn't, wouldn't, share hers.

Lily tugged her gaze from Rico and Carrie to find Johnny striding toward her. She opened her arms for a hug, but he frowned, shook his head, and led her away from the others.

She watched his face as he struggled, trying to tell her something. Lily put her hand on his arm. "I'll miss you, too."

He shrugged her off, kept trying to talk, but he was so upset, he couldn't utter the first word. Finally, he looked about a bit frantically, caught sight of a stick, and squatted to the ground. Then he glanced behind him to make sure no one was watching and wrote two letters in the dirt.

R.W.

Johnny looked up at her, back at the letters, then stood and kicked them into dust.

"He's gone, sugar. You heard that. I just wish I knew who killed him. I know I didn't."

He grabbed her arms, his face intense as he nodded. Understanding dawned in Lily.

"Do you know who killed him?"

"Y-y-y-yes." He paused, struggling. Lily held her breath.

Johnny released her. One beautiful, dark, long finger curled toward himself. Lily raised her gaze from his hand, to his face, then glanced past him to the others. No one looked at them.

Memories assaulted her one after the other— Johnny handing over her knife on Fat Tuesday, the cut on his hand, the blood on his clothes.

She cupped her palm over his hand and forced his finger back into a fist. "Shh," she breathed.

He shook his head and started toward Russell. Lily grabbed his arm and yanked him back. "No!" she insisted, harsh and low, for their ears only. "I don't know why you did it, but I'm sure you had a reason. They won't convict me. I didn't do it."

He pointed at himself. She slapped his hand. "Stop that! I mean it, Johnny. You stay here, and you take care of Carrie. And you keep your mouth *shut!* I need you to do that for me. All right? Promise?"

He shook his head. Lily put her hands to his face and stopped the movement. "For me? Please? Please!"

She stared desperately into his eyes, and at last he bowed his head in acquiescence. Lily kissed his brow. "Thank you. Don't worry. I'll handle this."

As she walked away, she muttered a sentence that was beginning to sound like a litany. "I'd do anything for you."

Reese showed up just as they were about to leave. A slight tilt of his head and Rico dismounted, ignoring the exasperated sigh of Russell as they walked a few steps away to talk.

"You going to be okay?" Reese began.

"Why wouldn't I be? I'm not a *bebé, capitán.*"

Reese grunted. "I can come along."

"No," Rico snapped. "You told me once I would have to stand up for myself."

"I think I was talking about Johnny."

"Sure you were."

Reese's lips tilted just a bit. Until he'd met Mary, that was as close to a smile as he'd ever gotten. "So how is going to New Orleans with Lily standing up for yourself?"

"Without her, there is no me. Or at least not a me I'm very proud of."

"We all thought there was something strange about Lily."

Rico stiffened. "There is nothing wrong with Lily."

"I didn't say that. But what if she did it?"

"Doesn't matter to me one way or another."

Reese stared at Rico as if he had never seen him before. At last, he nodded and put a hand on Rico's shoulder. "I had Jed check on this guy; he's a Pinkerton, all right. But watch him, anyway."

"Of course, *mi capitán.* I learned what you taught me."

"I think you finally might have." With a final piercing look, Reese spun on his heel and walked away.

Carrie ran alongside Rico's horse all the way to the outskirts of Rock Creek. Johnny caught up and took her hand.

"I love you, Rico!" she shouted. "And I don't hate you anymore, Lily."

Rico glanced at Lily to find her laughing, even as tears filled her eyes. She stared straight ahead, but Rico had to look back. Johnny and Carrie waved. Yvonne came up behind them and put a hand on each child's shoulder.

The rest of the town stood deserted except for

the figure of a man at the schoolhouse, another at the jail, and the last in front of the hotel. Each man lifted a hand, then lowered it. They'd be there if he needed them.

A short while later, Russell stopped his horse. "Lost already?" Rico asked.

"Nope. Just want you two to ride in front. I don't think you plan to kill me, but I'd feel better if I was watchin' you instead of the other way around."

"I don't know where we're going."

"Keep goin' until I say to turn. Sooner or later we'll hit New Orleans."

"A lot later," Rico mumbled. This trip was going to take weeks.

"Just get goin'."

Rico glanced at Lily, but she was already guiding her horse into the lead.

Johnny was acting funny. Carrie didn't like it. Not that he'd ever been a chatty sort, but since Lily and Rico had left, he wouldn't even play the piano, and that scared Carrie a lot.

Yvonne tried to get him to play something, anything. "Lily would want you to practice," she said.

Johnny gave her a disgusted look and locked himself in his room.

Though the emptiness of the saloon made Carrie sad, the last few days of school had raised her spirits. She and Millie Sullivan had become friends. Rafe and Teddy had taken to eating lunch with Johnny. Teddy whispered to Johnny quite a bit, and Carrie hoped he could get Johnny to start talking. After all, Teddy hadn't talked when he came to Rock Creek, either, so maybe he knew some talking secrets.

The five children together discouraged any teasing from the Sutton twins. Though after the way Carrie and Johnny had taken care of them, she didn't think Frank and Jack would come near any of them anytime soon.

But now that school was out, Carrie was bored. Sure, she had Gizzard to play with, but how much could you do with a lizard? No matter how many times she threw a ball at him, he would let it bounce off his nose without even trying to catch it.

Three Queens wasn't very busy, since Lily wasn't there to sing on Saturdays, but it was busy enough to keep Yvonne and the girls occupied. Carrie missed Lily nearly as much as she missed Rico, and she was sorry she'd ever been mean to her. She'd started to have a dream in which Lily was her mama and Rico was her daddy, and that dream was somehow better than the one she'd once had of marrying Rico. Now that she was nine, Carrie realized what a baby she'd been to even think that might happen.

One night when Carrie couldn't sleep, she got out of bed and crept into Johnny's room. A few times before, when the loneliness was bad, she'd slept at the foot of his bed all night, and he'd never so much as blinked to find her there in the morning.

Tonight, when Carrie sneaked in the door, her breath caught at the sight of the empty bed. If Johnny left her, she'd be completely alone. She ran into the hall, breath coming in hitching little sobs of panic.

"Johnny?" she called, and her voice broke in the middle.

Almost immediately, he appeared in the doorway to Lily's room, and she ran to him and threw her arms around his waist. "Don't leave me," she whispered. "Don't ever leave me."

Johnny's palm ran over her hair. The gentle touch soothed Carrie's fear, but when she looked into his face, what she saw there scared her. Something was very, very wrong.

Carrie took Johnny's hand and led him back to his room; then, just as they had the first night she'd been at Three Queens, they sat on the bed facing each other.

"Tell me," she demanded. He raised his eyebrows. "I mean it. Tell me what's the matter."

Johnny closed his eyes, swallowed hard, then opened them again. "I d-d-d-did it."

Carrie's mouth fell open. Not because of what he'd said but that he'd said it. His voice was hoarse, as if unused for years, but he had a voice.

She went up on her knees and put her arms around his neck to hug him. "You did, Johnny. You did do it. You spoke."

He shook his head and pulled her arms from his neck, then gently pushed her away. "N-n-no. I k-k-killed R.W."

Now Carrie couldn't speak—for a minute, anyway. "Why?"

"He w-w-was going t-t-to hurt Lily. I-I knew he'd d-d-do it. B-b-because . . ."

Johnny's shoulders hunched as he drew in on himself. One hand rubbed his forearm, and Carrie understood. She crawled across the bed and took his arm. Rolling up his sleeve, she exposed the scars. " 'Cause he hurt you." Johnny nodded. "We've got to tell Lily."

"I d-d-did."

Carrie frowned. "Then why didn't she tell the detective man?"

"Said she'd t-t-take c-c-care of it. Th-that I had t-t-to t-t-take c-c-care of y-y-you."

Without thought, Carrie climbed into Johnny's lap, where she felt safe, so she could think. He stiffened. "C-C-Carrie. Aren't y-you afraid of m-me n-n-ow?"

"Why would I be afraid of you?"

"I k-killed someone."

"For Lily. Because you love her."

"Yes."

"You love me, too. No one will ever hurt me while you're around."

Slowly, Johnny's arms encircled Carrie, and he hugged her for the first time all on his own. Carrie smiled secretly and laid her hands over his.

She'd never felt so protected or so loved. Lily had gone all the way to New Orleans to save Johnny, but Lily had left him here to take care of her. Carrie knew Rico loved her, and she'd figured Johnny did, too, but she hadn't been so sure about Lily. Now she was. Carrie was going to have that family she'd always wanted, and as Rico kept telling her, sometimes you had to go out and fight for what was important.

"You could talk all along, couldn't you?"

"Y-yes. S-s-sorry."

Carrie shrugged. She could understand why he'd kept silent. It was bad enough being the new kid in town—but the new kid who stuttered . . . The Suttons would have eaten Johnny for breakfast the very first day.

"It's okay." She patted his hand. "I understand you without the words."

"Lily, t-t-too."

"That's because we both love you. Now, this is

what we have to do. We'll go to New Orleans, and we'll tell them what happened."

"I-I don't know if I can t-talk in front of everyone."

Carrie turned so she could see his face. "I'll talk for you."

He smiled. "I'm su-su-supposed to take care of you."

"So take care of me. On the way to New Orleans. If we tell them the truth, everything will be all right. Rico will make sure of it."

"Y-you think?"

"I know."

Johnny nodded. "M-me, too. What d-do we d-do?"

"You think I had a fit to stay with Yvonne for nothing?" Carrie winked. "She's not as suspicious as Mr. Reese or as quick as Mrs. Mary. We sneak out tonight. We leave a note that we went on a picnic. She'll believe us. By the time they figure out we're gone, we'll be on a stage and halfway to Dallas."

The shadows still haunted Johnny's eyes—they probably always would—but the weight that had seemed to stoop his shoulders since Lily and Rico left was gone. When he smiled, Carrie's heart jumped with joy. He so rarely smiled all the way up to his eyes.

"You with me?" she asked.

"Always."

For a man who always knew exactly what was behind him, with a sixth sense some said was Comanche but Sinclair Sullivan knew could just as well be Irish, he had jumped out of his skin more times since Rico left town than he ever had in his life.

Sullivan couldn't figure out why. It wasn't as if they hadn't been separated before. Hell, there'd been months, once an entire year, when he hadn't seen any of the others. Until Rock Creek, none of them had stayed in one place for very long.

So why did he feel as if ten thousand ants were crawling all over him and every time the wind blew he spun about with his gun in his hand?

Sullivan stood in his empty jail, and he stared out the single window at the empty miles of land surrounding Rock Creek. Everything looked fine, but something wasn't right, and for the life of him, he didn't know what.

That feeling came again, and he twirled toward the door. His heart stopped at the sight of the huge man who blotted out the sunlight. "Bang, bang," Jed drawled. "You're dead, boy."

Sullivan scowled. "What do you want?"

"Eden said you were snarly as a wounded bear." Jed stepped inside and leaned on the desk. The old wood creaked with his weight. "What's the matter with you? Miss the kid?"

Sullivan shrugged. "I feel funny."

Jed's sharp gaze flicked to Sullivan's face. "Funny how?"

"Something's not right."

Jed nodded. "I know what you mean. That Pinkerton was too agreeable by half, letting Rico go along to New Orleans. But he checked out. He's a detective."

"He said he was sending a wire."

"Tried to find out what it was, but the telegraph agent won't budge."

"Really? Maybe I can budge him a bit."

"You think you can when I couldn't?"

Sullivan tapped his star. "Can't hurt to try."

"I'll just mosey along and see how it's done."

Ignoring him, Sullivan crossed the street to the new telegraph office. The telegraph operator, Vincent Crawley, was new, too—and unimpressed with the legend that went along with his visitors.

"I don't care who you are or what you did before I got here. You aren't invading the privacy of my customers."

Sullivan shrugged, pulled his gun, and pointed it at the tall, impossibly thin young man. "Hand it over."

Crawley's mouth opened, shut and opened again, but nothing came out.

"I could have done that," Jed pointed out.

"But then I'd have to arrest you. It works so much better when I do it."

"True."

Crawley found his voice. "Y-you can't do that. It's against the law."

"Since I'm the law and I'm all for it, I think you'd better hand over that telegraph."

Crawley did so in short order. Sullivan opened the paper and cursed. "I knew it. Where did you send this?"

"San Antone."

Jed snatched the sheet from Sullivan's hand, glanced at it, and cursed some more. "I'll send for Cash and Nate in Fort Worth. You tell Reese. We'll meet at the stable."

Sullivan hurried to the cabin behind the schoolhouse. When Reese answered the door, Sullivan handed him the paper. Mary appeared behind him. "What is it?"

"I've found Rico Salvatore," Reese read. "You can get him in New Orleans."

Mary gasped. "It's a trap?"

"Looks like." Reese glanced at Sullivan, and Sullivan was glad to see the command he'd always admired hardening Reese's eyes. "Send for Nate and Cash."

"Already done. This wire went to San Antonio."

"That's where the kid's from. I have no idea why he left, either. This could be about damn near anything, knowing Rico. I don't like it."

"That makes two of us."

"I'll get my things. We'll leave directly."

Sullivan returned to the hotel to pack. Eden stood at their bed, shoving clothes in his saddlebags.

"Did I do something I don't know about?"

"What?" She blinked at him, concern and confusion evident on her pretty, sweet face.

"You're kicking me out?"

"Jed was already here. He told me. You'd better hurry."

He pulled her into his arms. "You're not even going to ask me to stay?"

"What would be the point of that? This is Rico."

He kissed her, hard and fast. "I love you."

"I know. And you love him, too. Bring him back."

"We always do." Sullivan continued packing.

"You think Nate and Daniel will come?"

He tossed his saddlbag over his shoulder. "Why wouldn't they?"

"Daniel was pretty mad at Rico."

"Cash is always pretty mad at someone, and it's usually Rico."

"He said the six was two."

"He says a lot of things. He'll be there. I'd bet my life on it." She bit her lip, and he paused, not wanting to leave her when she was so uncertain. "You think four isn't as good as six?"

"I think any one of you is as good as ten. But I wouldn't bet *your* life on it."

He dropped the bags and pulled her into his arms one more time. "It'll be all right. Rico needs me, and after all . . ." They both sighed.

"We can't just leave him there," Eden finished.

CHAPTER 19

Carrie and Johnny nearly made it to Ranbourne. *Nearly*.

They'd packed clothes and food, written their false note, and freed Gizzard. The latter had nearly made Carrie cry, but she knew she couldn't leave him all cooped up with no one to love him. So free he was, and free he'd stay, though he'd looked at her with as sad a face as a lizard got when she put him by the river and walked away.

Borrowing the horses was so easy, Carrie wondered why people didn't borrow them all the time. The kid who ran the stable was snoring louder than a thunderstorm. He never so much as moved atop his bed of hay as she and Johnny led their mounts outside.

They rode all night and into the day; then, just as Ranbourne appeared on the horizon in front of them, three riders appeared on the horizon behind them.

Carrie knew who they were, so there was no point in trying to hide. She and Johnny exchanged glances and pulled to a stop.

"How do you think they found us out so fast?" she asked.

Johnny shrugged. He might be able to talk, but he didn't talk much.

Mr. Reese, Mr. Rourke, and Sheriff Sullivan reined in. All three stared at Carrie and Johnny as if they were ghosts.

"What in hell are you two doin' here?" Mr. Rourke demanded.

"You mean you didn't come after us?"

Mr. Reese rubbed his eyes. "No. We're going after Rico."

"Good. So are we. We can all go together."

"Like hell!" Mr. Rourke snapped. The sheriff sent him a glare, which made Carrie giggle. As if she hadn't heard that word before.

"You two turn right around and go home," Mr. Reese said. "We'll bring Rico back."

"We aren't worried about Rico; we're worried about Lily."

The three exchanged glances. "Why?" the sheriff asked.

Carrie looked at Johnny, who nodded. "Lily didn't kill that man. Johnny did. But only because he was the baddest man. He hurt Johnny, and he was going to hurt Lily, too."

"How do you know that?" Mr. Reese asked.

"Johnny said so."

Mr. Reese's mouth tightened the way it always did when one of the Sutton twins acted bratty. "Go home, Carrie."

"No, sir. We love Lily, and we love Rico, and we're going to go and tell the truth and make things right, and nothin' you can say or do will stop us. Right, Johnny?"

"R—r-right."

All three men stared at Johnny as if his horse had just spoken. Then Mr. Reese glanced at the others before returning his gaze to Johnny. "How long have you been chatting with Carrie?"

"Just since yesterday," Carrie answered. "Lily told him not to, 'cause—"

Mr. Reese narrowed his eyes on her. "Let him answer for himself."

"He don't like to talk unless he absolutely has to. It's hard for him, and kids are mean when you're different. Adults, too. So I said I'd do the talking."

"Well, he might *have* to do the talking in New Orleans."

Carrie grinned. "We can go?"

Mr. Reese sighed and looked up at the sky as if he wished God would help him out. "You can go."

Funny how New Orleans hadn't changed, even though Lily had. She never thought of herself as Betty anymore. Betty she had left in New Orleans.

The city had flourished for centuries. Why would it change now? What began as a small outpost of France in the New World had been ceded back and forth between France and Spain for decades, leading to a rich Creole culture. With the sale of Louisiana to America, New Orleans became the largest southern city. But she was never truly of the South. New Orleans was of France.

Lily, Rico, and Noah Russell crossed Canal Street into the American side of town, where Lily had always lived. When the Americans came to New

Orleans, they settled in what became known as the Protestant section.

Their houses were American, too, set back from the street and shaded with large, sweeping trees. They made up the Garden District and turned Canal Street into a hostile border between two worlds. Some Creoles boasted they had never crossed that street in their lives and they never would.

Exhausted after traveling so many miles for so long, Lily brightened at the thought that she might sleep in a bed that night. Though her bed might be in a jail, it wouldn't be on the ground. Lily sighed as disappointment flowed through her. She'd rather sleep on the ground next to Rico than in a feather bed without him.

On the trail, they'd grown closer—the two of them against the world, or at least Russell. To be truthful, the detective had been nothing but polite. He'd gotten them here, as he'd said he would, and no doubt would turn her over to the authorities, then disappear.

Up ahead Lily recognized R.W.'s place, the Hideaway. Now that she knew he'd had a wife stashed somewhere, the name made a whole lot of sense.

Russell stopped in front of the saloon and dismounted.

"Why are we here?" Lily asked. "I figured you'd take me to jail."

Rico scowled at her. "Don't give him ideas, *querida*."

"I was hired by Mrs. Ward, not the law of New Orleans. When I wired ahead to say I'd found Miss Lillian, I was told to bring her here.

Lily stared at the doorway. Inside the Hideaway she'd been treated as property. She'd believed that once she made her escape, she would never have to see the place again. Just went to prove that what you believed rarely happened. She should have remembered that lesson from her mother.

Sliding from her horse, Lily hung on to the saddle when her knees buckled. Rico was there in an instant to hold her up. Just the warmth of his hand at her waist steadied her enough to stay on her feet.

"I do not like this," he murmured.

"Me, either. But let's get it over with."

Russell awaited them at the door. Rico took Lily's arm, and together they joined the detective. Lily hesitated outside. She'd often thought of this place as her own private hell. Only the music and Johnny had kept her sane. Now she would go back without the comfort of music, without the calming surety of Johnny's presence.

"*Lilita?*" Rico's breath brushed her cheek.

She turned her head and met his dark gaze. What she saw there gave her the strength to walk through that door again, where she learned what hell really was.

The roomful of dour faces turned toward Lily, and from the rustle and hiss that rolled in her direction, she had already been found guilty.

"What the hell is this?" Rico demanded.

Russell appeared as confused as they were. He crossed to the gray-haired, sour-lipped woman seated next to the pompous-looking man in black.

"Mrs. Ward? What's going on here?"

Lily closed her eyes. That was R.W.'s wife? And she was sitting next to the judge. A feeling of doom settled over Lily like fog over a stormy sea.

She opened her eyes just in time to watch Mrs. Ward cast a triumphant glare her way before she waved Russell aside. "Is this the slut who killed my husband?"

Lily kept her face bland, though the words hit her like sharp kicks to her stomach. She should have expected no less. That the words surprised her only showed how quickly one could become accustomed to a better life.

"Shut your filthy mouth, lady, or I'll shut it for you," Rico snarled.

Lily put her hand on his arm. "Never mind," she whispered.

"Who is this? Your latest lover? I should have known a woman like you would be on to the next in a heartbeat. This one looks a little young for you, Betty. But then, why not? I suppose R.W. was getting old and that's why you killed him."

"I didn't touch him."

"From what I hear, you touched him a lot. And you're going to pay for it. Let's get on with this, Sherman."

"Ma'am," Russell broke in. "I brought her back for a fair trial. This looks like a vigilante committee."

"I paid you to bring her back. What I do with her afterward is none of your business. Besides, Sherman Oatley is a judge of this city. The trial will be legal." Rico snorted. Mrs. Ward looked his way and smiled. "Fair is a matter of opinion."

A chill went over Lily. Her fate had already been bought and paid for.

The mockery of a trail droned on and on. Since they'd been unprepared for the inquisition awaiting them, Lily had no lawyer. One was appointed for her. The guy had studied law as much as Rico had studied the priesthood.

Rico could have gone and hired a lawyer from the myriad offices uptown, but that lawyer would have known nothing about the case, and from the looks of Mrs. Ward's pet judge, it would make no difference.

Rico refused to leave Lily's side. He had a superstitious fear that if he did, that would be the last time he saw her. So he sat there as witness after witness was called to say that Lily, make that Betty, had not cared for R.W. but she'd endured him. That she was a schemer, a thief, an ambitious entertainer who had used Ward to get where she wanted and then killed him. With this many witnesses, the trial must be costing the widow most of her fortune.

"On the night in question, Miss Lillian, you say that the last time you saw Mr. Ward was in the saloon. Alive."

Lily nodded. She'd only answered the question ten times from ten different angles.

"Then how do you explain the argument that was heard? The fact that Mr. Ward shouted your name? How do you explain a dead Mr. Ward from a knife wound in his heart."

"I can't explain it."

"I have here the signed testimony of a Dr. Landsdowne, and I quote: 'The knife wound was one inch in width, leading to the assumption that a weapon of similar width was used in the murder.' Do you own such a knife, Miss Lillian?"

"Shit," Rico muttered.

At the same time, Lily answered, "Yes."

The prosecutor smiled and moved in for the kill. "The force of the wound indicates a murderer of lesser stature than Mr. Ward. A woman, perhaps."

Her lips tightened, but she said nothing more.

"Come, now, Miss Lillian, if you confess, perhaps you won't hang."

Lily gave him a withering look that said what she thought of that lie.

A commotion at the back of the room drew everyone's attention. Rico groaned at the sight of his five friends. Couldn't they ever trust him to handle things for himself?

"Rico!" Carrie ran down the aisle and jumped into his lap. Johnny followed slowly behind.

"Johnny!" Lily cried. "I told you to stay home."

"I thought you were watching Carrie," Rico said.

"He watched me. All the way here." Carrie hugged Rico so tightly that he had trouble breathing. He pulled her arms from around his throat, set her on her feet, and stood to meet Reese and the others.

"I can handle this," he said.

The four men at Reese's back appeared jumpy, and their gazes flicked about the room as if searching for someone. There was more going on here than met the eye.

"I don't think you can, kid."

Rico forgot about the odd behavior of his friends in the anger that flashed through him. Would Reese never believe he could take care of himself?

"I'll get Lily out of this."

"I have no doubt you will." The pleasure that rippled over Rico at those words dissolved on Reese's next. "That's not why we came. Haven't you seen anything funny, noticed anyone watching you?"

"Me? What do I have to do with it?"

"That's what we came here to find out."

"Judge, clear the room of these gunfighters!"

Mrs. Ward ordered. "They're going to take that Jezebel out of here by force."

"Shut her up," Nate mumbled. "Her voice grates in my head."

"Every voice grates in your head," Cash snapped. He glanced at Rico. "The shrew has a good idea. You want we should take the Jezebel out of here by force?"

"The Jezebel can speak for herself," Lily said. "I didn't kill R.W., and no one can prove that I did."

"Proof is as easy to buy as fair," Mrs. Ward said. "Sherman, do your duty."

The judge opened his mouth. The room went silent, awaiting his verdict. Into that silence came a hoarse, shaky voice.

"I–I d–did it," Johnny said.

"Aw, hell," Lily muttered.

Rico shot her a glare. "You knew that?" She shrugged. "When did you decide to start talking?" he demanded of the boy.

"Don't yell at Johnny," Carrie shouted. "He's doin' the best he can. That bad man hurt him. Said he was going to do the same to Lily. He deserved whatever he got."

Rico walked over to Johnny. "R.W. is the one who did that to you?"

"What?" Lily demanded, right behind him. "What did he do?"

"Not now, Lily." Rico gazed at Johnny until the boy ducked his head and nodded. "Then he's lucky he's already dead." He turned to the judge, stepping in front of the boy. "R.W. hurt this child. When he threatened to do the same to Lily, Johnny protected her."

"Do you have any proof of this?" the lawyer asked.

Johnny stepped forward and tugged at the sleeves of his shirt. His fingers trembled so badly, he faltered several times.

"What's he doing?" Lily whispered.

"There are scars all over his arms—bad ones."

"You saw them?" Rico nodded. "No!" Lily ran forward and stilled Johnny's hands. "You don't have to do this if you don't want to."

"I-I-I c-c-c-c—" He struggled with the word, mouth working, throat straining, but he could not finish.

Rico had been annoyed to discover that both Lily and Johnny had lied to him about the boy's silence. But seeing how difficult it was for Johnny to talk, he understood why. Rico would have done the same thing to save the boy such pain.

Johnny's face flushed dark. He shrugged free of Lily's fingers and yanked up his sleeves. The multitude of healed white scars were easily seen. The crowd shuffled and murmured.

"That doesn't prove anything," Mrs. Ward sneered. "He could have done that himself, or the slut with the knife could have done it."

Lily pulled Johnny's sleeves down. Her eyes were damp. "I would never hurt him," she whispered.

"You'll have to testify, Johnny. Tell them what he did."

The boy's face paled, but he nodded.

"I'll tell what happened!" Carrie shouted. "He doesn't like to talk."

"He'll *have* to talk," Rico said. "For Lily."

"No!" Lily stepped between the boy and judge.

"Lily, this is serious," Rico pointed out. "It won't hurt him to talk to the judge."

"Yes, it will. He can barely talk to me. I won't make him talk in front of an entire room. He shouldn't have to be embarrassed like that."

"R.W.'s the one who should be embarrassed—in hell."

"Johnny's been through enough. He is *not* talking in front of all these people."

"Even if they hang you?"

"Even if."

"The Jezebel obviously made up this story about R.W. hurting him. She practiced her wiles upon that child. She knew no one would hang a boy. Get on with this, Sherman."

The judge nodded. "I find the accused—"

"Hold on just a minute!" Reese said. "There's Russell. I wanna talk to you, Detective."

"Can't this wait?" the judge asked.

"No," Reese said shortly, and the judge relented. Most people did when Reese spoke like that. He went toe-to-toe with the Pinkerton detective. "Why did you send a wire to San Antonio saying you were bringing Salvatore to New Orleans? Who are you turning him over to?"

"What are you talking about?" Rico demanded. "Nobody's looking for me."

"There you are wrong."

Rico went still. The hair on his arms seemed to stand up on a chill wind that swept the room. Rico knew there was no wind, but as soon as he'd heard the voice, he was a child again and scared.

Rico managed not to gape at the man scowling at him from the doorway. "Father." He bowed. "I never thought to see you again."

"I am certain you did not, Rico. Yet here I am."

"Rico!" A young woman shoved past everyone in her path and launched herself into his arms.

Rico caught her. He had no choice. He also had no idea who she was—until she laughed with joy. Then his heart stuttered and seemed to stop. When she drew back to look into his face, Rico reached a trembling hand to touch her blue-black hair.

"Anna?" he asked. "How can it possibly be you?"

CHAPTER 20

Anna's laughter held the same depth of delight it had always held as a child. Rico had known her dead for so many years, he could not believe his eyes. So he kept touching her to make certain she was real, just as she kept touching him as if afraid he would disappear once more.

She was all grown up and beautiful—smooth, dusky skin, black hair, regal face and bearing—the image of their mother in her youth. Seeing Anna brought back all the pain of losing both his mother and his sister. Remembering all that had happened reminded Rico of the failure he had been.

"If you'd come home as you should have," his father began, "you'd have known Anna recovered. All of your life your rash behavior hurt those you loved and caused you to ruin all that you touched."

Well, his father hadn't changed. He still thought Rico worthless. Then why had he sent a Pinkerton detective after him? Why hadn't he been glad to see the last of the son who had always been a disappointment?

Rico's head spun with all that had happened, all that was happening still. His father had found him, his sister was alive, and—

"As I was saying," the judge continued, "the accused is found—"

"*Uno momento,*" the elder Salvatore interrupted. "I have here a letter from the governor, a personal friend of mine."

"Bring it here." The judge motioned impatiently.

Rico's father pulled the letter from his pocket and searched about for a lackey to deliver it to the judge. His gaze lit on Carrie. "You, urchin, come here."

Carrie glanced at Rico, who shook his head. Instead, Rico took the letter and strode over to the judge. One glance at the paper and Oatley stood. "Court is dismissed until the morning." He pointed at Russell. "Confine the prisoner upstairs and make sure she's here come tomorrow."

"Just one minute!" the Widow Ward shouted, but Oatley was already gone.

Rico's father looked pleased with himself, which meant trouble for someone else.

"What are you up to?" Rico asked.

"You shall see. We will dine at seven in the St. Louis Hotel. Do not be late, Rico. Come along, Anna."

Without so much as a hug, a pat, or spitting in Rico's eye, the man turned and walked away. The more minutes that passed, the more Rico saw how little anything had changed.

Anna kissed him on the cheek. "Come, please? I've missed you so."

"I'll come." He glanced after his father. "For you, *chica.*"

She smiled and hurried out the door.

"How come you called her *chica!*" Carrie demanded. "I'm your *chica.*"

"Of course you are." He picked her up. He had forgotten he'd always used the nickname for his sister. With Anna dead in his mind, he'd begun to use the name for Carrie. "She is my little sister."

"Humph." Carrie wrinkled her nose. "She didn't look little to me."

"No, she is all grown up."

With court adjourned, the crowd dissolved. Suddenly, Rico found himself surrounded by his friends. He looked for Lily.

"Russell took her upstairs," Reese said. Rico started to hand him Carrie, intent on following, but Reese held up his hand. "Hold on a minute. Just who is your father, anyway?"

Johnny took Carrie out of Rico's arms and led her to the piano, where they practiced an easy song Johnny had taught her.

"Adriano Salvatore."

"He knows the governor of Louisiana?"

"Looks like it."

"How?"

"I have no idea. I've been away."

"What does you father do in San Antone."

"Cattle."

"If I don't miss my guess, a whole lot of cattle?"

"Si."

"Are you rich, kid?"

"Not me. Him."

"Well, at least we know who was lookin' for him," Jed put in.

"You came all the way down here for me?"

"Not just you," Sullivan said. "I hate to see an innocent woman hang."

"Besides, we didn't have anything else to do," Cash said.

"And New Orleans has the best saloons in the South. Think I'll hang around awhile." Nate wandered in the direction of the bar.

"We may have to do something about this judge and the widow witch," Cash said. "Got any ideas?"

"You don't even like Lily," Rico pointed out.

"Hell, I don't like you. But there's right and there's wrong and this stinks."

Rico nodded. For once, Cash was right. "I'll take care of it."

"How?"

"I don't know yet. But for once let me handle my life."

Cash shrugged. "Suit yourself." He went to join the others at the bar.

Reese and Sullivan exchanged glances. Sullivan slapped Rico on the shoulder, which was as good as an entire conversation for him, and followed Cash.

Reese bent his head and spoke low so only Rico could hear him. "We'll do whatever you want. Whatever you need."

"I know."

"We took a vow to each other. If one calls, the others answer."

"Do you think I have forgotten?"

"You don't have to do this by yourself."

"This time I do." Rico looked at the staircase that led up to the second floor. He wanted to be with Lily now. "I love her. She is everything that is right and good to me. Carrie and the boy are like my own. I would give my life so they would be happy always."

He tore his gaze from the stairs to find Reese staring at him as if he'd just said his hair was purple and his pants were on fire. Slowly, Reese nodded. "Maybe you'll be all right, after all. Love is what matters. Family. That's worth fighting, and dying, for. But we're your family too, kid."

"My name is Rico, *Capitán*."

Reese raised his eyebrow. "All right. Then stop callin' me captain." Rico shrugged, and they shook on it. "Can I give you one last piece of advice?"

"I doubt I can stop you."

"Do whatever you have to do for them, whatever it takes. No matter what it is, no matter what anyone might think or say, do what's best for your family."

"That is exactly what I had planned." Rico started toward the stairs.

"And Rico?" Rico glanced back. "We'll always be here if you need us."

Rico didn't bother to answer something he'd known as the truth for years.

Upstairs, Russell sat outside the door. At the sight of Rico, he stood. He looked uneasy, not the cocky, full-of-himself detective they'd traveled to New Orleans with.

"I didn't know Mrs. Ward had this planned. I thought she meant to turn Miss Lillian over to the sheriff." He shook his head. "I should have known that with all her money she'd buy a judge and pay for a conviction."

Rico didn't think Russell was lying. He seemed an honest man, intent on his job, albeit a bit young and overly sure of himself. But then Rico could understand and sympathize with him. Sometimes the biggest braggarts were in reality the ones who liked themselves the least.

"You did your job," he said. "You believed Lily was a murderess."

"You didn't."

"Of course not. I know her. What I *am* curious about is me. How is it that you were hired by my father and Mrs. Ward, then conveniently discover both Lily and me in Rock Creek? That is much too good to be true."

"I wasn't hired by your father. He hired the agency to find you over ten years ago. But they lost track of you in the war."

"How did you know of me?"

"Open case." He shrugged. "We keep a record of folks we don't find. Just like we keep a rogue's gallery of outlaws on the loose. Every detective, regardless of the case he's on, can overlap into another if someone turns up."

"Lucky me," Rico murmured. "May I see Lily now?"

"Uh." Russell frowned. "Well, sure. Why not? No one said she had to be alone, only that she had to stay here."

Russell unlocked the door. Lily stood at the window. She didn't turn when Rico stepped inside.

The sight of her silhouette, stark against the bright sunlight, stopped Rico just inside the door. Her beauty hit him right below his throat, directly in the middle of his chest, with the same force it had the very first time he'd seen her. But now he knew the beauty didn't stop at her skin. Lily's courage was as much a part of her as her unruly black hair—a loner with the instincts of a mother, a lover with the innocence of a virgin. He couldn't get her out of his mind or heart.

The vow he'd once made with five men paled in comparison to the vow he made with himself now.

He would do whatever he had to do to make sure no one ever hurt her again.

Lily stared out the window as the last rays of summer sunshine banked over New Orleans. She had once loved this city as deeply as a person could love a place.

New Orleans was fashion and art, music, laughter and life. Now all she could think of was a dusty little town in Nowhere, Texas, USA. She wanted to be back in Rock Creek more than she'd ever wanted anything—more than fame, more than power or money, even control of her own life.

She'd just been give a lesson in how little anyone had control of anything at all.

"Go away," she said.

"Never."

Lily turned. Rico was so handsome, he made her eyes ache. Every time she saw him, she was struck again by the beauty of the man—a beauty that went deeper than skin. A strong man with a gentle touch, a boyish devotion to friends combined with the love of a father for any child who needed him. He had shown her how wonderful sex could be. He had changed her view of herself and her view of men—or at least of a few men.

"You thought I was Russell?"

"I knew it was you."

Confusion dropped over his face, erasing the smile she'd come to love. "Then why did you tell me to go away?"

"Because you should. This is going badly. The judge is going to convict me. I want you to take the children and the men and go home."

He snorted. "Not hardly."

"Why can't you just leave me alone?"

"Because I love you."

There was that word again. What did he *want* from her in exchange for his profession of love?

"I want to marry you, *Lilita*. We will be happy, I swear. We will make a life and a family together."

Her laughter erupted, too loud and too high, embarrassingly near hysteria. Rico's face revealed his alarm. He probably thought the stress of the courtroom drama had unhinged her mind when in reality her reaction was caused by one tiny word that could mean both so much and so little.

Well, at least she knew what he wanted for his love. Those things not in her power to give him— her life, her love, a family. Before he had her believing that miracles might come true, before he tore out her heart and crushed it to nothing beneath his boot, she had to get him to leave her behind. She had one secret left to share that would make him run away forever.

"If you marry me, you'll have no family." She didn't wait for his questions, plunging ahead with the truth. "I can't have children."

His face went blank at her announcement. He would turn and walk out now. Lily braced herself for the pain, even though it would be for the best. Rico deserved so much better than what she could give him.

"How do you know that?"

"I have never been with child. I'm barren."

He shrugged. "We've got two children. A place to call home. What more do we need?"

It was her turn to stare at him blankly. "What are you saying?"

"I don't care, Lily. I love you. No matter what. Why can't you hear me? How many times do I have to say it?"

"I'm going to hang."

"No, you aren't."

Frustration pulsed at the base of her skull. The man never listened to anything he did not wish to hear. She wanted to scream, rant and rail. She managed not to. Barely. "Where have you been all day? Mrs. Ward has the judge in her pocket."

"Trust me. I'll get you out of here." He took a step closer. "Say you trust me, Lily."

She backed up to the wall. The needy look in his eyes made her tell him the truth even though she should have kept her mouth shut. "I do."

"Tell me you love me."

He took another step, then another. There was nowhere left for her to run. So she used words to push him away. "I'm sure a thousand women have told you they loved you."

His small smile touched her heart. He knew what she was trying to do. "None of them were you. Tell me."

"Do you know how hard it is for me to say those words?"

Suddenly, he was right there, his long, dark, supple fingers brushing her face. "I have an idea, but tell me why, *Lilita.*"

She pressed her cheek along his palm, took comfort from his touch, took strength from him. "Man after man told my mother. She always believed them; they always betrayed her. She gave them all of herself, and inch by inch they destroyed her.

Man after man told me, too. Not one of them meant it."

"None of them were me. I mean it when I say that I love you. I will always love you. I will always be here for you."

"I've heard that before, too."

Anger sparked Rico's eyes, but Lily wasn't afraid. Not of him. Even when his mouth crushed down on hers, she knew in her heart he would never, ever, hurt her.

Being here, in this town, in this place where she had been a mere object and not a woman, had beat her down in the space of a single day. The despair Lily had felt only a short while ago disappeared as his kiss gentled.

She clung to him, the feelings that were theirs alone flowing between them, showing her that with him she could become the woman she'd always wanted to become because Rico already saw her that way.

His mouth traced her jaw; his lips brushed her ear; his fingers cupped her hip. She wanted to crawl inside him and never leave. She wanted to be a part of him forever, because with him she felt whole for the first time in her life.

"I will get you out of this. Believe me."

Miraculously, she *did* believe him. She trusted him. He would not let her die. She'd been foolish to think he would leave her behind.

"I believe you."

"It is all right if you don't say you love me. We will have a lifetime for you to get used to the idea. I will wait, however long it takes."

"I don't deserve you."

"You deserve so much better. But selfish bastard

that I am, I will not let you go. Unfortunately, I must now have dinner with my father."

"Oh, I nearly forgot. Anna!" She took his hand and held on tight. "She's alive. I'm so happy for you."

"I am happy for her." His sigh was sad, and his shoulders sagged.

"What's the matter? I'd think you would be so happy to see her."

"I am. But my father is another story. He is difficult"

"I wish I could go with you."

He smiled, though the expression did not reach his sad eyes, then ran his knuckle along her cheek. "Me, too, *querida*. Me, too. I could face anyone, or anything, with you at my side."

"Well, get me out of here and then you won't have to be alone ever again."

"Does that mean you will marry me?"

"I'll think about it."

"Think about this." He drew her into his arms and kissed her until she could barely breathe or stand, then he strode to the door and knocked for his release.

As the door shut behind him, she touched her lips and whispered, "I love you, Rico."

The words didn't sound so frightening, after all.

In the Creole section of New Orleans sat the stately St. Louis Hotel, one of the finest in the country. For years elaborate masked balls had been held there at Mardi Gras, making the St. Louis infamous as well as famous. Trust Adriano Salvatore to stay there.

Of course, being a descendent of the criollo,

the Spanish aristocracy who had immigrated to
Mexico, Adriano had always been above the peas-
ants—at least in his own mind. When he moved
to Texas, his opinion of himself had not changed.
As his ranch grew larger and larger, so had his ego.

In New Orleans, Adriano would never deign to
stay on the inferior side of Canal Street, where the
crass Americans lounged, even though they had
built a hotel there to rival the St. Louis and dubbed
it the St. Charles. Being of Spanish blood, born in
America, Adriano belonged in the First Municipal-
ity as much as any Frenchman.

Rico entered the St. Louis at a quarter past seven.
He would come to break bread with his father for
Anna's sake, but he just couldn't bring himself to
arrive on time. Petty annoyances like that had
always been his way to rebel against the iron-fisted
will of his father. Lifelong habits were hard to break
despite having been out of the habit for over ten
years.

"Rico!" Anna jumped up as soon as he entered
the dining room.

Their father gave her a disapproving frown for
her unladylike excitement. Anna sat down but continued to beam at Rico as he crossed the room.

They had already begun their first course. Rico
wasn't surprised. His father never waited for
anyone.

Rico tilted his head. He'd never thought of that
before. He'd been accused of selfishness and rash
behavior. He must have learned it somewhere.

After taking the chair across from his father and
closest to Anna, Rico kissed his sister. The pleasure
of that act spread through him as warm as Lily's
smile. Love might be different for different people,
but love was still love.

"Whiskey," he told the hovering waiter.

The voicing of his son's bourgeois taste caused Adriano to wince behind his glass of French wine. Anna clung to Rico's hand as if she would never let him go.

With a deliberate click, the elder Salvatore set his crystal goblet on the table. "I see little has changed. You are still an uncouth, low-class rake."

"I am glad you missed me, Father."

With narrowed eyes, Adriano contemplated his son. "You are my heir regardless of whatever else you have become."

"I was never the son you wanted or needed. That hasn't changed."

"We shall see. Let's eat together like a family; then we will discuss business later, as civilized people do."

Rico glanced at Anna, who shrugged, obviously as uncertain as he what their father was up to now. Funny, even though they'd been parted for ten years, the two of them slipped back into the roles they'd always held—the two of them against the world, or at least against their father.

In short order Rico's meal was chosen and delivered in suitable style, so he ordered a second whiskey. He didn't plan on having any discussion with his father, business or otherwise, while he was completely sober.

"I hear you have been riding with five men of questionable character for the past several years."

"You hear a lot. If you know so much, why did it take you so long to find me? And why in hell did you want to?"

His father scowled when Rico cursed at the table, then threw a glance at Anna, who continued to eat her dinner as if nothing on this earth could cause her to stop. She'd no doubt shared enough meals with their father to ignore all scowls, frowns, and blustering disapproval. Rico wished he had that ability.

"I've been looking for you ever since you left. Despite the sterling record of the Pinkerton Detective Agency, none of them managed to catch up to you until now. Staying in Rock Creek for the last several years changed all that."

"Foolish on my part."

"Perhaps. Since you are here, and so am I, I prefer to call your foolishness fate."

"Or bad luck," Rico murmured.

Typically, his father ignored what he didn't want to hear. "This Russell found out all that he could while he was in Rock Creek. Good man, Russell."

"Hell of a guy." Rico gave up on his steak and concentrated on his drink.

"You've done some good. I was pleased to hear it. Perhaps you could amount to something, after all."

Swirling his whiskey, Rico let his father ramble on, hoping what the man wanted would slip out eventually. His father had come here with a letter from his *amigo* the governor and stopped a bought-and-paid-for-judge from sentencing Lily—until tomorrow, anyway.

Rico smelled a deal in there somewhere. But he couldn't figure out what his father might want from him. Since he'd been old enough to understand words, his father had told Rico he was nothing. Adriano Salvatore's opinion didn't seem to have changed.

"Anna, it is time for you to retire."

"But, Papa—"

"Now," he snapped.

Anna stood immediately and leaned over to kiss Rico. "You can stay, *chica.*"

She touched the tip of his nose with the tip of her finger—the way she always used to. "You have been away too long if you think that is true." With a respectful nod to their father, she left.

Rico signaled for a third whiskey just for the enjoyment of seeing his father frown, if not because he'd most likely need another to endure any conversation between them.

While the waiter cleared their table, the two men studied each other—adversaries always, despite sharing blood and a name.

When they were alone at last, Rico sipped his whiskey and waited for his father to begin. One thing he'd learned from Cash: Waiting was sometimes the best method of attack.

With a growl of impatience, Adriano leaned forward. "Now that I have found you, you will come home."

"No."

His father merely smiled, which made Rico take another sip of his drink. He had just started to feel pleasantly unconcerned, but that smile sobered him in an instant. It was not a happy expression for whomever the smile was intended.

"You will come home and take your place as my son. You will manage the ranch. You will marry as I choose, and you will sire an heir."

"That will be difficult, since I love Lily and I'll be taking her and the children home to Rock Creek so we can get married."

"What children?"

"Carrie and Johnny."

His father snorted. "An unkempt urchin and an idiot piano player. They aren't your blood, thank

God; therefore, they aren't yours. And you won't be marrying that whore."

Rico put his whiskey down and leaned forward. "Call them that again and I'll conveniently forget you're my father."

"No son of mine will marry a saloon singer, especially one accused of murder. I plan to go into politics, Rico, and you will not ruin it for me."

"Because I'm not going to be anywhere near you."

They were nearly nose to nose across the table. Suddenly, his father sat back. "If a conviction can be bought, an acquittal can be bought just as easily. Or a quicker hanging. Whatever the situation warrants."

Here was the deal. Rico never would have guessed his father wanted him to return to San Antonio so badly.

"You've always despised me. Why do you want me back home?"

"You aren't the son I wanted, but you're my son. My only son. How would it look to Texas if I let you run with outlaws and marry a slut?"

Rico palmed his knife and flipped it forward to stick into the table directly in front of his father. "You will not speak of her again."

His father raised his gaze from the knife to Rico. "I won't if you won't. She will live if you agree to my terms, and then you will never speak her name again."

"What's to prevent me from breaking her out of that joke of a jail and disappearing."

"I'm not a fool." His father nodded toward the door. Rico turned to see a very rough looking character lurking at the entrance to the dining room. "You agree, she lives. You do not, she dies. It's as simple as that. One word from me and my friend goes to the judge. She'll be swinging from the nearest tree before you leave here; you can bet on that."

Panic threatened, and Rico's stomach roiled on whiskey and little else. He wished he'd kept a clear head. He'd never imagined something like this, and he didn't know what to do.

His beautiful dream of love, home, and a family was fading fast. To save Lily, he would have to give up that dream. But he had said he would give his life for her, and here he'd thought that meant he would only have to die. Returning to his father's house, living his father's life, beneath his father's thumb, might be worse than dying.

But it would be for Lily.

"Do you agree?" his father pressed.

Maybe he could agree, then have the others take her home and tell her what had happened. Then he would escape and return to Rock Creek. Hopefully his father would not be able to hurt them there.

But then he would be depending on others to save him. He'd never walk free or feel safe again. He'd be putting not only Lily and the children at risk but his friends, their families, and the town he'd come to think of as home as well.

Maybe he'd once been useless, irresponsible, selfish, but he could change all that. All he had to do was say . . .

"Yes."

CHAPTER 21

Lily spent a night dreaming of beautiful things—
a husband, home, and family. She could hardly
wait for the new day to dawn.

The second she saw Rico she would tell him she
loved him. She trusted him; he would save her
from this mess. He wasn't like all those other men;
he wasn't like any other man she'd ever met.
Because he was her man. And if she trusted him
with her life, she could trust him with her love,
too.

A subdued Russell led her into court. Rico was
nowhere to be seen, and neither were Carrie and
Johnny, which caused Lily to frown. But the sight
of the five men lounging with deceptive casualness
along the back wall made her tense with expecta-
tion. Perhaps they would rescue her at gunpoint.
She'd be ready for anything that might occur.

What she wasn't ready for was the judge, who
banged his hand on the table, announced, ''Case

dismissed," then disappeared into the commotion that followed.

Mrs. Ward gaped, then shouted, "I paid you good money, Sherman! Get back here!" Then she disappeared, too. The woman seemed to be forever chasing her bought-and-paid-for judge.

Suddenly, Recse was there, leading Lily outside, where, horses and Johnny awaited.

"Where's Rico and Carrie?" she asked.

"Let's get out of here while we still can," Jed grumbled.

While Lily thought it odd Rico wasn't here to greet her, she figured that if he expected trouble, he would have taken Carrie to wait outside of town. So she took Jed's advice and followed them out of New Orleans before anyone changed their mind.

But when they were out of town, on a road north, and there was still no sign of Rico, Lily stopped her horse. Reese held up a hand, and everyone else stopped, too.

"Where is he?" The look on Reese's face made her blood go cold. "He's dead."

She swayed in the saddle, and Johnny, who had not left her side since she'd emerged from the saloon, steadied her. She looked at him and saw anger in his eyes. "What is it?"

Johnny glanced at Reese, who cursed. "He's not dead. He's just gone."

"Gone?"

"Back home to San Antone. He took Carrie with him."

"B-but he asked me to marry him." She looked at each of the men in turn. When none of them would meet her eyes, she understood she'd been duped as badly as her mother had ever been. The despair that washed over Lily made her glad Johnny still hovered nearby.

If this pain was what her mother had experienced every time someone who'd said they loved her, someone she thought she loved and trusted, had betrayed her, Lily could see why a noose was better than feeling this way over and over again.

"He sent a note," Reese continued. "Told me you'd be freed and that we should take you and Johnny home."

"That was it?" Fool that she was, Lily still hoped for a personal message.

Just like Mama always hoped each and every man would come back? Lily flinched as the sarcastic taunt filled her mind.

Reese glanced at Sullivan. "Tell her," the sheriff said.

Lily didn't like the sound of that.

"He's going to take over the Salvatore holdings. Something about an heir to the family name. Hell, I never figured Rico gave a damn about anyone but himself. This isn't like him at all."

But it was like him. He was a man, wasn't he? And men always left when a better offer came along.

Lily's eyes burned, and she felt as if her pounding heart might just choke off her last hope of breath. He'd said he didn't care that she couldn't have children. Obviously that had been as much of a lie as his love.

Or maybe he'd loved her as much as he was able. But when offered an easier life and the possibility of a pristine wife and perfect little babies, barren Lily and her checkered past just hadn't been enough to keep that love from dying in an instant.

And that wasn't love. She'd at least learned that much.

"Maybe none of us knew him as well as we thought," she said, and prodded her horse in the direction of Rock Creek.

"I friggin' hate it here!" Carrie wailed.

Rico wanted to wail himself, but the deal was done. By now Lily hated him forever. She thought every vow he'd made to her a lie. Though he'd broken them *for* her, what difference did that make? There was no point in pouting over what might have been. But try telling Carrie that.

"Do not swear, *chica*. It makes my father angry."

"That's why I do it. I like to watch his face turn purple."

They were sitting on the front porch. They had been in San Antonio two weeks. Funny how it felt like two hundred years.

Rico had done as agreed. He became the right-hand man his father always wanted him to be. He learned about stinking, pigheaded cattle. He commanded lewd, crude cowboys. He endured each day despising nearly every waking moment. Still nothing was ever good enough for his father. Through adult eyes Rico was starting to see that maybe he wasn't as worthless as he'd been led to believe. Perhaps no one was good enough for Adriano Salvatore.

The only thing that kept Rico going day after day was having Carrie with him. He had refused to leave her behind, and that concession had cost him a last moment with Lily and any good-byes with his friends.

His father had preyed on his need for Carrie to get Rico to leave that very night. Adriano had thought Rico might tell the others what was going on and they would then be obliged to use their guns to gain his freedom. To protect them all, Rico had left New Orleans without a whimper. He'd said he wanted to take charge of his own life. He was doing a hell of a job so far.

Perhaps it was for the best that Lily hated him. Maybe then she could find another man to make her happy. The thought of any man loving her, living with her, knowing her strength, touching her hair, sharing her life, made his stomach burn in agony. Or perhaps that was just the burn of hatred for his new, or rather his old, life.

"While I can understand how much fun it is to watch my father turn purple," Rico said, "I would appreciate it if you didn't curse."

"But, Rico, sometimes only a curse word will do."

"So use the French curses Lily taught you."

Carrie's lower lip wobbled. Rico thought of a few choice curses of his own. He should know better than to mention Lily's name. Carrie had decided she loved Lily as passionately as she'd once hated her.

"Those words remind me of her. They make me wanna cry. I miss Lily. And Johnny and Gizzard." She stood up, fixed him with a tear-filled, yet defiant glare, and stomped her foot. "I friggin' hate it here!"

"Go to your room, Carrie."

"I hate it there, too."

"Do it anyway. I'll come up in a little while, and we'll talk about this some more."

"Why can't we go home?"

"This is our home now."

"Is not! Home is where there are people you love no matter what and people who love you the same. No one here loves me like that except you, and I can't love these people, Rico. I try, but I just can't."

"I know, *chica*, I know." He held open his arms, and she hugged him. Her scratchy new dress scraped his chin. He kissed her on top of her freshly washed and tightly braided hair. Since they'd come here, Carrie had been scrubbed, dressed, and feminized to within an inch of her life. She hated it nearly as much as he did. "Go on, now."

That Carrie went without further argument revealed how deep the sadness dwelt in her, as deep as it dwelt in Rico himself. The thought of being here forever made forever just too damned long. Yet forever with Lily had looked too short by far.

Gaining Lily's trust had made Rico whole. Breaking that trust had broken him.

"I hate to see you like this."

Rico glanced up as Anna took the chair Carrie had vacated. Though he ached every single minute in the place where Lily had lived, spending time with the sister he'd thought lost for so long gave Rico one more reason to get up every morning.

Anna was a gentle soul, a calming presence. Rico had no idea how she'd managed to grow up that way despite their father, but she had. Perhaps her brush with death had shown her there was little worth getting upset about in life.

"How do you know this isn't the way I always am?" he asked.

"I might have been small, but I remember you." She reached over and took his hand. "I adored you with all the love a little sister could have for her big brother."

"Then I let you die."

She laughed. "I'm not dead, Rico. You need to quit punishing yourself for something that never even happened."

"I was irresponsible, and you paid the price."

"What price? I lived here same as always. Of course, without you it wasn't really the same. But you paid for a sin you never committed."

"Father was right. If I'd faced up to what I'd done, I would have known it never happened. Being rash is what got me where I am today."

"You were a child. So was I. Forget it."

"Have you?"

"Yes."

Because he was watching her face so closely, he caught the tiny flicker in her eyes. "You're lying."

Anna looked away. "I only remember because you left, and I knew you left because of me. I've never forgiven myself for that."

"If it hadn't been that, it would have been something else. I was never meant to be a rancher. I learned that when I left."

"You were happy while you were away?"

He thought over the years he'd been gone. "I wouldn't say I was happy in the war, but I felt useful. And after, riding with the other men, that was good. I belonged with them."

"Were you ever truly happy?"

He thought of Lily. "For a little while."

"Then find that happiness again."

"I can't. I made a deal."

She leaned toward him, earnestness in every line of her face and body. "Break it. Do whatever you have to do. Lie, cheat, steal, hide, break your word."

"Being selfish and rash only gets people hurt."

"Going after love is all that makes life worth living."

"If I break this deal—"

"Lily could die?"

He blinked. "How did you know?"

"I made a deal once, too. I've been sorry ever since."

Rico studied her. She was only seventeen. What kind of deal had she made? "Anna—"

"Never mind me. Break your deal, Rico. Do it now before it's too late."

"I don't want to be looking over my shoulder for the rest of my life. I don't want Lily living that way. I don't want Carrie living that way, either."

"I live that way, too, but I'm looking over my shoulder, hoping to see just one more time the person I'll love forever." She looked deeply into his eyes. "It isn't any better my way, Rico. Believe me."

In her face he saw a sadness that echoed his own. "Even if I decided to go back, I'd never make it. Father would come after me with all the help he could buy."

"I'm sure I could find a way to delay him." Anna smiled as if the prospect amused her.

"You could come with me. I'd protect you, too. You could find the one you love and live in Rock Creek."

Her amused smile faded. "It's too late for me. Don't make the mistake I did and keep your promise to Father. I know it sounds dishonorable, but a promise against love isn't a promise worth keeping."

"I'll think about it."

"Don't think too long, *hermano*. Life has a way of moving on without us."

Anna went inside, leaving Rico alone with his thoughts.

Several hours later, as darkness settled over the land, he still hadn't decided what to do. How could he drag Carrie halfway across the state, most likely on the run? He loved Lily, but he loved Carrie, too. Even though Carrie wanted to go home, was it fair or right to put her in danger to get her there? Carrie was a child under his protection, and he would not make the same mistake twice.

Besides, Lily had never said she loved him. She wanted him, yes, but that wasn't love. Did he dare risk her life only to discover she couldn't care less if she ever saw him again?

There was no right answer. Was there ever a truly right answer? Uncertain still, Rico climbed the stairs to Carrie's room to say good night.

The room was empty, her bed unmade. He might have believed her out and about against his orders if there hadn't been a note on her pillow. Before he even read the childish handwriting, Rico knew the decision had been taken from his hands.

I want Lily to be my mommy. If you want to be my daddy, meet me in Rock Creek. Even if you don't, I'll still love you no matter what.

Rico stuffed her note into his pocket and barreled out of the room, only to bump into his father. "Where are you going in such a hurry?"

"Carrie has run away."

"Let her go. She's a foul-mouthed termagant."

"She's my little girl."

His father's eyes sharpened. "Is there something you haven't told me about that child?"

Rico shook his head. "She isn't mine by blood; she's mine by love."

"She's not a Salvatore, and she never will be. I

won't have her getting any of my land or my money. Do you hear me?"

"I always hear you, and sometimes I'm amazed at the idiocy that comes from your mouth."

Rico stepped around his father, who stopped him with a hand on his arm. "Let her go."

"No. She can't have gotten far. I'll be back before morning."

"You'd better be, or I'll come looking for you."

Nodding, Rico clattered down the stairs to find Anna on the porch.

"Carrie—" he began.

"I know. It's fate, *hermano*. Follow the child."

Rico looked back at the house. He thought of his father's words; he saw his life stretching before him, without Carrie, without Lily, without love, and in a flash everything became clear.

He wanted to be Carrie's daddy. He wanted to be Lily's husband. He wanted a family that was about love and nothing else. He wanted to be with the men who had been his only true family up until now.

He had done whatever he had to do to save Lily. But without her in his life, he wasn't really living, and if the same was true for her, he had to find out.

Sometimes you had to take care of yourself, so he'd tried to. But he'd forgotten that sometimes you had to depend on your friends, too. He hoped they loved him no matter what, because he was going to need them when he rode into Rock Creek.

"Anna, I love you."

"Of course you do." She kissed him on the chin. "Now, hurry."

He rode away as he had once before, but this time Anna stood on the porch waving to him, and instead of feeling as if his life had ended, he knew it had just begun.

* * *

Three Queens was doing better than Lily could ever have dreamed. Her notoriety increased their business. Then the atmosphere, alcohol, and entertainment kept the people coming back for more. Maybe soon she could begin the small theatrical productions she'd always dreamed of. At least more work would keep her mind more fully occupied.

She wasn't waiting around for Rico to return. She knew better than to hope for any such thing. If he'd meant to come back, he wouldn't have taken Carrie with him. Sometimes she hated him more for that than anything else. That child had needed a mother, and Lily had nearly talked herself into taking the job.

Tears sparked at the back of her eyes, and she put a stop to her maudlin thoughts right away. She had a place of her own; she had Johnny to love; she had friends; she had money. There was no reason Rock Creek should seem so dismal.

But tell that to the long faces that gathered in her saloon every day. As much as the men had whined about Rico being a pain, they whined now about his being gone.

As Lily finished her favorite sad song, she glanced at a table where three men pouted as only men could. If she hadn't already missed Rico and Carrie so badly that she thought she might die of it, those three would have made her cry just by looking at them.

Jed had never returned to Rock Creek, opting instead to split off from their group and join up with Russell to become a Pinkerton detective. Personally, Lily thought Jed just couldn't bear to come home without the kid.

Or perhaps he'd known what would happen if he did. Reese and Sullivan had promised to bring Rico home. Eden and Mary hadn't been too happy to find out they'd left him behind. According to Lily's friends, the two men had slept on the floor for a week.

"If you sing another sad song, Lily, I swear I will shoot the piano," Cash drawled.

"W-will n-not." Johnny scowled at him. For some reason, Cash didn't scare Johnny at all. Lily wasn't sure why.

"All right, boy, I won't. But play somethin' lighter before I take my own life in despair."

Johnny obliged. He was doing very well, though still quiet, and the stutter continued. He missed Carrie with a heart-wrenching depth that often brought tears to Lily's eyes. He'd hunted down Gizzard and brought the blasted creature home, where he treated it like a baby.

Since Lily often found herself dreaming she held Carrie close in the middle of the night and when she awoke her cheeks were salty with tears, she could hardly begrudge Johnny anything that soothed his pain for a single instant.

He refused to tell her all that R.W. had done to him. She assumed the knife wounds had been punishment for stuttering, but Johnny would not say. With the man dead and Johnny safe with her, there was no point in pressing him about it if he didn't want to share. Lily could understand hiding a secret. She still wished she'd kept her own secret to herself.

Nate and Reese played a haphazard game of cards with Cash. Nate had been awful sober of late, and that concerned everyone nearly as much as his drinking had. Because sober, Nate was haunted by ghosts he would not name, and as he grew gaunter and paler and quieter by the day, so grew the worry of everyone who loved him.

Sullivan came in the door. The others dealt him in without so much as a hello. Of all of the men, he appeared the least affected by Rico's defection. But, more often than not, the man who acted the least upset was the one bothered by something the most.

Being midafternoon of a weekday, the four men were her only customers. When the sound of galloping hooves stopped outside the saloon, Lily wasn't surprised when every single one checked to make sure she was safely behind the bar. They'd been behaving like hired bodyguards since they all rode out of New Orleans.

A dusty little whirlwind spun into the saloon screaming, "Johnny!"

He stood and caught Carrie mid-leap, swinging her around and around. Their childish laughter mingled. Lily had never heard Johnny laugh like that, and the sound made her smile until complete silence settled over the room and she knew Carrie had not come back alone.

How could Rico appear more handsome than the last time she'd seen him? Even tired and dusty, Lily wanted to kiss him all over and roll around on the floor. How pathetic. Like mother, like daughter, and that would not do.

He was probably already married and working on an heir. Hell, knowing Rico, he'd most likely impregnated the wife already and needed to dump Carrie on someone who loved her. *Fine.* Lily wasn't going to let the girl live unloved just because Car-

rie'd had the misfortune to fall in love with Rico
Salvatore—a malady that seemed to be going
around.

"What do you want?" Lily was proud when her
voice came out cold enough to freeze the Gulf.

Rico strode into the room, and she braced herself
against all the feelings the mere sight of him
revived. If he touched her, she wasn't sure what
she might do, say, or agree to.

But after one piercing, unreadable look, Rico
ignored her and crossed to the table where the
four men lounged. Lily should have known Rico
had not come here for her.

"I wouldn't blame you if you said no, but I'm
going to need a little help."

"Well, thank God," Cash said. "Here I thought
we'd have to drum up our own trouble. But the
kid is back."

They all stood and checked their weapons.

"Just like that?" Rico asked. "You don't want to
know where I've been? Why I left? What kind of
trouble?"

"Nope," they all answered in unison.

"Where to, Rico?" Reese asked.

A single gunshot from the street had them all
moving as one toward the door. Lily had never
seen them like this. Despite her sadness at the
proof that Rico had felt nothing for her beyond
lust, the sight of these men together gave her chills.
Only one word came to mind as five disparate men
molded into an invincible whole. *Magnificent.*

"Seems to be trouble right here and now." Nate
holstered his gun.

"Ain't it always?" Cash muttered as they filed
out the door.

Lily hurried over and peeked outside. Adriano

Salvatore and five mounted, armed men faced Three Queens. Rico and the others stood on the porch.

"We had a deal, Rico."

"Yes, sir."

"The woman's life for the entirety of yours." Lily's heart stuttered and seemed to stop. His life for hers? She couldn't seem to get her mind around what she was certain she'd heard. "Get on your horse and get your ass back home."

"No, sir."

Adriano's face turned an interesting shade of purple.

"I love it when that happens," Carrie whispered, slipping her hand into Lily's. On the other side, she hung on to Johnny as if she didn't plan to ever let him go. From the look on Johnny's face, that was all right with him.

"I'll have her arrested and hung right in front of your eyes."

"Your money means nothing here," Reese said.

"Then I'll have her hauled back to New Orleans."

"She was acquitted," Sullivan put in. "There's a little matter of the Constitution in the way of that plan."

"You all fought against the Constitution. Now you're throwing it in my face?"

"We lost that fight," Nate murmured.

Cash shot him a glare. "That's the only one."

"And now we kind of like the Constitution," Reese said.

"But we really don't like you." Somehow Cash had his pistol in his hand, and he checked the load with a deceptively casual flick of his wrist.

"What will you do, gunfighter?" Adriano sneered.

"Shoot us all? Some of you will die if I choose to say so."

"Wait." Rico stepped forward, making himself the prime target.

"No!" Lily shouted before she could stop herself. A glare from Cash had her biting her lip until she tasted blood. She'd been angry enough to hate Rico, but there wasn't enough anger in the world to make Lily stop loving him.

"This isn't their fight."

"Like hell," Reese growled.

"Quiet!" Amazingly, everyone listened to Rico, though none of them looked happy about it. "I'm not leaving here, Father. I'm not letting you touch Lily. Kill me if you want to. See what wonders *that* will do for your political career."

"He's goin' to turn scarlet now." Carrie giggled.

"This isn't funny. Rico could get hurt."

"No, he won't. Daddy can fix anything."

"Daddy?"

Carrie nodded. "When I ran off, I told him I wanted you to be my mommy." She tilted her head and fixed Lily with a soul-searching gaze. "Will you?"

Lily found herself nodding even before she'd thought things out. How could she not say yes? She loved this child. She'd mourned Carrie's loss as deeply as she'd mourned Rico's.

"I said if he wanted to be my daddy he should meet me in Rock Creek." She scowled. "But he caught up to me before I even got a mile out of that pisshole he called home."

"Carrie."

"Well, it was. Anyway, he said we could come back to you and Johnny, so here we are." She nodded sagely. "Daddy'll take care of everything.

You just have to believe in him and give him some time."

Lily stared at her for a long moment. Why couldn't she have the simple faith of a child?

"You are no longer my son." Adriano's voice was choked.

"I haven't been for a very long time."

"You will get nothing from me."

"Have I ever?"

"Scarlet *and* purple," Carrie murmured. "I never saw that before."

"If I ever find you near me or mine," Rico said, "I'll make sure your political career is as dead as Randolph Ward."

Adriano looked ready to explode. Instead, he whirled his horse and pounded out of town in a cloud of dust and hired help.

"I'll take that as an agreement to my terms," Rico murmured.

"Why didn't you tell us he was blackmailing you, kid?" Cash asked.

Rico continued to watch the cloud advance on the horizon. "This wasn't your fight."

"Since when has that mattered to any of us?" Reese said.

Rico turned and faced him. "You have a family now. So does Sullivan. I didn't want to bring trouble here."

"But you did, anyway. Why?"

"You told me I had to learn to stand up for myself—"

"But—"

"Let me finish, Reese. There is a time to stand up for yourself and a time when every man knows he must ask for the help of his friends. In this case,

I thought that six"—he glanced over at the men— "or five, is better than one."

Reese snorted. "How many times do I have to tell you that?"

"I think I understand it now."

"It's about damned time," Cash muttered.

"I might be slow, but eventually I learn. At least I know what I need now." Rico glanced toward the saloon. "I need her."

"Go get her, then."

"Hey, kid, I can still marry and bury," Nate said. Rico grinned. "Wait right here."

Lily backed away from the door in a hurry as Rico stepped onto the porch. Carrie and Johnny laughed and ran off, hand in hand, to see Gizzard.

He filled the doorway—dark, handsome, tall, and more confident than he'd ever been before. No more false bravado. Rico had found himself while he'd been gone, and maybe Lily had discovered herself, too.

For every step Rico took forward, Lily took a step back. Until he made one big stride and crowded her against the bar. "Don't run away, Lily."

All she could do was stare into his beautiful face and think that he had gone back to a place he hated, planned on living a life he loathed, for her.

"Can you trust me to keep my vow to you now that I've broken one to my father?"

"Wh-what vow?"

"I'll love you forever."

To Lily's horror, tears filled her eyes. "Aw, Rico, you broke my heart. I thought—" Her voice cracked, and she couldn't go on.

He placed his palm very gently on her hip but made no other move to touch her. "What did you think?"

"That you left because I couldn't give you an heir. I felt so worthless."

"*Querida*, you are worth everything to me. You are perfection."

"I can never give you children."

"I heard you the first time. I didn't care then, and I don't care now. Still, never is almost as long as forever. We shall see what we shall see." He nodded at Johnny and Carrie. "Blood doesn't make a family, *Lilita*. Love makes a family. All I need is you and them. I wouldn't blame you if you turned me away, but I must tell you, I will not go. I will spend the rest of my life convincing you to love me."

"I already love you."

He blinked, shocked at her easy admission. "When did this happen?"

"I think it was when I kicked you in your Texas-sized ego."

He winced. "I remember. You really must stop that."

She reached up and kissed him, hard and deep, pouring everything she felt for him into the embrace. When at last they parted, she held his gaze and repeated the vow that had become theirs.

"I'd do anything for you."

Dear Reader,

I hope you enjoyed Rico's story. The man really grew on me. He has that gift, among quite a few others.

I fell in love with all the characters in this book, more so than usual I must admit. Carrie and Johnny became near and dear to me; Lily is one strong and interesting lady, and, of course, each one of the Rock Creek Six is special in his own way. I'd be very sad to leave them behind. Luckily for me I don't have to, since just about everyone returns in my next Rock Creek Six tale *Nate,* which will be available in January 2002.

I love to hear from readers. You can reach me at P.O. Box 736, Thiensville, WI, 53092. Or check out my Web site for news of upcoming releases and contests: *www.lorihandeland.com*

Enjoy *Savage Destiny*
A Romantic Series from
Rosanne Bittner